CARIBBEAN RIM

CARIBBEAN RIM

RANDY WAYNE WHITE

G. P. PUTNAM'S SONS
- - - - - - - - - - - - -
NEW YORK

G. P. PUTNAM'S SONS
Publishers Since 1838
An imprint of Penguin Random House LLC
375 Hudson Street
New York, New York 10014

Library of Congress Cataloging-in-Publication Data

Names: White, Randy Wayne.
Title: Caribbean rim / Randy Wayne White.
Description: New York : G. P. Putnam's Sons, 2018. | Series: A Doc Ford novel; 25
Identifiers: LCCN 2018002132| ISBN 9780735212787 (hardcover) |
ISBN 9780735212800 (epub)
Subjects: LCSH: Ford, Doc (Fictitious character)—Fiction. | Marine
biologists—Fiction. | BISAC: FICTION / Crime. | FICTION / Suspense. |
GSAFD: Suspense fiction. | Mystery fiction.
Classification: LCC PS3573.H47473 C37 2018 | DDC 813/.54—dc23
LC record available at https://lccn.loc.gov/2018002132

Printed in the United States of America
1   3   5   7   9   10   8   6   4   2

BOOK DESIGN BY MEIGHAN CAVANAUGH

For Saylor Grace White,
a Floridian saltwater-born

Imagine your grave on a windy winter night: you've been dead seventy years; it's been fifty since a visitor last paused at your tombstone—now explain why you're in a pissy mood *today.*

—S. M. Tomlinson, *One Fathom Above Sea Level*

A valid point Darwin didn't make but could have made: In most dimorphic species, males are interchangeable, so expendable. Perhaps that's why male vertebrates inherit the war gene.

—Marion D. Ford, "Sexual Dimorphism in Gulf Fishes"

[DISCLAIMER]

Sanibel and Captiva Islands and the Bahamas are real places, faithfully described, but used fictitiously in this novel. The same is true of certain businesses, marinas, bars, and other places frequented by Doc Ford, Tomlinson, and pals.

In all other respects, however, this novel is a work of fiction. Names (unless used by permission), characters, places, and incidents are either the product of the author's imagination or are used fictitiously. Any resemblance to actual persons, living or dead, or to actual events or locales is unintentional and coincidental.

Contact Mr. White at www.docford.com.

AUTHOR'S NOTE

This novel was seeded many years ago on my first visit to Cat Island, Bahamas, and was augmented by a recent hopscotch seaplane journey from Sanibel Island, Florida, to Andros, then southeast to islands known and unknown. We landed as needed, and even when we didn't need to, we landed and fished anyway. I am unaware of a more intimate way to explore a vast blue schematic of salt and karst geology, for an amphibious plane fires the wanderlust in those who inhabit remote places and brings them on the run, always equipped with advice and a wealth of local knowledge. Tales of piracy, old and new, are as common as opinions on where to eat, sleep, rent a boat, and as compelling as rumors of witchcraft—obeah, it is called—and of Spanish coins that a friend or relative came *this* damn close to finding. What makes it fun is, in the Bahamas, the rumors are sometimes true.

For this book, a key source of fact and lore was Captain Mark Keasler, an eco-fishing guide who has lived on Cat Island for more than thirty years. We met in 1995, and were the first to dive a spot known locally as the Horse Eating Hole because, we were told, it was where dead livestock was dragged by day, and was eaten overnight by something—a dragon, old-timers claimed. "A crocodile, more likely," Mark suggested, and not only provided a rubber raft but joined me in the lunacy of hacking our way to a pond that locals avoided day and night—no footpaths, no litter, no human spore of any kind. Just Mark, his brother Andy, my young son Rogan, and myself.

As I described the place in my column for *Outside* magazine:

> Horse Eating Hole is encircled by mangroves so dense that even on a bright Bahamian day the light seems to have been leached away by shadows and stillness. It is a brackish water pond that lies off a sand trail at the north end of the island and below a network of caves from which, each day at dusk, emerge thousands of fruit bats. En masse, the bats create smoky contrails over the mangroves, ascending charcoal strokes above a tree canopy of waxen green.

Get the picture? Spooky? You bet.

We paddled out. Mark took the lead by using the anchor to sound for depth. Over and over he tossed and measured. Rarely was the water deeper than a swimming pool. But then, at a spot near the mangroves, sixty feet of line peeled through his hands, and the anchor snagged something solid below. Because exploring

----

the pond was my idea, protocol demanded I pretend to be courageous. Worse, I had to get in the damn water. Wearing snorkel gear, I followed the anchor line down through a darkening gloom until I lost my nerve and surfaced. "Too murky," I told my buddies. "Let's go home." Who were we to sneer at a century of Cat Island legend? The creature—whatever it was—could've been down there in its hole, seriously peeved at having been awakened by the rude thunk of our anchor.

Mark didn't give up as easily. When he jackknifed toward the bottom, we waited for what seemed too long for a man without tanks to be down there in all that blackness. Then he came shooting to the surface, wide-eyed, yelling, "Our anchor landed right in the mouth of the cave. It's clear, man. You get down close to the bottom, the water turns crystal clear!"

Incredible. I swam down through thirty feet of murk into a lucent world of bright-green-and-yellow rock, all domed in a huge bubble of clear saltwater. There was our anchor, sitting smack in the horse-sized mouth of the cave. Not far away there was yet another, larger cavern.

No wonder research for this book began with a phone call to Capt. Keasler, or that Cat Island became my base of operations. Uncle Mark, as he is known to every child on the island, patiently fielded questions about local history, language, and customs, and provided a key plotline hook when he explained why he started a free program to teach children how to swim—Team Barracuda, it is called. "Seventy percent of Bahamian women and almost as

- - - - - - - - - - -

many men never learn," he told me, "so they tell their kids to never wade in deeper than their waist. Generation after generation, it's been that way. Maybe that's why there are so many legends about monsters in places like Horse Eating Hole—a way to keep the kids safe by scaring them away from the water."

Child by child, things are changing on Cat Island. If you'd like to fish or explore with Capt. Mark Keasler, contact him at: bwanacat@yahoo.com or call him in the Bahamas at: (242) 474-0840.

This book has much to do with finding shipwrecks, and there is no better resource than my friend Capt. Carl Fismer, a legend in a business that has many pretenders but few true pros. During his forty-year career, Capt. Fizz, as he is known, worked over three hundred shipwrecks in Florida, the Bahamas, the Indian Ocean, and Central and South America, and recovered millions in Spanish gold, silver, jewels, and other artifacts. For years, he partnered with treasure historian Jack Haskins, and he was Mel Fisher's choice to direct part of the salvage diving of the *Santa Margarita*, sister ship to the *Atocha*, so no surprise that he was awarded the Mel Fisher Lifetime Achievement Award in 2010. Fizz provided valuable guidance as I researched this book, and also an authentic voice (I hope) to my fictional character, Capt. Carl Fitzpatrick. While the two men share many admirable qualities, I want to make it clear that Fizz cannot be faulted for Fitzpatrick's negative qualities (if any) nor the fictional character's choice of language or misstatements of fact. To learn more about Capt. Fismer, I highly recommend his book *Unchartered Waters: The Life and Times of Captain Fizz*. Or go to http://www.carlfismer.com.

As stated, this novel is a work of fiction, but the scaffolding is based upon fact. Therefore, before thanking others who contributed their expertise or good humor during the writing of *Caribbean Rim*, I want to make clear that all errors, exaggerations, or misstatements are entirely my fault, not theirs.

Insights, ideas, and medical advice were provided by doctors Brian Hummel, my brother Dan White, Marybeth B. Saunders, Peggy C. Kalkounos, and my nephew, Justin P. White, Ph.D.

Pals, advisers, and/or teammates are always a help because they know firsthand that writing and writers are a pain in the ass. They are Jeff Carter, Gary and Donna Terwilliger, Ron Iossi, Jerry Rehfuss, Stu Johnson, Victor Candalaria, Gene Lamont, Nick Swartz, Kerry Griner, Mike Shevlin, Jon Warden, Phil Jones, Dr. Mike Tucker, Davey Johnson, Barry Rubel, Mike Westhoff, Col. Joe Kittinger, Capt. Tony Johnson, Commander Dan O'Shea, Steve Smith, Garret Anderson, Mark Futch for seaplane advice, and behavioral guru Don Carman.

My wife, singer/songwriter Wendy Webb, not only provided support and understanding but is a trusted adviser, as are my daughters-in-law, Oceana Blue and Rachael Ketterman White. Bill Lee and his orbiting star, Diana, as always have guided me safely into the strange but fun and enlightened world of our mutual friend the Reverend Sighurdhr M. Tomlinson. Equal thanks

----

go to Albert Randall, Donna Terwilliger, Stephen Grendon, my devoted SOB, the angelic Mrs. Iris Tanner, and my partners and pals, Mark Marinello, Marty and Brenda Harrity.

People I met at Cat Island's Fernandez Bay and nearby one-room eateries—The Starlite, Hidden Treasures, and Four Brothers— were as generous with their stories as they were with local recipes. Due to my laziness and poor penmanship, I will thank them by first names only: Wendylee, Marlene, Sheena, Karen, Erica and Dan from Fern Bay, Desha Star, Dahnay and Eugene of New Bight.

Key to this novel's plotline is the long history of Freemasonry in the Bahamas, a uniting influence that continues to join people of disparate backgrounds with trust and a potent bond. My fraternal brothers Dominique Gibson of Nassau, and Jovann O'Neil Burrows of Mount Alvernia Lodge, Cat Island, donated a lot of time, information, and fun to the writing of this book—a kindness I hope to repay.

Much of this novel was written at corner tables before and after hours at Doc Ford's Rum Bar & Grille, where staff were tolerant beyond the call of duty. Thanks go to: Liz Filbrandt, Capt. Tommy, Kim McGonnell, Tyler Wussler, Tall Sean Lamont, Motown Rachel Songalewski, Boston Brian Cunningham, and Cardinals Fan Justin Harris. Chefs Sergio and Dustin, my friends Allyson, Alex, Amanda, Andy, Ashley, Becca, Brenda, Casey, Caroline, Carle, David, Gina, Heather, Jerry, Jim, Jon, Mandi, Mary, Michelle, Patti, Peter, Rachael O, Ray, Sara W, Sarah, Samuel, Scott, Tiffany, Terri, Whitney, Yamily and Yvonne, Abbie, Brian,

----

St. James, Jim and Lisa, and hostesses Briana, Carolina, Samantha, Shelby, and Tall Cheyne Diaz.

At Doc Ford's on Fort Myers Beach: Lovely Kandice Salvador,
Reyes Ramon #1, Reyes Ramon #2, Netta Kramb, Sandy Rodri-
guez, Mark Hines, Stephen Hansman, Kelsey King, Brandon
Cashatt, Timothy Riggs, Jessica Del Gandio, Bre Cagnoli, Drew
Acord, Jaqui Engh, Karli Goodison, Reid Pietrzyk, Alex Wyatt
Hall, Justin Voskulhl, Brian Westheimer, Eric Westheimer, Rachel
Lane, Zeke Pietrzyk, Samantha Wylie, S'iva Goodman, Amel
Hadzic, Jordan Veale, Kirby Miller, Jose Mata, Nicole Volberg,
Krystian Martinez, Carly Cooper, Kelsey Collins, Denise Beckham,
Rich Capo, Rocky Olah, Gabby Moschitta, Shae Conrad, James Pat-
terson, Austin Edward, Alexis Terran-Cortez, Tony Anderson, Ste-
vie Cooper, Mitchell Arimura, Jade Beuth, Annette Williams, Nora
Billheimer, Eric Hines, Timothy Riggs, Jeff Bright, Eric Munchel,
Violet Vetter, Shelby Fleshman, Ryan Schlottman, Chantel Mari-
neau, Carlos Rios, Jessie Fox, Consuelo Parra-Hermida, Jordan
Kryzk, Kassee Buonano, Edith Lopez, Lizet Leon, Tayler Glavin,
Nick "The Man" Howes, Jon Healey, Raul Muniz, Hector Rodri-
guez, Carlos Rubi, Nick Dowling, Edgar Zapata, Daniel Castaneda,
Louis Gyenese, Cody Brown, Alam Nabil, Seth Wiglesworth,
Aiden Collins, Ross Pinkard, Cadin Kin, Eroll Brackman, Nelson
Rojas, Bronson Janey, Kandice Salvador, Meredith Rickards, John
Goetz, Andrea Aguayo, Baltazar Lopez, Adrian Uscanga, Oralia
Ramos, Enrique Hernandez, Catalina Ramirez, Nicolas Cardona,
Jaime Rodriguez, Zeferino Molina, Julio Cruz, Cristian Ramos,

AUTHOR'S NOTE

Juan Vargas, Jose Perez, Ramon Luna, Carlos Cano, Jorge Cuevas, Jose Mixtun, Reyes Ramon, Roni Martinez, Jose Vaegas, Carlos Marcial, Luis Cuevas, Joseph Bodkin, Jose Gutierrez, Alonso Ramos, Adrian Trinidad, Evodio Lopez, Enrique Tello, David Leon, Yadiel Velazquez, Heriberto Ramos, Roberto Deleon.

At Doc Ford's on Captiva Island: Big Pappa Mario Zanolli, Joyous Joy Schawalder, Hiya Shawn Scott, Adam Traum, Alicia Rutter, Ally Llanos, Amanda Schaefer, Bob Butterfield, Chris James, Christina Teixeira, Daniel Leader, Donald Yacono, Dylan Wussler, Edgar Mena, Erica DeBacker, Heather Walk, Joey Wilson, John King, Jon Economy, Amazing Josh Kerschner, Matt Ginn, Ray Rosario, Ryan Body, Ryan Cook, Sarah Collins, Sue Baker, Shelbi Muske, Tony Foreman, Yakhyo Yakubov, Lovely Cheryl Erickson, Ko-Ko Heather O'Dell, El Capitán Steve Day, Karla Garatchea, Krystal Bovan, Skyler Muske, Adrian Medina, Garrett Hartle, Ivan Riverol, Jose Sanchez, Miguel Pieretti, Robert DelGandio, Sam Uscanga, Oscar Baltazar Ramirez, and Guitar Czar Steve Reynolds.

My sons have typed or retyped and sent the last two words of every Doc Ford novel since 1990, so once again my loving thanks go to Lee and Rogan White for helping me finish yet another book.

—Randy Wayne White
Sanibel Island, Florida

CARIBBEAN RIM

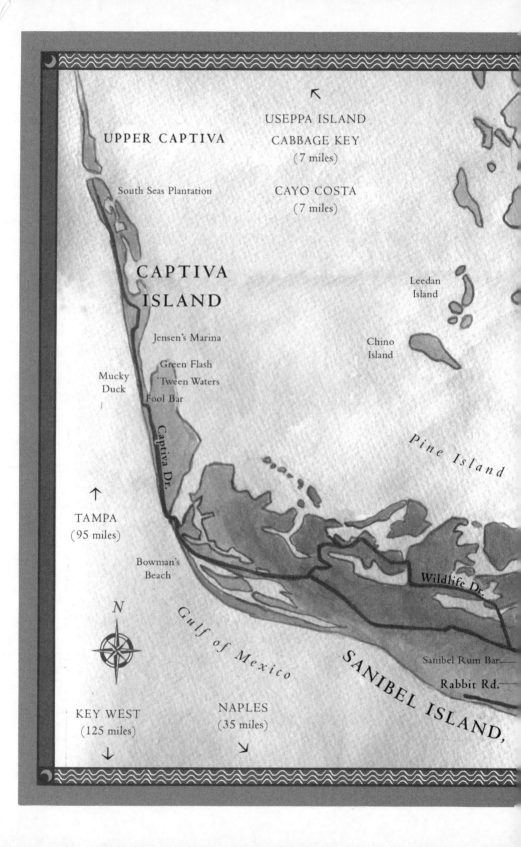

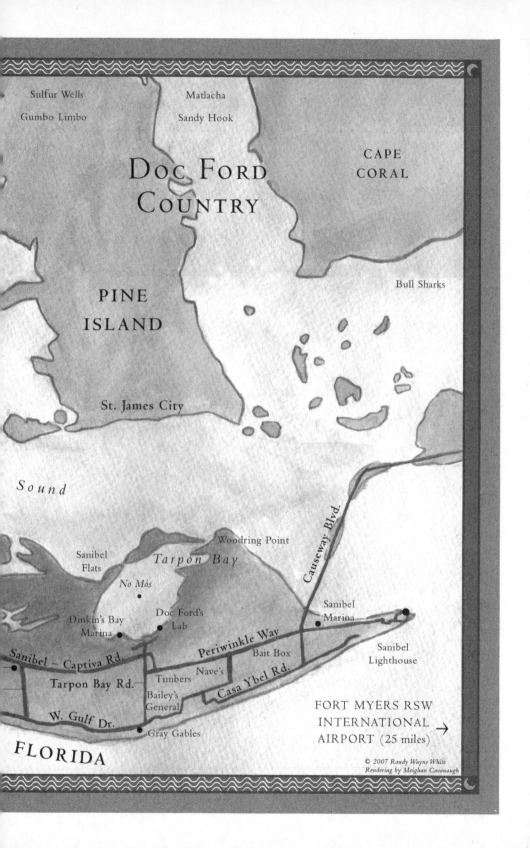

Marion Ford spent Friday battling traffic, romantic issues, and writing automated replies to thwart future intrusions, and by Tuesday was in the Bahamas distanced by a turquoise sea.

Isolation. He craved it at junctures, the skin-on-bone reality of a tent, zero electronics, miles of beach to run, the indifference of saltwater, tide, wind. Two books, minimal supplies, a fire starter for abundant driftwood. The process, not time, was spatial. Whatever was enough to quell his own sense of drifting, the weakness granted to sloth, pointless emotion, guilt. Love, too—if "love" existed beyond the chemical bond that, in his experience, clouded reasonable behavior.

Family was different. Those bonds were inviolable. The same was true of friendship—a select few.

After a week, he packed his seaplane, a Maule four-seater, and returned to Andros Town not refreshed but newly focused. Luck is an illusion embraced by those who are unprepared. Ford seldom was. Two days later, he struck the trail of the man he wanted to find but had no reason to hurt, let alone kill.

Someone on the island, he discovered, possibly did.

The man, a professor turned bureaucrat, was too caught up in Lydia, his former student, to give a damn about being followed, or anything connected with the past. To hell with the past. To hell with bills, his job, his unhappy wife, and the new boss, too, a supercilious business grad—not a qualified maritime archaeologist—who wore Polos to show off his tattoos, for Christ's sake, and was ten years younger.

"There's nothing wrong with a tat or two," Lydia, no longer a student, had counseled, "or smoking weed, for that matter. You can't smell it on his clothes? I did when I came to your office yesterday to apologize. The real problem is, he's just another ambitious shark. They scare people like us. Admit it."

This was eight months ago after he'd almost had her arrested for using a metal detector in Ocala National Forest. And he would've done it, called a ranger, if she hadn't . . .

Well, there were a couple ways to explain why he had fallen under her spell. He remembered her from Advanced Anthropology, a night course for working students. Lydia, bland-faced, thin, always on time, always in the back row, off by herself. They were alike in that way—outsiders, solid, responsible, both subdued by what the mirror had failed to promise every morning since puberty.

He was five-eight and bald. Lydia, an introvert, averted her eyes while speaking. A slow, voltaic awareness evolved.

The girl often lingered long enough in the parking lot to call, "Good night, Professor Nickelby." And twice had waited with him for Triple A to jump-start his pathetic old Volvo. Their clumsy small talk was memorable only because she hadn't brought up Indiana Jones. Lambasting Hollywood was how the socialite types denounced a fantasy that had, in fact, flooded archaeology with their kind.

Not Lydia. The notebook she'd turned in was fastidious. Legible cursive with footnotes in fine block print. No copy-and-paste plagiarism, the new academic norm. And not a single goddamn emoji or doodled happy face.

One exchange *was* memorable. The Triple A guy had been busy with paperwork when, out of the blue, she'd asked Nickelby, "Do you ever wonder if things might be fixable? Like your timing's totally off and it's up to you to change, to . . . I don't know, do the unexpected. Something totally . . . *risky*."

"I can't afford payments, so I'm stuck," he'd replied. "The

- - - - - - - - - - -

timing belt was serviced at seventy thousand, just like the manual says, and, safety-wise, I did the research. Volvos are the least risky when it comes to . . ." He'd rambled on in lecture mode even after realizing he had totally missed her meaning.

The silence that followed lasted seven years. He married. He changed jobs, although remained an adjunct professor because the State of Florida didn't pay crap. More than once, alone in the stucco confines of a home he couldn't afford, he had replayed that conversation in his head.

Do you ever wonder if the way things are might be fixable?

Jesus Christ, he'd been an idiot. The Volvo's timing belt had nothing to do with it. The girl had wanted to explore bigger issues. Archaeology as a profession, possibly. Or she was talking about life. Her life, his life. All screwed-up lives.

It's up to us to change. To do something . . . risky.

This was a tantalizing fragment. Had she been addressing their age difference? Him close to tenure, her not yet twenty years old. If so, my god, it was the way a shy student might attempt to seduce an older man without compromising his career.

That brief voltaic awareness took root as his marriage crumbled. Humiliations he suffered in the bedroom sought refuge in fantasy. The girl, rather cute, not bland at all, came alive in his mind. She had glistening brown hair, a thin body, but not so thin her clothes—jeans and tank tops often—didn't reveal taut hips and small stiletto breasts. Sloped valleys, too, one night in the

----

parking lot when she'd knelt to retrieve a book, then stood as if to prove he was taller.

The fantasy motivated him to finally do the legwork.

Lydia Johnson had dropped out midway through her sophomore year. She had forfeited an academic scholarship and a housing grant based on economic need. It made no sense. A straight-A student on the fast track who also had minority status—an unexpected twist. DNA results proved she was nine percent Native American. Documentation had been provided *after* acceptance.

This was an eye-opener. Sweet, shy Lydia was also damn savvy. In academia, minority status was the golden umbrella. So why the hell had she left all those perks behind?

He dug deeper, and it all began to unravel.

Campus police and a court hearing had been involved. No details. Her record, if any, had been expunged, and the file sealed. A theft of some type, possibly, but more likely drugs—selling, not just using. The dorms would be empty otherwise.

Fantasy could not tolerate the realities of Dr. Leonard Nickelby's respectable, stuffy world.

Seven years passed. When he thought of Lydia, which wasn't often, he winced at what might have happened that night in the parking lot. Then, a year ago, there she was in Ocala National Forest, wearing earphones, sweeping a path with a metal detector. He didn't recognize her at first. Not consciously. Then she turned and flipped him the bird in response to what he'd yelled, which

- - - - - - - - - - -

was, "That's a felony, you idiot. Don't bother running, I've got you on video."

It took her a long moment, too. "Professor Nickelby?" The way her face lit up caused him to fumble his phone. Thank god, because he had park headquarters on speed dial. He wouldn't have heard her add, "You have no idea how many times I've thought about you."

He'd stammered something pompous about switching jobs, and she should consider herself damn lucky to be his former student. Five minutes of talk was all he could spare. Steaks were on, and a group of lobbyists awaited him at a nearby pavilion—a picnic intended to win the ear of government officials.

"A meat eater," she'd chuckled. "I used to wonder if anyone else saw that side of you. Congratulations. I always knew you'd be a big success."

Huh?

The fantasy could not end with another question mark. After three sleepless nights, he would've phoned if she hadn't shown up at his office to "apologize," then suggested they meet the next day.

"I can't," he told her at the door.

"You will," she replied. "What worries me is, you'll never understand why."

Lydia and her cryptic remarks.

Yet she was correct. They were alone on a riverbank when she referenced his boss, a handsome shark who smoked weed. "They

----

scare us—people who think doing exceptional work will be enough, but it never is. Admit it."

What he wanted to talk about was that night in the parking lot. Instead, he nodded wisely. "I'm certainly not frightened of him or any of my colleagues, but, for argument's sake, let's say you're right. Is that why you dropped out of school?"

No, Lydia had been asked to leave—she offered no explanation—and went to work for a treasure salvage company based in West Palm Beach. The company's founder was in jail after refusing to reveal where he'd hidden four hundred million in gold bars and coins.

"Not surprised, professor? In your new job, you must deal with treasure hunters all the time. They're not all thieves."

The job wasn't new, he'd been at it six years. He knew enough about the guy to say, "Maybe not, but they're all con men, the way they think, the way they live. You worked for Benthic Exploration? Jimmy Jones must've hired you, so you understand why he's in jail, right?"

Jimmy and her eighteen months with Benthic were not topics to be discussed. "Benthic was a good group to work for at the time, that's all I know. I learned a lot."

Lydia's stubborn deference irritated Nickelby. "What? You'd rather be a thieving pirate than sit behind a desk, I suppose, and enforce state statutes."

"It would be a lot more fun than what I do now, which is

----

doctor cattle for a bona fide creep. Here, relax—" She produced a joint that was twisted at the ends not unlike pre-Columbian cordage.

"You work on a ranch?"

"For a vet clinic. My boss is a hormone pusher, the type cattle barons love." Lydia exhaled through her nose and passed the joint to him, a man who didn't drink or use drugs.

Nickelby felt as if he was dreaming. Stared at the joint between his fingers and worried about residue accumulating on his skin until she said, "Your beat-up old Volvo—do you remember the night we waited for Triple A? I wanted to talk about it then, how to deal with being like us. You know, smart, dependable— conformists by nature—but not other people's idea of . . ."

"Fashion models?" he suggested when her voice faltered. "You're wrong. I've always found you quite attractive, but—" In a daze, he put the joint to his lips, inhaled, then had to deal with a coughing fit, before explaining, "I was too darn stuffy to take the chance. To do something risky. Those were your exact words."

Her eyes actually began to tear. "You remember."

"Of course I do. Almost every night for I don't know how many years." He took a more aggressive hit. "But the age difference . . . If you meant what I think you did in the parking lot, why would you . . . Why me?"

"I don't date boys," she replied, studying him in a way that meant something. "I never will."

"Oh come on. You didn't wait all these years just because—"

- - - - - - - - - - -

"I didn't say that. Waiting and not moving ahead are two different things. I've seen the future too often. Women like me, with brains, and the train wrecks they end up marrying because they're too fat or too thin, or their background isn't quite suitable. Whatever. Another caged bird, professor—that's the way I felt when I met you."

Her face, framed in smoke, was suddenly lucent in the sunlight. The sense of loss Nickelby felt was numbing. "I . . . I don't know what to say. But, at your age, you truly have no idea of the responsibilities that come with my—"

"Shut up, Leonard. I'm the only person you've ever met you can say any damn crazy thing that comes into your head, and it'll be okay—as long as it's the truth."

Her boldness, so unexpected, wasn't an epiphany. More like a kick in the butt toward a door he'd never found the courage to open. "You shouldn't speak to me that way."

"I just did. After class, all those nights I walked you out, I felt like a fool because—"

"You don't think I wanted to?" He puffed, held his breath, coughed. "Goddamn right, I wanted to. I was an idiot back then. A coward, okay? Who followed every rule because that's what I've done my entire fucking life. Risk jail and my career for an underage student? Brilliant. But that's exactly what I should've done. I just wish to heck I would've—"

"You still can," Lydia said. She took a step back, stripped off her tank top, and unsnapped her bra, then held it to her chest,

----

watching him all the while. Several seconds passed before she did it, bared her body for him to see—ribs beneath pale skin, erect nipples—then stood nose to nose. "Do you like?" she whispered.

"Oh my god . . . Beautiful, yes."

"I'm not and I never will be. Don't ruin what's real by saying crap like that."

"You are to me."

"No more talking." Her fingers found his belt buckle, a metallic sound as it popped free. Next, his zipper as she knelt. Shaded by trees, the river flowed while Lydia made it all become real.

Eight months later, he was still married but willing to risk everything when she produced a chart of the Bahamas and said, "The next step is, we need money."

2

Mars Bay, South Andros, is a mangrove village born of a freshwater spring, not commerce or ease of access. Ford arrived on a Wednesday, mid-July, and started asking around.

"I don't understand why people care 'bout a loud-mouthed little fella like that," the dive shack owner said. "He was nice enough, kind of fun even, but that voice of his. Sort of high-pitched, like a bird, you know? But formal in an educated way."

"I'm not the first to ask about those two?"

The owner's name was Tamarinda Constance, according to the sign. Tamara, for short, she'd told him. She was big-boned, observant, and had appeared slightly bored standing outside her tin-roofed dive shack, beachside. Ford had spent half an hour on pleasantries, discussing local dive spots, before risking a question about the runaway archaeologist who was also a thief.

"No, sir. A few days back, there was a big fella—well-dressed, he was—with an accent. Cuban, I thought at first, but he had money, so he could be from South America. Spain, maybe. He asked did a man claimed to be an archaeologist come to rent tanks and regulators. What's so important about him?"

"The guy," Ford said, "supposedly he's the quiet type. Leonard Nickelby. Are you sure we're talking about—"

"Same name on the dive card he used to rent equipment. Doctor Nickelby, is the way he said it. Bald fella who got louder and louder when him and his girlfriend, or niece—could be, she's so much younger—when they started drinking rum punches over there at the Turtle Kraals Café." Tamara's eyes swept bayside to a thatched *palapa*, where there was a driftwood bar, stools upturned on tables, shaded by palms. Overhead, in the high green fronds, parrots rioted in the tradewind heat.

"Hard to believe someone like Dr. Nickelby would cause trouble."

"What he caused was a party, mostly local folks since not many tourists are around this time of year. Shoulda seen that little man playing drums and leading a conga line around the fire."

"That seems out of character."

"Partying? You don't know the Bahamas very well."

"I mean he works for the Florida Division of Historical Resources, Underwater Archaeology. Or did. Supposedly, he's as straitlaced and sober as they come. We have mutual friends, so I wanted to say hello since I'm in the area."

"Florida Division of . . . ?"

"They monitor treasure hunters, usually from behind a desk. It's not what you'd call exciting work."

Tamara nodded as she processed the information. "Shut up in an office, he's just that kind. Reminded me of a nervous little dog who'd been caged and coming here was his first taste of freedom. Barking for attention and running wild. Like that. But loud drunks, I got no use for them no matter their reasons."

Ford felt the same, and wanted to learn more about the Cuban-sounding man who'd inquired about Nickelby. It was probably nothing to worry about unless he'd been misled about what was at stake. On the *palapa*'s wall a chalkboard read *Fresh Snapper, Lobster, Conch.* "If the food's any good, maybe I can buy you dinner tonight. We can talk about the wreck you mentioned, and how you got started."

"Not unless you want me to cook it, too. I work the grill when my shop closes. On this island, a woman's gotta do what she can to make ends meet. This the slow season, sir, and money's hard to come by."

It was a statement, not a veiled invitation. He decided he liked her. A pragmatist, Ford relied on instinct more than he cared to

----

admit. He also had a soft spot for people who hadn't been gifted with wealth or physical beauty yet battled on toward whatever success their secrets embraced.

"What about tomorrow? If you're available, I want to hire your boat. Let's talk about it over a drink after you get off."

"Talk about this fella you're after, you mean," she said, suddenly not so friendly. "I got a five-year-old child at home and get back too late as it is."

"Invite your husband to come along."

"My husband got nothing to do with the subject, you don't mind me saying."

When he tried to apologize, she interrupted. "I trust who I want to trust. The other fella, he had a hard look and treated me like I was stupid, so I sent him on his way. With you, well, I've enjoyed our conversing, but this here's a professional business I run. People's privacy on the island, why they come, that's none of my affair. First thing I shoulda asked, I guess, is are you some kinda po-lice?"

The cautionary awareness imprinted on blacks and whites in the U.S. did not exist in the rural Bahamas. That wasn't the issue. From a shoulder bag he removed an envelope embossed with the crest of the Bahamian Ministry of Fisheries. "Maybe this will help."

She unfolded an ornate document. It granted this pleasant, solid-looking American permission to spend a month in the islands taking coral samples and doing research on something

----

called Conditioned Auditory Response of Marine Fishes, Subclass *Elasmobranchii*.

"You're a scientist," she said, impressed. "Marion D. Ford, P-h-D. That's a very pretty name for a man. What's the auditory response thing?"

"How sharks respond to the sound of boat engines."

"Oh, Elasmo . . . another word for sharks, huh? I've heard that's true."

"About boat engines? It's a fairly recent issue. Guides who specialize in marlin, sailfish—the deep-water trolling species—they say ocean-going sharks have figured out what they're doing. Not just here. Throughout the Caribbean. You know how a boat has to back its engines when a big billfish takes a bait? They claim, fish or no fish, all they have to do is throw the engines into reverse and sharks appear."

"Hmm, then I'm glad I use a sailboat on my dive trips." She pursed her lips, still reading. "Coral samples, too. Collecting coral is illegal for most folks. You must know some powerful people, they give you papers like this."

Ford, a marine biologist, did. He had used similar credentials often enough to know they were useful, but not enough to disguise an obvious lie. "Leonard Nickelby has nothing to do with my project. He supposedly knows a lot about wreck sites in the islands, and diving wrecks is a hobby of mine. My friends thought he might give me some tips."

"What kinda wrecks?"

"Any kind, as long as they're not too deep. I'm pretty new at it. That spot you told me about sounds interesting, the one you haven't figured out yet." He was referring to a sandy basin where she claimed to have seen what looked like dinosaur bones even though dinosaurs had never roamed the Bahamas.

Tamara indulged him. "That's smart mixing business with pleasure. Collect your coral and study sharks while doing what's fun. This man, Nickelby, let me ask you something . . . Well, it don't matter. Been lots of experts show up on this island and they're all after treasure of some type. No one ever says what they're really looking for." Her eyes, when they made contact, added, *Including you.* "Come on now, sir. There's nothing illegal about hunting other valuables that might float up here."

"Such as?"

"You serious or playing dumb?"

"I'm asking."

"Oh-h-h, people look for lots of things. Glass fishing floats, they can still be found. Others collect rare wood that sometimes floats all the way over from Africa. Or bottles that wash up on the windward side. Someone like you, though, might have something else in mind."

Ford looked at her blankly.

"Come on. The gray rock, you know? That's where the money is."

"The what?"

"Amber wax. Floating gold, as old-timers would say. Most come here these days, that's what they're after. It's a recent thing."

"Never heard of it."

"Truly?"

"Are you talking about cocaine?"

She rolled her eyes like a teenager, meaning he was way behind the times. "Ambergris. Ambergris from the belly of whales. You're a scientist and don't know that? It sells for more than gold to perfume makers in France. Stuff washes up on the reefs, if you know where to look, sometimes balls of forty, fifty pounds. New Providence used to be the best place, which is why no one bothered with the south islands 'til recently. No need to pretend with me if that's your reason, sir."

Ford was familiar with ambergris, its origins and content, but was more concerned with losing the confidence of a woman who might be a useful source. And not just because of the wayward archaeologist.

"Tamara—mind if I call you that? I'm going to trust you with something I should've told you right off. Dr. Nickelby stole a logbook from a friend of mine. That's not the main reason I'm here, but I would like to find him."

"I knew it," she said. "I'm almost always right about such things. Like a ship's log from a boat?"

He added a few details. The logbook belonged to an aging treasure hunter who had invested forty years of travel, hard work, and research in the notes the book contained.

"Why didn't you tell me before—"

"Because we just met and I want to keep this out of the news.

Nickelby's a respected public official in Florida. His wife's worried. She wants him home safe. I happened to be in the area anyway, so why not try to talk some sense into the guy before the police have to get involved?"

That won her over. Temporarily. "Bet she's mighty angry, too, him and that teenage-looking girl he's acting the fool with. What exactly's in your friend's book so important you gotta show me those government papers, then pretend to like wreck diving?"

"I'm not pretending," he said, and tucked the research permits away. "Let me charter you for the day and I'll tell you the rest of it. That spot you mentioned sounds like a good start. What I'm looking for is bleached coral. I'm sure you're familiar with it, a disease that has nothing to do with bleach. Thermal bleaching, it's called, very common on reefs around—"

"Tell me this now," she interrupted. "That little man's an archaeologist? Explain something. I told him about the same spot, what I'd seen—a big tusk-looking bone from dinosaur times—but he wasn't interested. That doesn't make sense. Spanish wrecks, that's what he's after, and you know it. Either that or amber wax."

"Like you said," Ford replied, "everyone's looking for something."

Her thin smile was either a ruse or that of a willing conspirator. "Sounds like this book you're after might be valuable. It contains wreck numbers, I suppose. Or what did your friend do, draw maps? Like, X marks the spot? Mister, I can count how many of

----

those I've heard about. You plan to steal that logbook back, I suppose."

Ford's laughter sounded genuine. "If I had the nerve, it might be fun trying something crazy for a change. But, no, I just want to talk to the guy before he screws up his life more than he already has. It's kinda weird, though, I'm not the only man looking for him. Remember anything else about the foreign guy you mentioned?"

"Screwin' up people's lives," Tamara said, "is what a lot of men are good at. The same's true of you, I suppose."

His expression asked, *Me?*

Her dubious snort replied, *Don't play innocent.*

Ford had to laugh again, because she was right. "I've done too many dumb things to list, but the life I screw up is usually my own. Are we on for tomorrow? I'll pay cash."

The frankness of that seemed to go over okay. She got around to saying, "First light, meet me at the dock. If you change your mind once you see my boat, I suggest you hire your treasure hunter friend."

3

- - - - - - - - - -

arl Fitzpatrick, past retirement age but fit-looking in khaki shorts, his eyes bleached gray by the sun, said, "Nickelby's wife scares me more than him running loose in the Bahamas with my logbook. She called yesterday out of the blue. That's why I had to see you. Did you warn Doc?"

Ford's pal, Tomlinson, couldn't look at the man without hearing the Buffett song in his head, "A Pirate Looks at Forty," but more like seventy-something in Fitz's case. Him with his beat-up SUV, a compressor and dive gear in the trunk, and business cards that read

Professional Treasure Hunter
As Featured in Miller Lite Commercials

&

National Geographic

Oh yeah, on the back, *Argosy, True,* and a few other magazines that had gone tits-up decades ago. Plus, a link to a documentary featuring Fitz, Mel Fisher, and Jack Haskins, a trifecta of treasure hunting pros, although Mel had been the only one to make it big.

"I didn't see the need for a warning, just shared with Doc what you said. A reporter, a writer of some type, might already be in the Bahamas looking for Nickelby. So what? But, you know, to keep his eyes open. Oh, and explained I'm leaving a day late because you wanted to—"

"Reporter, my ass. What, she's threatening Leonard with an exposé in the *Key West Citizen?* Horsefeathers."

Leonard—Nickelby's first name, which took a moment to connect. "That's my point," Tomlinson said. "There's no need to put Doc on serious alert for something like this."

"But there is. I'm worried it's someone pretending to be a reporter. And if it's the guy I'm thinking of—"

"Who?"

"Did you follow the stories about the SS *Panama?* It's a deepwater wreck, sank in 1877, with literally tons of gold ingots. The guy who found it was a MIT grad shyster who built an underwater robot—"

"Jimmy Jones, the hotshot treasure hunter," Tomlinson said. "I haven't heard that name in a while."

"Professional conman and thief, more like it. Gave us all a bad name."

"Wasn't he beaten to death in—"

"Jimmy, yeah, in prison about a month ago, and no wonder. He surrounded himself with the big-money crowd, the greedier, the better—including his hired help. But smart in his way, I'll give him that. The *Panama* went down in water a mile deep—the Tongue of the Ocean. So he built a big-assed robot, and salvaged what no one thought would ever be salvaged, then ran off with—"

"I know the story," Tomlinson said. "How does this concern Doc?"

"Because the guy I'm thinking of worked security for one of Jimmy's investors. Ex-military turned cage fighter, I heard, probably an ex-con, too. His name . . . maybe it'll come to me, but a Latin-looking tough. He wanted to get into movies and maybe did, but mostly he kicked whoever ass he was told to kick. The whole salvage group was dirty. Now do you see?"

Fitzpatrick's voice had mileage, a gravelly wisdom like the old prospector who'd played opposite Bogie in *The Treasure of the Sierra Madre*. But Tomlinson was in a skittish mood he'd been battling for weeks and he lost the battle now. "Goddamn it, Fitz, what's the connection?"

The old treasure hunter sat back. "Geezus, shallow up. I thought it was obvious. Nickelby was one of the so-called govern-

----

ment experts who helped send Jimmy to jail. So the guy shows up claiming to be a reporter, what does the wife care if he's legit or not?"

"You're guessing. Nickelby's wife didn't say—"

"I'm being careful. I've talked to jealous wives before, but never one as fired up as her. On the phone, she asked where to send the reporter—whatever he is—after Nassau because she'd paid five hundred in expenses. Like that's a big deal. I said, 'Lady, there's a thousand miles of islands between Nassau and Port of Spain, you got off cheap.' Which really pissed her off. That's when she started making threats."

"Threatening you?"

"Oh yeah."

"After her husband ripped you off?" Tomlinson's tone—*No way.* "Dude, come on. There's got to be something else involved if you expect me to believe—"

"That's what I'm trying to explain."

"You admit it, then."

"Yes, shit. Okay—" Fitz sighed and rubbed his temple. "I didn't tell you everything because I was hoping . . . Anyway, now that Nickelby's wife is involved, I've got no choice. You need to hear the whole—"

"Leaving shit out isn't cool, man. There's got to be a reason she was ballsy enough to say shit like . . . What exactly did she say?" Tomlinson got up and began to pace.

Fitzpatrick gave him a concerned look. The hipster was usually

----

laid-back, not jittery, constantly tugging at his hair like he was now. He was more likely to wander off on philosophical tangents. "Hey . . . are you okay?"

Tomlinson realized he'd overreacted. "Oh, a little pressed for time, maybe. Why do you ask?"

"Save the manure for your new crop of weed. It's the way you're bouncing off the walls. Are you doing speed again?"

The barb produced admiration. "Fitz, you haven't lost your junkie radar. Good ol' Key West, huh? You learn more there by accident than shrinks learn by design. Meth, no. What I tried was this nasty shit flakka, a synthetic amphetamine. The street names vary, but Five Dollar Insanity sums it up." He silenced the man with an open palm and took a seat. "Yes, I had my reasons. In fact, smoking a gram of flakka was a well-planned experiential decision. Totally appropriate for the circumstance. That was four months ago—not that I'm counting."

"Looks to me like the monkey's still got you by the nuts. You know my rules about diving and doing business with stoners who're still using."

Rules in the treasure biz? This was news to Tomlinson, but he said, "A residual echo is what you're seeing. Trust me, one visit to Flakka Land was twice too many. A hit of that shit, wow. The descent was like parachuting into a forest fire after a snort of propane." A brittle smile offered reassurance. "Ancient history, man. Sorry if I was sharp. Uhh . . . what were we talking about again?"

Fitzpatrick tugged at his collar and looked around, seeing fish,

----

sea horses in aquariums, and rows of beakers and other stuff on shelves, but no refrigerator. "Is there someplace we can get a beer?"

They were in Marion Ford's old stilthouse, the side he'd converted into a lab. Windows opened to the bay, water from every angle, including a boardwalk that led to shore. Tomlinson got up. "The dog, that big retriever swimming around outside—if he wants in, open the door or he'll bust right through the screen. You want a glass or just the bottle?"

"Zonk, you sure you're feeling up to snuff? What it comes down to is, I'm embarrassed at being so damn stupid. That's why I didn't lay it all out for you right away."

Zonk, a nickname bestowed by treasure hunter friends in Key West.

"I'll bring two and ice down a six-pack," Tomlinson answered.

"Meth heads," Fitzpatrick muttered as the screen door closed. "Like I don't have enough to worry about."

I t was late afternoon, sleepy time at Dinkin's Bay Marina, the docks empty down the mangrove shoreline. Tomlinson crossed the breezeway into Ford's home. It was more like a ship's cabin. There was a galley, bookshelves by a reading chair, ceiling fans above a wooden floor, and a bed behind a curtain where there were more bookshelves and an old Trans-Oceanic shortwave radio.

A counter separated the galley from a table that seated four. Earlier, after feeding the fish and the dog, he had brought in Ford's mail and stacked it there. He was a reluctant snoop who, out of respect, only snooped in the hope of better understanding his friends—or protecting them, which was a more palatable excuse.

Three letters, all hand-addressed, Tomlinson now placed in a separate pile. Ford had a son and a daughter by different mothers, in different parts of the world. One of the kids was having serious problems—exactly who and what, he would have to pretend not to know. It was best to wait until he delivered the letters personally.

A fourth letter was from Ford's sometime lover, a local fishing guide, Hannah Smith. Hannah was strong-willed, independent, and as devoted to honesty as she was to her Christian convictions. The woman was also very, very pregnant. Tomlinson added Hannah's letter to the pile.

From the fridge, he took two bottles of Hammerhead Ice, a local beer. He chugged one, then opened another.

Hopefully, Fitz wasn't waiting with more bad news in the lab.

Two weeks ago, on the phone, all Fitzpatrick had said was that Nickelby, a government drone, had confiscated his logbook on some bullshit technicality, then split for the Bahamas with a younger woman who wasn't his wife.

Fitz didn't want the police involved. His business required dealing with the Bureau of Archaeological Research, so why risk a bargaining chip he might use down the road when negotiating

----

with the stuffy bastards? The reward for helping to recover his logbook, he'd said, was partnership in a hot new wreck site he'd found.

Tomlinson didn't care about a reward. He did care about a friend who had spent decades, from Florida to the Caribbean to the archives in Seville, perfecting his craft. A pioneer, as Tomlinson viewed the man, who loved boats and history as much as he did and also despised tight-assed bureaucrats. He and Fitz had had many fun, beery nights together in Key West. So he had pitched the idea to Ford via email—join forces and have some fun while they tracked down Nickelby. It was a long shot, but a small favor to ask, and the timing was ideal.

When Tomlinson returned to the lab, Fitzpatrick was fussing with his iPhone. Didn't even glance at the cold beer at his elbow. "Here, I looked up his web page."

"Who?"

"The guy Nickelby's wife claims is a freelance writer. There's only one page, sort of amateurish. Looks fake to me. Oh hell . . . need my glasses. Maybe you can figure out this damn gadget."

Tomlinson accepted the phone but laid it aside. "I wouldn't worry about Doc."

"You haven't heard the rest of it yet. Doc's doing me a favor. You both are."

"What you don't understand is . . ." Tomlinson stopped himself. What Fitzpatrick didn't understand about Marion Ford could not be shared. Not openly. But a hint or two might put the old guy at

- - - - - - - - - - -

ease. "Look, he wanted to get out of Dodge anyway, so he took off last week to do some bonefishing, which, in his world, could've meant a trip to Colombia or Fumbuck anywhere. Or maybe he was already in the Bahamas when I sent the email. In other words, you did him a favor."

"I don't follow."

"Exactly. That's the way Doc plans it whenever he disappears. See, his girlfriend, it's possible she's about to dump him again, and he's got some other heavy family kimchi coming down, so the man was antsy. Plus, he truly loves this sort of thing. Poking around, doing intel-psycho assessments of total strangers."

"Psycho . . . ? You lost me."

"Get used to it. It's the Gemini in him. Or could be he'll use this as an excuse to . . . Hell, let's not even explore that nest of snakes. Anyhoo, looking for Nickelby is small potatoes compared to what you might call Doc's usual research trips." Boney fingers bracketed the phrase in quotes.

Fitzpatrick missed the inference. "That's what I mean, a nice guy like Doc, he might be in way over his head. What if the wife sent that cage fighter security freak? I feel guilty enough about not going after Nickelby on my own. And with you still in withdrawal—"

"Stop saying that. I'm right as goddamn rain," Tomlinson snapped, then calmly pulled up a chair. "So it's official, you can't go, huh? Doc will understand. He knows about that mess you got into a while back."

At a certain age, bitterness is buffered by amusement. "Which mess? Colombia dropped the charges two years ago, but *that* story didn't make the headlines, of course. The government still won't release my damn boat—the Chris Commander I rebuilt with twin Cats and blowers. And the Bahamas, after all the *plata* I put on the deck off Nassau, they flagged my goddamn passport. That's where I was, at the consulate in Miami, and they, this guy with a smirk and a pressed suit, he laughed in my face. I'm a marked man in every country a Spanish galleon made landfall. Florida's the worst, no surprise there, which is why . . ." He reached for the briefcase, then decided, "I'll get to that in a bit."

Tomlinson nudged him along. "Most pissed off wives go to an attorney. I still don't understand why she called you."

"Probably because she spent twenty years trying to change Leonard and suddenly he wasn't the man she'd married. Why does it always surprise them? Becca, that's her name. She blames me for her husband screwing around with a college girl, I guess, then the two of them bugging out. Like I'd planned the whole shebang."

"His wife should know better. There would be no such thing as adjunct professors if it wasn't for the perks," Tomlinson said. "It happens all the time. Gotta tell you, amigo, so far Prof. Nickelby doesn't sound like the straight arrow you described."

"No shit. For years he was an officious jerk to anyone, kids, old retired farts, it didn't matter if they owned metal detectors. Treasure hunters, especially the few old pros around, we despised

----

the guy. Called him Nick the Prick. Then all of a sudden"—Fitzpatrick shrugged—"he went middle-aged crazy, I guess. Or woke up one morning, saw his wife, and packed his shit. It was a day or so after he vamoosed that I realized I'd been robbed."

Tomlinson said, "Do you know anything about the girl?"

"Just that she was his student for a while. Only found one old photo—Lydia Johnson, a skinny, mousy little thing. She's about as interesting as a paper bag. Which makes sense, at least. Nickelby—I'd describe the little dweeb as about the same. That bastard chased me off more wrecks than bad weather."

"His wife has to have something against you. Or on you. Let's have it, Fitz. Offering a government suit a bribe would've been just plain damn stupid, so it can't be that."

"Hell, I would've had I thought it might have . . . But, no, he approached me back around Christmas. Called me on my cell and asked if we could meet privately. That was surprise number one. Then hinted around like he might be willing to cut a deal if we could just speak confidentially."

"Geezus, you didn't fall for a rookie gambit like that." Tomlinson chewed at a strand of hair, readying himself for the worst.

"Pissed me off, is what it did. Sure, I figured it was some kind of sting, but he kept after me, so we took a boat ride. Then another and another. That's how he finally convinced me. Money problems, sick of being paid jack shit for years of work, and he'd lost a promotion to a younger guy who's now his asshole boss. Oh, and his car. He bitched about driving the same shitty Volvo while

- - - - - - - - - - -

us treasure hunters were out getting rich. That part cracked me up, it really did."

Fitzpatrick moved his briefcase from the floor to his lap. "Anyway, I finally listened to his offer. Nickelby said he'd fix the papers while I dove a couple of off-limits spots. In return, I'd teach him the treasure diving business—open up my files, so to speak. That, plus half of whatever we recovered."

"And you fell for it."

"Goddamn, give me some credit. I did a couple of test runs first. Let him find a few trash coins I'd seeded, then some pot shards and one of my best ale bottles. You've seen them—black glass, torpedo-shaped. Fairly rare. They're mostly from the sixteen hundreds. That's what sealed it. You know that look an amateur gets? A kind of greedy-assed glow. Man, I could tell the hook was set. After that, we hit a couple of real spots and split the profits from a nice little bronze cannon and a couple of Dutch coins. The deal seemed to be working out okay—until he took a powder. Among other things."

"Another government suit run amok."

"I know, I know."

"Small people with power, man, never trust them. Now Nickelby will either narc you to the feds if he ends up in court or sell your GPS numbers to the competition. Or . . . Wait, is he any good? Could be he'll dive the spots himself."

"You haven't heard the worst. The idiot took his laptop but left behind a hard drive with enough evidence to put us both in jail.

All the details and numbers in a row, plus pictures—X-rated, I guess—of his new girlfriend."

"Oh shit."

"Yep, his wife found it." Fitz rubbed his forehead. "That's how she knew we'd worked out a secret deal. It must've taken her a week to figure out the password, and that's what she's threatening to do—put us both in jail if I don't . . . Well, I'm sick to death worrying about it. Take a look at these before you hear the rest."

He opened the briefcase and placed several coins on the lab table. They were in plastic sleeves, clumps of three or four fused together by centuries of black oxidation. This indicated the metal was silver, not gold.

Tomlinson fetched a magnifying glass. A light brought a single coin into focus. It was heavy, round but imperfect, the die hand-struck, a king's head in profile. Date, 178-something, the last digit indecipherable.

"You and Nickelby found these?"

"Just me, almost a year ago. I didn't get a reply from Seville that confirmed the source until a few days after Nickelby split. Thank god, or all the details would've been in my logbook. These coins could have changed American history, and that's no bull."

They'd been commissioned in 1782 by King Charles the Third, he explained, to fund Spain's holdings in the Americas. About thirty million dollars' worth out of the Mexico City mint.

"That's by today's bullion prices. Most believe the manifest left Vera Cruz on a single ship, the *El Cazador*, which sank in the

----

winter of 1784. If she'd made New Orleans, Spain wouldn't have gone broke and ceded Louisiana back to France. Think about how that would've changed everything."

Tomlinson's brain raced ahead. There would have been no Lewis and Clark Expedition, no Louisiana Purchase, no Hollywood, no Bogart-and-Bacall classics, or even a decent cup of Starbucks coffee. In his mind, the domino effect erased seventeen U.S. states and a lot of good times. Goodbye Yellow Brick Road, an entire generational hoedown from Berkeley to Boulder, a golden era of hopeful discord that in recent years had withered like a flower, the movement poisoned by a self-righteous myopia that had once infected only the enemy.

"There would've had to have been a bright side," he mused.

"Huh?"

"Had that ship not sunk. For instance, Texas shit-kickers would need a visa if they wanted to breed with human beings. But, yeah, changed history. For sure."

Fitz ignored that by producing another sleeve of coins. "Check out the die marks on the one you're holding. These and a bunch more could be yours if you help dig me out of this mess."

On the coin's obverse side was a Spanish coat of arms braced by pillars. Or cannon. "How deep?"

"The *El Cazador*? Too deep for nitrox, about three hundred feet, but don't worry. That wreck's already been picked clean. A few years back, a Louisiana shrimper snagged his nets and winched up a few hundred of these. All black as tar, of course—I'm not

----

making this up. Nets full of what they figured were seashells and junk. The captain 'bout had a heart attack when he realized what he had."

The captain had played it straight and sort of smart, Fitz added, but not smart enough. He'd hired a crack maritime attorney before contacting the feds—and lost more than half of what he finally dredged up for being so damn honest.

"What the pinheads don't realize is, pros like me have discovered more important wrecks than all the archaeologists combined. And we'd keep sharing information if they'd just cut us a fair deal." Fitz had a whole speech on the subject. Lots of bitterness based on personal experience. It went on for a while.

Tomlinson returned the coins to their sleeves before interrupting. "But these didn't come from . . . where?"

The man's eyes sharpened. "The *Cazador*'s sister ship, and the letter I mentioned confirmed it. The so-called experts didn't believe she existed because they were too lazy to do their own research—that's always been the difference between us. I spent most of a decade in Seville learning to read and write archaic Spanish. The sister ship, I call her *La Escaponda* because that's what she was doing, I think—'running for her life.'"

"The Runaway," Tomlinson said, a loose translation of the name.

"Your Spanish is pretty good. What I think happened is . . ."

Fitzpatrick had a theory. The captain of the sister ship had seen the *El Cazador* go down in a hurricane. By the time he'd saved his

----

own ship it was too late to help, but not too late to change course and steal the manifest.

"Picture the poor bastard and his crew, barely alive, eating wormy salt beef but carrying a ton of newly minted coins. How his mind might view the situation, you understand. If neither boat arrived in New Orleans, the big shots in Madrid might figure they both sank in the storm. Risky, but the chance of a lifetime, right? So he and his crew said screw it and headed for the islands to live like rich men."

A few hundred miles later, the sister ship sank, too. Damage from the first storm or another hurricane came along—or it was captured by privateers, not uncommon in those days.

"I know where she is," Fitz said. *"La Escaponda."*

"The Bahamas," Tomlinson said in a flat tone.

The treasure hunter tried not to react. "I've got forty years of hard work recorded in that logbook. Trips all over the Caribbean where I dragged magnetometers, and marked wrecks that I didn't have time to dive. Or didn't have the money. Or the weather went to shit. Wrecks, some of them, I matched up later with the archives in Seville. You wouldn't believe the potential dollar amount if I told you."

"I'd believe it but don't care. Will Nickelby know what he's reading?"

Maybe not. Fitz had his own system when it came to writing GPS numbers. All salvage pros did, just like fishermen. Add or

----

subtract a linchpin number in case someone peeks over your shoulder.

"The coordinates will confuse him unless he figures it out. He might. Nickelby's smart. And he's dealt with enough archaic Spanish to understand some of my notes. It's my sketches he'll focus on first: the way reefs lie, the trees and the towers, the anchorages—you know how triangulation works. The less important sites, I didn't bother writing everything in code. That's where I think we'll find him."

Tomlinson was running out of patience. "Where exactly? Are you talking about the whole damn Caribbean Sea?"

"Yeah . . . no . . . a couple of places. Islands, shallow-water areas with promising spots not far from shore. He'll try those first. Don't worry, I'll stay in touch by phone."

That did it. "The hell you will. The cell towers down there suck. It's text messages only, unless you're close to Nassau. And that's on a good day. Doc's already poking around Andros because that's what you suggested, and I'm supposed to fly out tomorrow. *If* I fly out. Damn it, Fitz, I'm not dumb. You want to use us like chess pieces to block Nickelby from finding something. The question is, what?"

Fitzpatrick evaded by repeating a tired old maxim—*The first rule of treasure hunting is to trust no one*—then withdrew into himself while Tomlinson's hollow, haunted blue eyes probed the man's cranial bone.

Truth is multilayered. It is tangled in roots and often caged in lies. Patterns of thought formed in Tomlinson's brain as a topo map. There were contours of varying intensity.

"You're worried about Nickelby," he said gently. "Worried that someone might kill him to get your logbook. No . . . to get their hands on something else. Talk to me, Fitz."

The older man stared at the floor. "Him and the girl, if they're still together, they might start around the Elutheras, but probably Andros, the southern tip, like I said on the phone. There're a couple of promising wreck sites there. Not great, but okay. That much of what I told you is true. Hopefully, Nickelby stops there. But I doubt it."

Tomlinson pictured white sand and ballast rock, a remote expanse of turquoise water. "Before the Bahamas flagged your passport, you were onto something really big, weren't you?"

The treasure hunter in Fitzpatrick sidestepped that, too, saying, "There's more I left out. Don't get pissed. Along with my logbook, he stole something else—three primo Spanish coins. Very, very valuable. So, in a way, you're right."

"Right about what you found?"

"I'm talking about the coins. Nick the Prick stole a gold doubloon that could get them both killed."

- - - - - - - - - - -

4

Tamara's boat was an Abaco dory, 18 feet of lapstreak with a heart-shaped transom and enough sail to haul sponge divers offshore. That's what the boats had been built to do before the hurricane of '29 wiped out the sponges and most of the local fleet.

"Gas is expensive," Tamara remarked, sculling away from the dock. The sun had just topped the trees. "I like sailing better anyway. And if what you're researching is true 'bout the sound of boat engines and sharks, probably safer, you think?" She watched Ford nod, then continued, "I've kept this 'un in fine shape since my gran'daddy passed along. If you're hungry, there's sliced mangoes, water, beer, and such in the cooler. Mullet jerky, too. Made it myself."

The sculling oar required both hands. She lifted, tilted the blade, and took another long stroke, before saying, "The beer—I brought two bottles, which I'll have to charge extra for. That's up to you."

Tamara's attitude was aloof but congenial. She possessed a lifetime of local knowledge and navigated with languid confidence. Even so, Ford paid attention to landmarks as they sailed, asking the names of coral banks and channels to fix them in memory while, overhead, frigate birds soared.

Wind-sheared mangroves flattened aft. The sky settled around them blending into a horizon of saline air and heat, a jade desert without quadrants.

He slid closer to the helm and watched the compass. Questions about the Cuban-sounding man who'd asked about Nickelby could wait until he had Tamara's full confidence.

It's the way his mind worked. No matter where, or who you're traveling with, always, always be prepared to find your way back alone. If someone was tailing the archaeologist, he—or they— might first try to derail any competitors. Unlikely, but possible, depending on the value, real or imagined, of Fitzpatrick's logbook.

Which is why Ford had to wonder who else she had told about a biologist with papers from the Bahamian government?

Miles offshore, still inside the reef, Tamara swung into the wind, saying, "I'll use the oar from here."

"We're close to where you saw the dinosaur bones?" He had put on his picnic persona, easygoing, having fun with a claim he knew couldn't be true.

"I hear that smile in your tone," she replied. "Give me a few minutes, Mister Scientist, then maybe you can explain what it is I saw."

They had talked on the long sail out. She was a certified dive master thanks to a government program that had fast-tracked her and a dozen other Bahamian women. In a nation where seventy percent of females never learn to swim, they were newbies in a business dominated by men. A grant had financed her little dive shop, but finding good spots to dive had been left to her.

Tamara was determined to excel. That's what she'd been doing, out in her boat alone, drifting, using a glass bucket as a lens, when she spotted a pile of rubble where there shouldn't have been rubble. Among the litter was a long, curved object that resembled a photo she'd seen in *National Geographic*. A mastodon or woolly mammoth tusk, possibly—animals that, like dinosaurs, had not inhabited Andros, or any other island in the Bahamas. It had been too late in the day to risk a dive, so she'd been waiting for the right client and the right weather to return.

That was three weeks ago.

The sail came down. As a range marker, she fixated on an expanse of rock where seawort and a single battered palm grew. A twelve-foot paddle sculled them closer while the woman's eyes darted from the tree to coral heads below. Whitecaps outside the reef provided a triangulation point.

"This is it," she said after a while. "Hang on, sir, while I set the anchor. Wouldn't leave my boat untended most charters, but you seem to know what you're about."

Twice they had stopped at near-shore coral banks. Checkout dives. Ford had done just enough to prove he was competent, but not too much. He'd also taken a few samples from brain corals that showed symptoms of thermal bleaching disease.

She went over the side cradling the flukes of a Danforth. A trip buoy tracked her progress across the bottom until she reappeared. "It's shallow enough, have a look around first. After that, we'll use tanks if you don't think I was dreaming what I saw."

Ford tumbled backward into water. It was salt-dense, blueberry-tinted, clear, and twenty feet deep. Coral flamed with lavender fans and clouds of iridescent fish. A basin of white stood apart. Sand was thatched with the outline of what might be timbers beneath. Nature abhors straight lines. Scattered ballast rock confirmed the unexpected.

Impressive. No sonar gear, or GPS, yet the woman had put them directly over a remnant of shipwreck. He no longer doubted she'd seen something that resembled a prehistoric bone.

Back on the surface, he got his bearings. They were five miles from the southern tip of Andros Island. It was a barren archipelago that constituted land—a long swim if something went wrong. The silhouette of a vessel in the distance mitigated the sense of isolation. The vessel exited Jack Fish Channel and turned, possibly toward them. A plume of black smoke suggested heavy diesel engines. His attention shifted and zeroed in on the rubble scattered beneath his fins.

Tamara wore a baggy white dive skin with a hood over a T-shirt and shorts. A Japanese pearl diver came to mind, a dancer in a white gown, a fluid underwater ballet. Leg strokes, long, strong, her body a slow missile in ascent. No wasted effort, no pointless splashing, when, after separating for ten minutes, they compared notes on the surface. She was excitable, a woman who loved discovery.

"Yeah, man, didn't I tell you! This here's a wreck of some type or part of a litter trail. Could be we're the first to dive it. You see any beer cans or fishing lures?"

No, the area was pristine. An acre of sand dunes, the dunes spaced washboard-like between rocks and gardens of coral.

"You're good luck, that's what you are, sir. I would've heard the rumors if there was something worth diving in this area. That hurricane a few months back must've shifted the sand away. You see all the ballast rock? I didn't notice it first time I was here."

Ford, smiling, waved her closer. "I found it."

"Ballast rock?" Her expression brightened behind her dive mask. "Wait, you don't mean . . ."

"Exactly as you described. But it's not from a dinosaur or a mastodon, or anything else prehistoric. I can't figure out how the heck it got here, but, by god, it can't be anything else. Come on before I lose the spot."

Tidal current was deceptive, a steady force that would've swept them away had they been unaware. It flowed northeast over a mile of shoals, then spilled into a chasm twenty miles long and six thousand feet deep. The Tongue of the Ocean, the trough was called. In this current, next stop was Spanish Wells or Nassau—if sharks, tigers, and oceanic white tips didn't find them first.

She braced him on a series of bounce dives. Wedged beneath a litter of staghorn, there it was: a log of ivory curved like a sword. Ford clung to it and fanned away sand. The object was longer, heavier than a fence post, mossy with age and barnacle-encrusted on the pointed end. With a knife, he'd already scraped away enough patina to expose what might be scrimshaw but could be scars from a machete.

They surfaced. "It's an elephant tusk," he said.

She hooted with delight, then sobered. "Elephant? It can't be. Like from a circus? Not in these islands."

"From Africa," he said. "Not the whole animal, just the ivory. Could be Dutch or British, a ship headed for the States to do some trading, probably under sail because of all the ballast. Or a steamer, maybe. I doubt if there's anything really valuable, but—"

"Valuable enough," she laughed. "Come on."

For twenty minutes, their world glazed. Near the elephant tusk

----

were shards of glass that turned purple when exposed to the sun. Hogfish rooted among the detritus as they kicked away more sand. The underwater world wasn't silent. It was relentless motion and noise. Whales chirped from the distant depths, fish groaned an octave lower. A multitude of crustaceans crackled like a blazing fire. Gradually, Ford's radar broadened to include a diesel rumble he'd ignored too long.

He went up to check. The vessel he'd seen earlier was closer than expected, much closer, coming toward them at speed. It was the commercial variety, powered like an ocean-going tug and scarred by rough use as a barge. If someone in the wheelhouse didn't wake up—or sober up—it was on a collision course with the little sailboat.

Tamara surfaced nearby, whooping with laughter. "Looka what I found. We gotta mark this spot and get our tanks. See?" She held up a simple copper bracelet—it was open-ended, with Arabic-looking knobs, the patina jade green—then pushed her mask back, concerned by his expression.

"What's wrong?"

"Who are those idiots?"

She snapped out of her daze when she saw the trawler bearing down and the size of its wake. "Drunk bastards . . . Damn him . . . Or just dumb, stupid, mean. Hurry. We've got to get back and pull anchor or he'll swamp us for sure."

Ford grabbed her wrist. "We're safer here. He's bound to see your boat."

"That's the problem."

"You know who it is?"

"Swim for the shallows," she told him. "I've got to get back and free that anchor. He's crazy enough, he might stop and do worse when he sees you."

What the hell did that mean?

Tamara set off alone, her fins low, sleek like an otter. Ford followed, swimming on his side. The trawler was almost on them by then, the bow huge through his prescription dive mask. It had a high steel rail adorned with tire bumpers that banged against a rusted hull of white. SANDMAN, the name stenciled portside. The vessel's speed, its course, guaranteed what was about to happen.

"Tamara, goddamn it, come back here!"

Roaring diesels masked all sound.

Crawl-stroking, he went after the woman in earnest. After what seemed a long time, he almost caught her fin, missed her a second time, then got a grip on her ankle not far from where the dory sat prettily at anchor. By then, it was too late. He snatched her down and kicked toward the bottom expecting an explosive impact. Instead of steel crushing wood, they heard the dory's hull slam the surface after it went airborne, then what resembled the snap of a brittle tree as diesel engines thrummed overhead.

Wait—Ford used his open palm to communicate. Framed within her mask, the woman's eyes widened while the trawler's shadow blotted out the sunlight, then sailed past like a black cloud. On the surface, cresting waves awaited. From atop each was a view

----

of the trawler's stern. Drifting in the opposite direction, the dory had broken free. Its mast was a wild metronome battling to stay upright in the waves.

"Snapped my anchor line," she yelled and took off after the thing.

It is a common error, often fatal, to chase a drifting boat when land is nearby. Again, he caught her from behind. "Listen to me. Wait for the wake to settle down and let's see what she does in this tide."

"You crazy, man? We'd die out here all alone, and that fool sure isn't gonna help." She meant the trawler. A couple of men were up there in the wheelhouse looking back, maybe laughing, but already too far away from them to be sure.

"We could die chasing your boat, too, the way this tide's running. Maybe the anchor pulled loose. Give it a minute and let's watch. If you're convinced you can out-swim the tide and the wind, we'll both go. But we're not splitting up."

"I'm the dive master," she snapped. "It's my boat."

"And I'm your paying client. Wouldn't do your business much good to lose a client, now would it?"

As one, they watched the Abaco dory. Its lapstreaked hull was red, the mast black mahogany. The little vessel settled like a duck on rolling waves that pushed it away. An easterly trade wind turned the bow while the tide tractored it north toward the Tongue of the Ocean, where that ledge plummeted a mile deep.

"This is bad," she muttered after a few seconds. "We'll never

----

catch her. And god help us out here at night on that little bitty piece of rock. Local fishermen, they don't hardly never come this way."

The lone palm tree was suddenly half a mile away. The tide had swept them east at a different angle from the boat. They were drifting toward a rip line where the shallows transitioned to purple, then black. Wait much longer, they might not make it back to the only high ground for miles. Ford was about to say just that when the dory jolted, spun away from the wind . . . jolted again, then swung hard into the tide and stopped drifting.

"Maybe you are good luck," Tamara said, meaning he'd been right. The anchor had snagged another piece of bottom. They kicked along side by side, not leisurely, but not panicked either— until the anchor pulled free again. Wind caught the boat and pushed it away faster than the flowing tide.

Ford put his head down and swam. Below, through his mask, he saw sand funneling into a valley. An indigo crevice appeared. At the edge of the drop-off, a slow carousel of sharks awaited tidal effluvium. Reef sharks, a few black tips. In water this clear they ate fish, not mammals. But a thousand feet below, in the darkness, larger predators might be scanning the surface for larger prey.

He looked back only once. Tamara lagged far behind. At the boat's transom, he battled the current with his fins to slow the hull and waited for her to get a hand over the gumwale. She was breathing heavily.

"After you," he said.

- - - - - - - - - - -

"That was close, man. I don't think I'd have made on my own."

"You'd have managed."

She gazed down into the darkness before pushing her mask back. Whatever it was she mumbled was rushed and had the flavor of panic.

Ford searched beneath them, seeing only rays of sunlight. "What's the problem?"

"I don't like hanging here, that's all. No telling what's looking up at us. Diving's different. I'm like a fish if I know where the bottom is."

"It's always straight down," Ford replied. "Hop in, we've got to check for damage. I'll help you."

No need. Fear launched her over the side while he took his time and enjoyed the sensation of drifting above the abyss.

Aboard, they removed their gear. She opened bottles of water and thanked him too many times for slowing the boat enough for her to catch up. Her breathing had returned to normal, but her adrenaline was spiking, and she felt the need to explain.

"It's not often I get scared like that."

"I didn't notice."

"That supposed to make me feel better? I wasn't afraid exactly, it's just something got put into my head a long time ago. Wall dives, they don't bother me neither, but black water like this . . . It's because, well . . . Uh-oh." She got up and searched around her feet while patting the pockets of her baggy tunic. "The bracelet," she muttered, "I must've dropped it when I climbed in."

48

Ford watched her peer over the side. No way was she going after the thing.

"It's a normal response," he said. "Dark water scares everyone. Me included."

"Now you're lying to be nice. Damn it all—" On her knees now, she continued to search. And she kept talking. "I'm not making excuses. It's the way I was raised. I didn't learn to swim 'til high school. Move your feet for a sec."

He did. And he provided her an excuse by referencing the government program she'd mentioned.

"Stop pretending you understand because you don't. My grandma used to switch me if I went into water over my waist. Bathtub-deep, we call it. She said I had the ears. It's an expression here. *You got the ears, Tamarinda, don't make me cut a switch.* Meant I was destined to drown."

"Your ears look fine to me. Switch you, as in—"

"You know, whip me with a switch. That's the way it is on the islands. They tell children they got the ears so as to scare them away from deep water. Older folks can't swim—most of 'em anyway—so that's what they do."

"Only girls?"

She lifted a dive bag, moved his fins, still searching for the bracelet. "Everyone, the boys, most of them, too. Even the ones with daddies who fish for a living. Sounds silly, but what child doesn't believe what their grandfolks tell 'em? It's a story keeps getting passed down. *If a child's got the ears, he'll die eating sand.*

That's another expression. Everyone on these islands, we've all got some family member who drowned. Me, it was two cousins I hardly knew and my Uncle Oxley. Then my . . ." She left the sentence unfinished, with a sense of sadness. "Black water, it used to give me dreams."

For an instant, he got a glimpse of Tamara as a little girl. Timid, too big-boned to be pretty, but with a mind that was open and wanted more. And still wrestling with childhood demons, as most adults do.

The bracelet was gone. "Damn it," she said again, but several minutes later, as they checked the boat for damage.

T he mast was cracked. Under partial sail, it was sunset before they reached the channel to Congo Town and Mars Bay.

The long sculling oar came out. She'd been talkative on the trip back. Ford had learned more about Leonard Nickelby and the stranger who'd asked about him. He also knew where the trawler *Sandman* was moored when in port.

"Why you care about that? A lot of men on the island, they're jealous, that's all. Don't like the idea of women dive masters. They think the government gave us special treatment, so they play their little jokes to scare us out of the business."

Strangers who survive a near-death experience, imagined or not, are never again strangers. Ford used the bond to say, "He recognized your boat and you recognized who was steering. Tell me or not, it's up to you."

"The police won't do nothing, if that's what's on your mind. And you don't want to trade words with the man we saw up there laughing." She watched the biologist clean his wire-rimmed glasses. "Is that what's in your head? If it is, don't. It would be a dangerous thing to do, Mister Scientist."

Ford went silent to let her know he was waiting.

Ten minutes of silence was enough. "His name's Hubert Purcell, but Sandman's what everybody calls him. Even before he started running boats. What he did was . . . I . . . I've never told anybody this before. It's not like I've had a lot of men bothering after me in my life, so folks might not have believed—"

"I'll believe you," Ford said, already aware of the possibilities. Purcell, he suspected, was her ex, lover or husband, possibly the father of her child.

Wrong, but close.

"Sandman—Hubert—he wanted his way with me once. This was a year or so back, and I said no. Didn't let him touch me. Some men are the type to hold a grudge, but I really think what happened today was jealousy over what I do."

"Wanted? Or tried to force you?"

"Bullied me with words, that's all, when his idea of charm didn't work. He'd been drinking. Of course, he's always drinking, but he was drunker than usual. Hubert, what you don't understand about him is, he does dive trips on the side. That's how he

----

makes his living. No license, but tourists, a certain type, never bother to ask." She said this in a way that invited questions.

"Tourists like Dr. Nickelby?"

"The type that think they know everything there is about diving, yeah. Him and his girl, they chartered the *Sandman* 'cause they said a sailing dory was too slow for what they had in mind. And too small, is what they said, because they had a lot of gear. No sense arguing. The three of them had too much fun in the conga line that night."

There was no hint of jealousy in her voice. Ford abandoned the subject and asked if she had shared the same information with the Cuban-looking guy who'd come asking about Nickelby.

"Already said I didn't trust him—had kind of a cold, mean way, superior-acting, you know? Besides, I didn't find out who Dr. Nickelby hired until later. Tend bar at the Turtle Kraals, you hear just about everything there is to hear. Three full days, him and that girl were aboard Sandman's boat. I don't know where it is they went to dive. That part's strange. Captains usually got no reason to keep the information private, which might mean something to you."

It did. Ford said, "You need to involve the police or he'll run you out of business. At the very least, tell someone you trust. Your husband, maybe."

A bitter half laugh prefaced "This sort of thing, I can take care of myself. Promise you won't do nothing stupid?"

"Confront Hubert and another hard-assed local? No thanks. I'm not the type."

The biologist's easygoing manner tried to convince her while Tamara scrutinized his face. "I can't say I've ever met your type. You're a nice man, I think, but I've been wrong before. You also know a lot more about boats and diving than you let on. I wonder why that is?"

"I didn't say I wasn't a good swimmer."

"Not in words, maybe. More in a polite way so I'd feel like the expert. Which is sweet, I guess, unless you were being tricky. I don't like tricky." After a sharp look, she shrugged. "Either way, I've changed my mind. I'd be pleased to have that drink tonight when I finish work."

They were in range of a cell tower by then. His phone chimed. Instead of accepting her offer, he read a text message. She ignored him as if, yes or no, his answer made no difference, but said as he put the phone away, "Your wife's probably worried and I don't blame her. She back in Florida?"

"It's from a friend," he said, "a guy named Tomlinson. He and that treasure hunter I mentioned, they were supposed to rent a boat out of Cay Sal and sail north, but the Bahamian government won't let . . . Anyway, I'll get back with him later."

Tamara found this interesting. "A sailboat big enough to make a trip like that costs money. They rich, these friends of yours?"

"Tomlinson, probably—he wrote a best-selling book years ago.

Kind of a self-help philosophy thing for hippie types. The other guy, I've yet to meet a rich treasure hunter. What about you?"

"Answer him back while you can," Tamara said. She used her weight to thrust the dory toward a dock, several small boats visible in the distance. "We're close enough, I might also suggest you have one of those beers in the cooler. No charge."

As Ford dug through the ice, she added, "Open one for me, too. I wouldn't mind hearing more about that logbook."

- - - - - - - - - - -

5

F itzpatrick had been worried about Tomlinson, the abrupt
mood swings. After a break at the marina to watch the sunset, he began to feel more at ease. Mentioning the stolen
coins had softened Zonk's attitude, perhaps because he had
yet to hear the details about why Nickelby and the girl were
in danger.

Fried-fish sandwiches and a sociable lap around the docks
hadn't hurt either. Whatever the reason, the jittery hipster was
showing signs of his laid-back old self. This included the sort of
oddball remarks that had launched more than one of their drinking buddies toward the door.

"Since your birthday party," he told a woman who lived aboard an old cruiser, *Tiger Lilly*, "I've amended my précis on aging. The most beautiful women in the world are at least thirty-five because complexity takes time. But when it comes to dirty dancing, add a decade or two and save me a seat." A big grin. "What do you think?"

Oh, she loved it. Outrageous, what the hipster could say to women and get away with.

Then to a little Cuban named Figgie, "Fidel's dead, and your right to be a dumbass died with him. It's time to strap on your spikes and apply for a credit card."

In Key West? Anyone but Zonk, *pow*, a broken nose.

A true meth addict was incapable of insight or shifting gears. Fitz found the change reassuring. On the other hand, the hipster was known as a freaky clairvoyant to those who believed in such nonsense. Zonk had weathered many chemical storms and fooled many a cop. A test, Fitz decided, was in order. His financial future, maybe even his life, was on the line.

He waited until they'd returned to Ford's house. It was dark by then. The dog, a blockheaded retriever with yellow eyes, came and went without pausing to sniff a crotch or wag its tail. This provided an excuse to bring up medicine via a reference to veterinarians. Soon the door was open to all pharmaceuticals.

"Speaking of drugs, the one you told me about, the synthetic crap? Key West started an all-night clinic for those pathetic flake heads. No offense. You know that area off Duval near the old shrimp docks? I'm surprised a counselor would tell you a beer or two is okay after rehab."

"I would've kissed him right on the mouth," Tomlinson replied, getting up, another bottle of Hammerhead beer empty. "How about a couple more?"

Fitz was flummoxed. He grumbled an affirmative, not pleased with the test results thus far.

This time the hipster returned with glass mugs slick with ice and a nautical chart rolled under his arm. "To qualify for rehab, I would first have to be habilitated. Or is it habilitory? I'll look it up. Anyway, that horse threw the jockey years ago. What I did was, I kicked the habit the old-fashioned way—eight days of the shits and sweats, offshore, alone, on my boat. It was tolerable because no one could hear me . . . Well, let's just say truly savage noises are involved. The pathetic mewling that comes later is an embarrassment, so I stayed out two full weeks. The choice of music is important, of course. As you may remember, I've got quite the library aboard my boat. Vinyl, not that inferior iTunes shit."

"Cold turkey," Fitz said. "What sort of music?" It was an amateur attempt to assess stability while he pretended to rearrange his briefcase.

Tomlinson sweetened the set with Roy Orbison and waited. He was eager to return to the subject of the coins. Maybe the matter was more serious than Fitz had led them believe. If so, it was time to get the evening back on an even keel, but slowly. The

----

old treasure hunter had been spooked by too many questions early on.

The briefcase snapped closed. Fitzpatrick controlled the conversation while Tomlinson unrolled a chart of the Bahamas. "You don't have anything more detailed? You're pissed because I won't show you my private honey holes, then give me half the Western Hemisphere to work with."

"Just the fun regions," Tomlinson said, "Florida to the Caribbean Rim." Glass beakers were used to anchor the chart before he made room. "Ever notice how beautifully the islands flow from Bimini to the Gulf of Venezuela? A thousand miles like petrified vertebrae, every bone awash in blue saline."

"Blue, sure. Who hasn't?"

"All too few people, I fear. There's a mysterious pattern in this world, my man, and I'm starting to piece it together. A sort of repetition of form that suggests—"

"Get out of my way," Fitz said. "I'm going to need my glasses again."

"Ah, sarcasm. You doubt? Then explain this." A skinny finger traced the sweep of islands. "A flying dragon. Its skeletal remains, if you let your eyes blur. See how the tail curves west toward Colombia? Grand Bahama forms the head, and Andros . . . I guess Andros would be the beard."

"Dragons don't have beards," Fitz countered. "My daughter and grandkids live near Disney World, so don't tell me. I've seen dragons. Here's what we should be talking about."

The briefcase snapped open. A manila envelope was produced. "I put together a file on Nickelby and the girl. If you're going to find them, you need to know what they look like. There's a bunch on him. Next to nothing on her. She blends in like those paintings people buy to cover a hole in the wall."

Fitz paraphrased what the envelope contained. "High school, she graduated with honors, then did a year and a half of college where Nickelby taught. That's it. Nothing after that on social media, except—get this—she was a member of her high school metal detector club. That's where I found the picture. Isn't that a kick? A pot hunter and Nick the Prick. Lydia Johnson, twenty-six years old." He spun the envelope onto the table. "Leaf through it and I'll fill in the blanks."

Tomlinson relegated the envelope to an outboard area of the desk. "Show me where you found the coins or we can spend the evening comparing shark scars."

More grumbling, but a nautical chart—any chart—turns a treasure hunter into a hapless moth near a flame. The older man locked onto familiar shapes and clusters. "A thousand miles of coral," he mused. "Almost every one of those islands I've either been ashore or close enough to piss on the trees. Some too salty for trees to grow. Like this area right here."

Fitz indicated Cay Sal Bank east of Cuba and a massive shoal to the north. Three no-name Spanish galleons had gone down there in the 1500s, he said. It wasn't unusual for clerks in Seville to reference ships only by type because the names were repetitive,

----

always saints or kings, so were sometimes changed for the duration of a voyage.

"This is Hogsty Reef," he said, "twelve square miles of coral atoll. In 'ninety-six, we lost two of our three boats there to Hurricane Lili. Broke my arm and my nose, too, but that's okay. I'm still good-looking." A grin formed while his memory reached back. "The next day we rescued a dozen Haitians who were adrift. Yep, they would've died if it wasn't for our shitty luck. Now that you mention it, I guess things in this world do have a way of working out."

A good man, Tomlinson thought, and let him talk. Fitz's stories were always footnoted with details acquired over decades. Lots of personal asides and jargon familiar only to treasure hunters. Cartagena Bay, Port-au-Prince, Salinas Reef, the Berry Islands. Hunting treasure was an obsession, with many landfalls and close calls that blended history with hydraulics and mechanical expertise. The man truly knew his shit.

Finally, Fitz got around to saying, "Nickelby and the girl probably flew to Nassau first—most tourists, it's the easiest way—then worked their way here." His finger moved to Andros, one hundred and twenty miles off Florida, then east to the Exumas. "There are several shallow-water sites I didn't bother to disguise in my logbook. Nickelby might've found a couple already. But the spot I'm worried about most is—" Reluctantly, his finger stopped south of Eleuthera. "It's an unnamed island close to here. I'm

----

talking about a multimillion-dollar glory hole if he figures out my code. Your base of operations would have to be out of here."

The man was referring to Cat Island, a long, narrow spine of land with a boot at the end like Italy.

Tomlinson had to restrain himself. Fitzpatrick had found something big. "Perfect. I'm tight with a woman who was born there. It's like God's stamp of approval, you know? Way, way back, as I wrote in my book—apparently—a waterfall doesn't mean a river has no destination."

The treasure hunter didn't like the sound of that at all. "God-damn it, speak English. You can't tell anybody about this, especially some woman you slept with. I don't care if she's your best friend's sister and her father's a priest. Not one word, understand?"

This, in Tomlinson's view, was another green light. Not only had he slept with the woman, there was a family connection. Sorta. She was the daughter of a man who had conned his way through the Caribbean and sown a lot of wild seed. At least one seed had rooted on Cat Island and produced the woman in question.

"You ever meet Tucker Gatrell?" Tomlinson asked.

"What's that tricky old bastard have to do with the price of bait? He's dead, so who cares?"

"He was Doc's uncle."

"I know, and it's still hard to believe they were related . . . Hold on, here." A long look of suspicion followed. "The answer is

----

no—especially if the woman is connected with Tucker in some way. What don't you understand about you can't tell a damn soul?"

"Just a thought." Tomlinson returned his attention to the chart. "Maybe Cat Island is where I should start. Is there a big-money marina there where Nickelby might try to sell your coins?"

Fitzpatrick said nope, it was all farmers and fishermen because the cruise ship casino monsters hadn't discovered the place yet. Then he finally took the bait.

"Know what galls me more than anything?"

"Trusting people?"

"For Christ's sake, pay attention. What galls me is, I'm paying for that suit's vacation. For all I know, he's already gambled my money away, him and his new squeeze. That little prick shacking up in some thousand-bucks-a-night resort."

"I don't remember you saying he swiped your credit cards."

"I'm talking about my damn coins. You're right. If he hasn't sold them, he will. I was a fool to fall for his story. But a guy as straight as him? You know? I never saw it coming. Way too shrewd for an academic stiff."

"Could've been the girl," Tomlinson suggested. He opened the envelope and let the man talk.

Nickelby had finalized the con by calling Fitz with what he claimed was last-minute insider information. State cops, he said, had been assigned to raid the houses of three suspected night-hawks. *Nighthawk* was trade jargon for divers who scavenged wrecks illegally. Maybe Fitz was on the list, maybe not, but

----

Nickelby insisted he had less than an hour to move anything shady to a safe haven. Afterward, Fitzpatrick was supposed go back to bed and pretend to be surprised when the cops showed up.

"That was around seven on a Sunday morning," Fitz said. "He could've been watching my house with the phone to his ear, for all I know. If he was, he got quite a show. Less than an hour, Jesus—I went banging into walls, throwing shit in a duffel bag. Then I slammed the goddamn safe on my hand. Look at this mess." His fist sprouted five bruised fingers. "Damn door has to weigh two hundred pounds easy. Why'd I buy his bullshit? Because I figured his ass was on the line, too. Thank god, my wife was spending the week with her sister."

If Nickelby wasn't viewing it all from a window, he was somewhere close enough to watch Fitz stagger around his backyard looking for a hiding place. The high foliage of a poinciana tree was a good spot for the duffel bag. He'd used rope and a ladder. His best items, though, the logbook and three prized coins, were worthy of extra effort. Those went into a waterproof bag, double-layered, then into a crab trap attached to a Styrofoam buoy.

"I love soft-shelled crab," he said. "I sunk the trap in the canal behind my house with some other traps. Figured it was the safest spot in the world."

The cops didn't show. Fitz had checked his hidey-holes visually but didn't retrieve his goods until after dark the next day.

"I'd locked the ladder in my van—that's why Nickelby didn't get the duffel bag. The little priss probably never climbed a tree in

----

his life. But the crab trap, I almost vomited when I saw my bag was gone. Him and the girl had probably already left on their island vacation, all expenses paid, by then. You know the rest."

"What are the coins worth?"

"A lot."

"Have it your way." Tomlinson began rolling up the chart.

"Okay. But you can't write any of this down. Just listen."

The most valuable was a gold Tricentennial Royal doubloon struck in 1714. The others were silver, off the *Atocha*, from back when Fitz was working with Mel Fisher. A pair of eight-ounce Spanish reales with near-perfect die marks. Ree-AL, he pronounced the word.

Doubloons were gold. Reales were silver. A simple demarcation.

Fitz said, "At auction, those would go for—"

"Auction doesn't matter," Tomlinson cut in. "How much on the street? A state narc like Nickelby will have a list of black market buyers."

"Oh . . . minimum, twelve, maybe thirteen grand apiece. They'd retail for three times as much. That doesn't include the Tricentennial, of course. Only four of those are thought to exist." After a pause for effect, he added, "But I guarantee there are at least five, and he stole one of them. A year ago, a Tricentennial sold at Sotheby's for half a million. Four hundred and eighty-five thousand, to be exact. Look it up."

How the hell had Fitzpatrick gotten his hands on that?

Tomlinson played it cool. "You're luckier than you realize."

"Luck like that I can live without."

"The short-term picture, amigo. Think about it. You might be financing Nickelby's trip, but not for more than what he gets for the silver coins. A buyer with thirteen thousand in cash wouldn't be too hard to find. But half a million? That could take months, even years—as you probably found out when you tried to sell the thing."

Dead serious, Fitzpatrick shook his head. "I'm not that stupid. If word got out I had a gold Tricentennial, finding me would've been worth the price of a plane ticket from anywhere in the world. *You* think about it. They'd beat the information out of me, then kill me. You don't know as much about treasure hunters as I thought."

"Because it was stolen?"

"Because I found it."

"Found the coin or—"

"Both. A wreck people have been looking for three hundred years. I think it hit the same reef that sunk the *El Cazador*'s sister ship in 1784."

Fitz was satisfied with Tomlinson's reaction, which was *Holy shit*. But the hipster was also confused. "Then why only one gold Tricentennial? No, wait, you said four were known to exist."

"The others can be traced back to Vera Cruz, a mountain area where they were minted—stolen, most likely, by some poor bastard who worked there. Where the ship went down—" Again, his finger tapped an area near Cat Island. "Well, there's a reason I only did one quick dive."

"Too deep?" Tomlinson was thinking about Nickelby, an amateur diver.

"No. Thirty feet, max, on a ledge that drops down damn near a mile. Sharks were the problem. I've never seen so many in my life. And it lies off an island where the people aren't exactly friendly. But if Nickelby flashes that coin around, sharks are the least of his worries—and even a lying thief doesn't deserve to be murdered just for being dumb. I planned to fill you in after we got to the Bahamas. That's why you've got to—"

Tomlinson, preoccupied, motioned for silence. "Hang on a sec," he said. "I've got to check on the dog."

He went outside and texted Ford.

6

F ord read the message and was pleased on a perverse level by the content. The search for Leonard Nickelby had been a pleasant diversion. Now that he knew the girl's name—Lydia Johnson—the task had an unexpected edge.

He replied, *Tell Fitz no more surprises. Bring my mail.*

The phone, ringer off, went into a tactical bag suspended from a hook. He'd found a comfortable hammock with a starlit view of the docks. The trawler *Sandman* was there, stern to the seawall, between a derelict boat and the quay. Dark windows framed the wheelhouse and the helm, electronics dark within.

Turn his head, the view changed. The road to Mars Bay was limestone, a single lane along the beach. A distant strand of party lights marked a shed-sized restaurant—plywood, propane stove, beer buried in ice. Reggae music was amplified by a massive speaker in the middle of the road. Volume had increased in proportion to beer sales. No car traffic. Only people, animated silhouettes, fewer and fewer as time passed, until only drunks and those with something to celebrate remained.

Hubert Purcell, owner of the trawler, was among them. His partner—deckhand, more likely—had walked the same direction after rigging sloppy spring lines and pretending to mop the deck. Last call was midnight, probably later. Tamara had said the same was true at the Turtle Kraals Café.

This gave Ford almost two hours. He believed himself to be a patient man, which was true if he had something to occupy his time. An article on brain corals, "Meandroid Tissue Integration," and a flashlight, provided a diversion until the music was loud enough.

He crossed the road, stepped aboard, and went up the ladder as if he owned the boat. He could have. The cabin wasn't locked, keys dangled from twin ignitions. His weight activated a bilge pump below. A watery three-second discharge sounded like a cow pissing—no need to locate the main battery switch after that. The *Sandman* was powered up, ready to go.

Wearing gloves, he closed the curtains and used the same flashlight. A red lens preserved night vision. Above the helm was an electronics cabinet—old equipment jury-rigged, tangled wires, and tape. The Garmin GPS chart plotter was the size of a small

- - - - - - - - - - -

TV and new enough to contain a mini SD memory card. The SD card, in a converter sleeve, slipped easily into Ford's laptop. A default Garmin firewall was breached by software created by an agency Ford had worked for—and sometimes still did.

The download would take several minutes. He used the time to search. Bags of groceries told him Hubert and the mate would soon leave on another trip. Possibly tonight. Cabinets contained nothing unexpected, including haphazard entries and a lot of empty pages in the vessel's logbook.

The most recent was in pencil, four days ago: *Prof & Lidee. $$$.* A number was written to the right, area code 242, a Bahamian exchange.

Professor Nickelby and his girlfriend had purchased a phone locally, apparently, before paying top dollar to charter the *Sandman.*

Ford photographed the page, and a few others. When the download was complete, he used a scrubber program to delete all waypoints on the GPS chart plotter. *Waypoints* were Hubert Purcell's private entries. They marked favorite fishing and wreck locations he had saved electronically but hadn't bothered to log in writing.

In the charter business, GPS numbers are considered monetary assets. Ford had just stolen Purcell's life savings and deposited them in his personal account.

The SD card went back into the Garmin. Curtains were re-opened, cabinets closed. A photo taken upon entry confirmed everything was as he'd found it. The odor of diesel, foul ice, an

----

ashtray, trailed him to the door. And something else . . . a chalky bacterial stink he should have recognized but didn't take time to process.

He closed his bag and left.

At the Turtle Kraals Café, Tamara was behind the bar with a mop, lights dimmed, but still a few stragglers slamming dominoes under the palms. Her aloofness suggested she'd been awaiting his arrival but didn't want the locals to know.

"You gentlemen carry yourselves on home," she warned the men, "lest I tell your wives when I see 'em at church." As proof, she killed the music. Ford kept his distance until the stragglers had been displaced by the murmur of waves, frogs, an east wind off the sea.

When she acknowledged him, it was by speaking loud enough for the shadows to hear. "Last call, sir. Kitchen's closed, but we do have two kinds of beer. Kalik is what most visitors like, but some like Sands. New to the islands. It's very nice."

Tamara looked heavier in shorts and an apron, not fashionable, but confident, leaving no doubt who was in charge. Nothing like the frightened girl he'd gotten a glimpse of earlier in the day.

"A six-pack to go, I guess. Is there someplace I can—"

"Can't drink it here," she replied. Then, after making change, handed him a sack, close enough to speak privately. Her murmured directions were followed by, "Give me fifteen minutes."

She didn't want to be seen with him. Why? The city of Nassau aside, Bahamian whites, blacks, Asians, East Indians, and every possible combination, had intermingled since British land grant days and the collapse of slavery. Isolation had funneled most rurals into one small church or another. That bond, passed through generations, had resulted in an amicable tolerance, even a harmony, that Ford had observed in few other places in the world.

Perhaps a jealous husband was the problem.

The beach was through the trees, on the island's windward side. There was a picnic table and a fire pit, probably where Leonard Nickelby, a nerd reborn, had led a conga line. Ford didn't open the sack until Tamara was sitting across from him. She wore a fresh white blouse and slacks. The forethought this required was touching. It also demanded a peremptory approach. He asked about her child, and mentioned his own children, a subterfuge that hinted at him having a wife.

"Don't you worry about my personal affairs," she said. "I'm here to discuss what we found . . . Marion." Saying it for the first time amused her. "A pretty name, sure is, but somehow it just doesn't feel right." She removed two bottles, opened one, then the other, while deciding. "Think I'll stick with calling you sir."

That quickly, all subtext of seduction was neutralized.

"Call me Doc. I want to show you something." He opened his laptop. "Is it okay if I sit next to you?"

"Doc . . . sorta fits the way you are," she said, scooching over to make room even as she warned, "but not too close. On this island, a pigeon coos and every dog for miles starts barking. Understand? *Sip-sip*, is what we call gossip, and tote the news is what folks love to do. Now"—the computer brightened her hazel eyes—"what did you find? Something about elephant ivory, I hope."

No, he had screenshots captured from the *Sandman*'s chart plotter. There were a dozen, which he wanted Tamara to view in reverse chronological order. He opened the first. It was a Google Earth–type chart overlaid with lat/long lines that had been recorded this morning.

"Does this look familiar?"

After a second, she banged her bottle on the table harder than necessary. "You had no right. You didn't tell me you were carrying a GPS because you knew I wouldn't allow it. That's a picture of where we anchored when—"

"It's not mine. It's from a commercial chart plotter. Take a closer look."

The Garmin had been programmed to track *breadcrumbs*. These were dotted lines that traced a vessel's course on the chart plotter's display screen. After the near collision, *Sandman* had continued west, then south to a seamount that nearly breached six thousand feet of water—but only after Hubert Purcell had marked where the dory had been anchored. A solitary red diamond served as the icon.

Tamara used her finger without touching the screen. "That's

----

my wreck, where we were diving"—the date stamp caught her attention—"at the exact same time that fool just about swamped us. If it wasn't you who marked this spot, then it had be—"

"That's right," Ford said.

She faced him no longer angry, just serious. "Where'd you get this picture? No . . . how did you get it. I know darn well Hubert Purcell didn't invite you aboard his boat, and . . . Wait—" Her tone and expression changed. "Something tells me you went and did what you promised you wouldn't. Did something stupid, and I'd be a fool to ask."

Ford didn't bother with pretense. "I've got some earlier shots from when Nickelby and the girl chartered the *Sandman*. The dates seem to match anyway. I don't know these islands. You do. I'd appreciate your opinion on—"

"Hold it right there. Hubert finds his GPS missing, you know where he's gonna come, don't you? Straight to me. He saw us out there diving today, man." She shushed Ford's attempt at a denial. "Those papers of yours, they had the Crown imprint made with one of those"—she flexed her hand as if using an embossing stamp—"so they aren't fake. That much I know. The Crown's approval, it *means* something in the Bahamas. People from the States wouldn't understand, so maybe what you did was . . . *Legal*'s not the word . . . *authorized* . . . Maybe you are, but I'm the one he'll come looking for."

"Fine," Ford said. "I want you to introduce us."

It scared her. This scientist, so calm as her boat drifted away,

----

had also wanted her to believe he was a novice diver. Now this. "You're up to something," she said. "Why are you really here?"

The man's puzzlement was genuine. "I told you."

"Not the part about stealing Hubert's GPS, you didn't, and using me for bait. I don't want any trouble with the law. Especially where a man—you, maybe—could get hurt. I won't tolerate violence."

"You think I . . . No, you're confusing two issues. Purcell could've killed us today. You're afraid of him, right? You can't go to the police even though he's trying to ruin your business. So I came up with something that might help us both. No guarantees, but first let's stick to the—" He angled the laptop so she had a better view. "These dotted lines are water he covered over the last week or so. His boat did a lot of circling in shoal areas. Even if they had trolling lines out, that makes no sense. And why would Nickelby want to travel seventy miles east to dive when it would've been easier to charter a boat out of . . ." The biologist lifted his wire glasses and squinted, suddenly pleased with something. "Cat Island. I'll be darn."

"What about it?"

"An odd coincidence, that's all. I've got a cousin—that's what she claims anyway—who grew up on Cat Island. She reminds me of you in a lot of ways."

Tamara pushed the computer away and started to get up. "I hope she's been luckier in life than some of us born on Andros. I

- - - - - - - - - - -

believe our conversation is done here, Doc, or Marion, or whatever your real name is."

"Hold on, it's true. I had an uncle who—well, he doesn't matter now—but a few years back this woman—his daughter, it turns out—she showed up at my door and—"

"That's not the part I don't believe. Use your cousin if you need bait to put Hubert in jail—I want nothing to do with it. I came here expecting to talk about my wreck, how the elephant tusk got there, but you tricked me into—"

"Tamara, at least hear me out." Ford's voice was soft, very low, oddly calming. He waited until she was seated again. "Let me explain something. I want to help you, not hurt Hubert Purcell. There are ways to change a man's behavior that don't include threats, jail, whatever it is you picture. If you're protecting him for a reason, well, I'm just going to come out and ask. Is he the father of your child?"

This was an insult that also struck her as funny. "Sandman?" She took a sip of her beer as if to wash the image out of her head. "You sure don't think much of me to say such a thing. Of course, you didn't have to meet Hubert to steal his GPS or you'd know better."

Ford focused in a way that to her was better than an apology. "I figured he was the reason you didn't want us to be seen together. Or your husband. That's why I said to invite him if—"

"I wish you'd drop that subject," she said, oddly terse. "I already

----

told you how the sip-sip gossip spreads here. Go off with a tourist this late at night? That's something a lady wouldn't do. Besides, one of the fellas at the domino table, he's minister at our church. But Sandman? My god." Her frown faded and she laughed.

"Tell me about Purcell."

"He's an idiot. What else you want to know?"

"Details. You'll understand, if you give me a chance. The nickname—why Sandman?"

"Most everybody on the island is called something from childhood."

"How'd he get it?"

"Depends who you ask. What he claims is, one punch, he's put a lot of fellas to sleep. Big and fat as he is, tourists believe him. But the truth is, he got the name 'cause he's so blessed dumb. Makes your ears tired when he's talkative, you know? And the biggest crybaby around as a boy, scared to death of the dark. That could be another reason."

"Scared kids grow up to be bullies," Ford reasoned. "Does he get into a lot of fights?"

"Yes, probably . . . Well, no. Doesn't need to, a man his size, but there's been plenty of close calls. Hubert's nasty side comes out when he's drinking. And he's jealous of any tourist he sees with local women, especially since the night I turned him down. But catch him sober—good luck on that, by the way—he can be sorta sweet. Either way, my god, he doesn't have the brains of a child. Like today, I doubt it crossed his mind he could've killed us."

"Dumb, as in mentally challenged, or—"

"Not like he got dropped on his head as a child. Just slow, you know? But acts fast without stopping to think."

"If Nickelby wanted to sell some Spanish coins, how would Purcell react?"

"What?"

"You heard me."

"That's a strange thing to ask. Selling salvaged coins would be illegal," Tamara said, but was thinking about the possibility.

"Is he smart enough to work out a deal with a buyer? I'm still trying to figure out why they traveled seventy miles to—"

"You mean coins they found diving here? Rest your mind on that. Hubert woulda kept everything for himself."

"The ones I'm talking about were stolen from my treasure hunter friend. I didn't find out until tonight. Nickelby didn't mention anything about coin dealers when he rented equipment from you?"

"He should've, rather than trust that big fool. You asking if Hubert's a thief? Sure, if he thought he could get away with it. He's too simpleminded to plan anything tricky, but he runs with some bad folks. Not from this island. They Haitians. To be honest, Haitians never been welcome in the Bahamas—men who'd cut your throat if the price was right. How much these coins worth?"

"More than I can afford," Ford said as if amused. "There are two eight-ounce silver reales, very good condition, and a third coin I don't know much about."

- - - - - - - - - - -

"Are you saying you're not rich or you don't trust me? Either way, it's not what a girl wants to hear."

"You're better off not knowing all the details."

The woman seemed to accept that and concentrated on photos from the GPS. "Where a lot of rich folks live is here"—her finger indicated Staniel Cay—"which would've been an easy stop on the way to Cat Island. Do you know for a fact they—"

Tamara went silent when Ford's attention shifted to the trees. She watched him open his bag and take out a small scope. The lens cast a greenish light as he put it to his eye. "What in the world you doing?" She swung around to see. There was Hubert Purcell, the man's girth unmistakable in the darkness against the white sand beach. "Uh-oh, you best skedaddle. No violence—you promised."

Ford remained seated and cleared the laptop screen. "Don't stand up, just listen. Wait for an opening and bring up the subject of computers. Tell him I'm an expert. Yours is broken and I'm showing you how to do a reboot. It's possible he'll ask for my help."

The woman's half laugh was not intended to reassure. "What's possible is, you'd better swim toward Africa. The only computer around is ten miles down the road. Pointe Lodge, the bonefish camp."

She hadn't exaggerated the man's size. Purcell stopped, recognized Tamara, bellowed something about his boat, and lumbered toward them.

"He's bad drunk. I can tell by the way he's walking. What if he knows you stole his GPS?"

Ford was using the green lens again, focusing on a different area. "Someone's following him . . . hiding back there in the trees. Looks like he's carrying a . . . machete?" The biologist got up as if to pursue but changed his mind. "Guy ran off. I wonder if—"

"Don't be a fool," she hollered to Purcell, who was close enough they could hear his wheezing. Then asked Ford, "What else you got in that bag?" He had opened a rear zipper like he was reaching for a weapon.

Ford said, "Come up with another reason we're here, then let me do the talking."

"Like what?"

"Be creative." He didn't add, *Or you're not going to like how this goes.*

t didn't go well until Ford took a stab at diplomacy, his hand close enough to pull the 9mm Sig from his bag. "Me and a client of yours have mutual friends," he said. "That's what Tamara and I were discussing. Remember Leonard Nickelby?"

The change that came over Purcell was remarkable. "You *know* the professor?"

"Enough to charter your boat if you stop threatening to kick my ass."

The man appeared to visibly shrink. "Why didn't you say so?"

"I was scared. Why else?"

"Really?"

"Who wouldn't be?"

Purcell was flattered. "There you go, shows you got intelligence. Wish the professor had as much sense—he's the meanest little man I ever met. Look here what he done to my face."

"We can't see in all this darkness, you fool," Tamara said. "Stop spinning 'round like a ballerina. That don't help, plus we don't want to look at your face. Just say what you got to say and scoot."

In Velcro, next to the pistol, was a flashlight. Ford handed it to Purcell, who was six-six and weighed over three hundred pounds. "I wouldn't mind having a look."

Purcell's sweaty shadow loomed over the table until the light came on. Ford cleaned his glasses and put them on again. "Are you sure we're talking about the same Dr. Nickelby?"

"Yeah, the professor," the man said, and posed, offering a side view of his melon-sized head. One purple eye was swollen shut, a bandage under it, and his lower lip was crusted with blood. Injuries from a fight.

Tamara's laughter started softly and got louder. "That little fella did that? No one's gonna believe you."

"It ain't funny. My dogtooth, I think it's loose. No amount of beer I drink helps my headache neither. And it was even worse when it happened four, five days ago."

"Oh Lord, Sandman, get used to it. Did he have to climb on a stool to reach you?"

"Don't you be running your mouth about Professor Leo, that's

----

my advice. Man's got a temper. What happened is, he hit me when I wasn't looking—with his damn fist, due to a little misunderstanding. And him being a doctor, as you say."

"Leo?" Ford asked.

"That's what his girlfriend calls him. Her name's Lidee, something like that. Or she calls him the professor, too." Purcell touched a careful finger to his jaw. "I'm starting to worry. Think the bone might be broke?"

"That's not what worries you," Tamara said. "I expect the man's in hospital now. Or dead by the time you got done wiping the ground with him. Is that why you come here with your drunk talk, making threats before the constable hauls you off?"

Purcell staggered a little as he placed the flashlight on the table. "Never touched the professor after he attacked me. I couldn't."

"'Cause he's so small? I don't believe that neither."

"Believe what you want. Most fellas run away when I get mad, so I just stood there after it happened not sure what to do. Surprised, I guess, 'cause no one ever had the spine to hit me before, which is what I told him. You know, in a threatening way to scare them both. That's when he hit me again. Damn near put me down."

Tamara had to slap the table.

"Stop your damn laughing. Friends of mine was on the dock and saw it happen. Ask them if Professor Leo is a man to cross. They'll tell you. That witch of a girl he's with, she's just as smart, and meaner, in her way. I think she hexed my boat somehow."

"How?"

"I called her a witch, didn't I?"

"Funnier and funnier," Tamara said. "You best get used to laughter. The only hex on you, Sandman, you put there yourself."

"All I'm saying is, I had nothing but bad luck since. One thing after another, then tonight, as I fired the engines, my GPS was blank as a roll of butcher paper. No indeed, I don't want no more trouble from that pair."

Ford, closing his bag, getting to his feet, tried not to show amusement. "I've done work on marine electronics. What kind of GPS do you have?"

Purcell was too busy seeking sympathy to respond. "All my waypoints," he said to Tamara, "the best fishing and dive spots around, spent years marking those places. Guess my only hope is to apologize to the professor and ask him to fix it right. Trouble is, that little misunderstanding I mentioned, those two might not feel charitable toward me."

Tamara wanted to know what kind of misunderstanding, but Ford interrupted. "Take me to your boat. I'll fix your GPS."

Purcell, startled, turned—comical, almost, the hopeful look on his face. "I'd do most anything if that's true, sir."

"We'll see." Ford started toward the road. He didn't speak again for a while. Purcell's amended persona was deferential and dumb—an act, possibly. There were a lot of dangerous men with low IQs who were animal shrewd and had a gift for manipulation.

And who had been hiding in the trees with a machete? When Tamara was far enough behind, he began to probe.

"Your buddy should've joined us instead of running off like that."

"Who you talking about? If it's the boy I pay as mate, he too drunk to run anywhere 'bout now."

"You came alone?"

"Hell yeah, man. Why I need help dealing with a tourist such as yourself?"

Ford stopped and said, "Gotta take a whiz."

From the bushes, he used the NV monocular to confirm they weren't being followed. A little later, he asked Purcell, "Where are Dr. Nickelby and the girl staying?"

"At a hotel, I guess. That's what most tourists do."

"On Andros?"

"Nah, think they left days ago. I ain't seen them anyway. I sure am sorry, sir, 'bout giving you a hard time back there. I didn't know you and the professor was friends."

"We aren't. Just mutual friends, is what I said. That's why I'm looking for him. Did he happen to mention a couple of coins he wanted to sell?"

Purcell took his time formulating another lie. "Coins, hmm. Don't think so. You a collector, sir?"

"I'll pay a finder's fee if they're worth buying. You had to drop him and the girl somewhere. If they're not on Andros, which island?"

"Hard to even remember, my head feeling like it does. Besides, that's something I'd have to get the professor's permission to share. When you say finder's fee, how much we talking? Wouldn't want to waste my time making inquiries for less than my time's worth."

"So he hasn't sold them."

"No. Well . . . maybe one of the coins. You carry that much cash on you?"

Ford illuminated his phone and showed Purcell the phone number he'd copied from the boat's logbook. "Call Nickelby and tell him I'm interested. It's a Bahamas area code, your phone will work."

Purcell recognized the number. There was no doubt. "Tell you what, sir, fix my GPS, we'll talk about it. That sound like a fair trade to you?"

Like a threat, is how it sounded.

"You haven't asked how much I charge," Ford said, a mild threat of his own that Purcell misunderstood. The man was still bemoaning his list of gambling woes as they boarded the *Sandman*.

There was a cell tower close enough. Ford's text to Tomlinson read *Here's the number. Talk Nickelby in before he gets hurt.*

7

efore the phone rang—a stranger named Tomlinson calling—Lydia was on the porch of their beach house. Below were tiki torches that illuminated a private pool. She had been counting money, hundreds and fifties, but stopped when Leonard exited the bathroom and posed in front of the mirror. It made her feel good because he looked good, tanned, with a hint of muscle definition after seven months at her gym near Gainesville. That and some veterinarian magic used to bulk up Angus bulls.

The clinic where she'd worked stocked a big selection.

Prof. Leonard Nickelby would never be mistaken for a

bull—or an athlete, for that matter—but try to convince him of that after twelve days in the Bahamas.

"Where's my brilliant little sea wench?" Leering, he turned, nothing but a towel around his waist.

God, it was hard not to laugh when he said stupid stuff like that. His silliest line was *I've got the grog if you've got the stein*, whatever the hell that meant. Well, it meant he was horny, but he was always horny—another change in Prof. Nickelby.

Lydia gave herself credit for the change. Injections of vet-grade testosterone had played a role, but there was no anabolic fakery in the way their bodies meshed. Since losing her virginity at twenty-one, she'd been with only three others, all bigger, younger, although not much younger, but none of them compared to the happy little bald man leering in the next room. The transformation had been so seamless it felt like they'd always been this way. That was not the case. Reassembling the man's shattered ego had required tenderness—and an objective.

"We have reservations, Leo," she said, the prelude to a game they played.

"Cancel 'em."

"What about dinner?"

"Had it yesterday."

"You'll be hungry."

"By tomorrow, who cares?"

"We could do room service."

"Precisely, my beauty. Then eat later at the bar."

Lydia, for the first time in her life, felt unexpected moments of being loved, safe, and in control, yet, inevitably, reality yanked her back into a mess of her own design. But Leonard was now ready, his towel on the floor.

Afterward, he lingered in bed while she showered. The bathroom was spacious, marble with gold fixtures, double doors opened wide so they could converse.

"You know, maybe you're right," Leonard said from the next room. "Maybe I should get a doctor to take a look at this hand. Doesn't hurt—not much—but the damn thing still looks swollen."

His right hand, the one he'd used to hit the charter boat captain five days ago. Leonard was like a kid with a trophy he didn't want to lose—a child whose timidity had produced scars only on the inside. This was another similarity they shared. Yet something Lydia had not experienced was the methodical humiliation by a spouse. Mrs. Rebecca Nickelby was a hundred pounds overweight and had tried to destroy her husband emotionally and sexually as punishment for her own self-contempt.

Lydia, the armchair shrink, was also a rescuer. How else could she rescue herself? She felt a surge of unwelcome emotion, so turned her face in to the shower before replying, "What's the problem, prof? Can't hear you."

"My damn knuckles. I can't help thinking about the look on

87

Purcell's face when I punched him. What the hell'd he expect? I hated to do it, but even my patience has a limit. The big oaf had it coming."

"Leo the Lion," she called out. "Yes he did. But honey? Try to keep your temper in check from now on, okay?"

"I didn't start it. Then the jerk threatens you? Makes me mad just thinking about what else I should've done."

That's not the way it happened. Leonard had caught Captain Purcell going through a waterproof Pelican case that should have been locked, and probably was. It contained the stolen logbook, their last silver Spanish real, and one extraordinarily beautiful gold doubloon. The stricken look on Leonard's face, pure terror, as the captain, giant-sized, had stepped toward him. Then *smack*, like a cornered animal, Leonard had fought back, before fleeing to the stern of the boat.

Purcell had stumbled along in pursuit. Then glowered at them both—that's all—before Leonard swung another wild fist. Again, the sickening sound of bone on skin. Blood, too. The giant with a bewildered expression, while six of his buddies, watching from the dock, whooped and laughed.

On the ferry to the resort, Staniel Cay, Leo the Lionhearted had vomited, he was so overwrought with nerves, but did it privately. Lydia had pretended to be unaware. Then, after a shower and three margaritas, presto, another transformation. Leonard had rallied on the beach by stripping her naked in moonlight and taking her from behind.

Was this really the same nervous little man? His wolf-like growling had been unexpected. Very sexy, in a way, but it had also scared her. His inflated confidence still did—Capt. Purcell could've crushed both their skulls with one bare hand. Lydia had helped create the new Leonard Nickelby. Now the problem was, how to keep him under control and safe?

She exited the shower and selected a towel of Egyptian cotton while speaking through the open doorway. "Point is, we don't want to draw attention to ourselves. I think the locals got the word loud and clear about who not to mess with. That's all I'm saying."

"The coconut telegraph."

"You don't need to prove yourself again, prof. What time are we supposed to meet that man?"

"Who?"

"The coin dealer. Or collector. Or whatever he is. I'm still a little miffed you didn't include me in the decision."

"There's a good example, for you," Leonard said. "Primitive communication is always underestimated. Columbus, in his journals, wrote about the Taino people—Indios, he called them, *una gente en Dios*, meaning 'a people of God.' Why? Because they were naked. Savages, the Spaniards considered them. Isn't that a laugh from so-called explorers who slaughtered an entire race?"

Professor Nickelby, archaeologist-historian, lectured on until he finally got to his point. "They used drums and signal fires. The Indians along the Florida coast knew about the Spaniards forty years before they actually landed. Now it's cell phones. Same

----

concept. Did you see the way the security guy looked at me when we checked in? I think they already know. Probably Purcell's pals—the story of our little fight has spread from here to Nassau."

The pride the little man felt was obvious.

Lydia stepped out wearing a black sleeveless dress, local pearls, and high heels of raspberry red. She'd paid cash at the resort boutique, an outfit that cost more than the dented Toyota she'd left behind at the airport in West Palm. "The coin dealer, Leo. What time?"

"My god, you look delicious. Come here, I want to show you something."

The stolen logbook, leather-bound, lay open on a desk. A chart of the Exumas—three hundred islands, most of them deserted—was nearby. "Fitzpatrick is a shrewd old bastard, but the amateurs are all alike in one way. They can't see the bigger picture. Not just historically, but in terms of hydrogeology. But why am I telling you? You worked for Benthic. Oh yeah, the great Jimmy Jones. Mr. Big Shot Con Man until a few weeks back when his cell mate—"

"I know, I know, let's not go over that again," Lydia said. News of Jimmy's death had catalyzed too many barbs, an equal number of lies, and had led to their only blowup thus far. Jealousy was new to her. Flattering, in a way, but enough already. Her hand massaged the professor's neck as she seated herself on the arm of the chair. "Show me what you found."

Leonard hadn't found anything. He had hijacked an idea and formulated a theory. It was based on two small chunks of

----

ambergris that Capt. Purcell had plucked from the sea. Both were found in shoal areas, as directed by the logbook, but miles apart.

Ambergris was a strange substance. It resembled gray volcanic rock yet floated on the surface like Styrofoam. Profitable—very profitable—because Lydia had insisted on a fifty-fifty split. This was before the "big fight." God, the stuff stunk, which is why a buyer in Nassau had paid only six dollars per gram, half the wholesale rate. Thirteen pounds equaled almost six thousand grams—$37,400 cash, Bahamian dollars.

It was Capt. Purcell who had stumbled upon the idea. After losing his sixteen grand playing roulette at the Hyatt, he had suggested, "Could be that book of yours is better at finding amber wax than some damn ol' wreck where there's sharks and other shit. Me? I don't like the water."

Locals called ambergris by several names. Often it was a humorous reference to whale feces.

Leonard was terrified of sharks, too, but had become more assertive after two days aboard the filthy trawler *Sandman*. "Have I asked you to get in the water? Just punch in the numbers and run the boat like you're paid to do. There's a little reef ahead I want to check out."

"A captain does more than steer," Purcell had replied, "and he sure don't take orders. You got something against money? By rights, the way the law of the sea works is, the boat gets a third, the captain gets a third, and that's what you and the missus shoulda got. Not half."

"More for you to gamble away, in other words."

"Whatever I want to do, that's none of your business. What I'm saying is, let me have a look inside that book, maybe I'll find us another good amber wax spot."

This was the first sign of trouble. Leonard had been oblivious, already seeking a connection between wreck sites and coral intersections that had snagged blobs of ambergris.

The results, paid in cash, now lay on the desk of their expensive beach house, far from the main resort.

'This is what your common treasure hunter types would've never figured out," Leonard said. "I'll show you." He re-folded the chart to display only the southern tip of Andros, Staniel Cay, and the leeward rim of Cat Island. Several miles west lay a pair of tiny islands, unnamed. They were joined like beads in a trough called the Tongue of the Ocean.

"Think they're inhabited?" Lydia asked.

"Doesn't matter, because we won't need a dock," Leonard said. "See how the currents carom toward deep water? Fitz and his goddamn fake GPS numbers. But he was sloppy when it came to magnetometer readings in shallow areas. The same with his notes on triangulation, most in Spanish, but some in English like these spots."

In pencil, Leonard had drawn arrows to indicate tidal flow where, years ago, Carl Fitzpatrick had marked possible wreck sites. The arrows formed whirlpool vortexes around several reefs.

"Picture a Spanish galleon being beaten to death in a storm.

Hydrology, there's something called the venturi effect. Current accelerates through constricted spaces—imagine water shooting out of a garden hose. Then it explodes in reverse if the flow's deflected by a reef." He tapped the chart for emphasis. "Thermoclines—denser water—have an effect, too. In a storm, tidal velocity would have accelerated. See what I'm getting at?"

During her eighteen months working for Benthic Exploration, Lydia had risen from deckhand to Jimmy Jones's "smart little geek." Soon, she was his secret adviser that no one else on the project bothered to give a second look. At Jimmy's insistence, she had tended to his less savory needs as well. The concession had allowed her freedom to learn a great deal about finding small objects on the bottom of a big blue sea.

It had also helped her appreciate Leonard, a man she might be falling in love with—something she hadn't planned. "I feel dense, Leo. I hate you spending so much time on ambergris when we both know what we really want."

Their own private island. That was the late-night fantasy they'd chattered about like kids. Somewhere safe. Remote. A sunny place where they could be themselves without apology.

"Working our asses off to find what Fitzpatrick never found in the first place isn't the only way," Leonard replied. "You don't see it, do you?"

She listened patiently while he explained what she already understood. The whirlpool vortexes that positioned sunken objects along a reef also directed floating objects onto a reef.

"Then Capt. Purcell was right," she said.

"Purcell? Christ, it was a lucky guess. You don't really give him credit for—"

"That's not what I mean. What worries me is, Purcell made the connection. Those friends of his watching from the dock when you hit him? They were scary. Gangster-looking. They liked seeing his blood. And, my god, the way they humiliated the man by howling like animals. What if they know?"

"About the logbook?"

"Any of it. The equipment we brought is worth a fortune to people like them. Purcell knows we're carrying a bundle of cash. And the coins—are you sure he didn't see them?"

Nickelby wasn't sure but replied, "How many times do I have to tell you? Yes, they were in the Pelican case, but in their own little box, just like always. Stop being such a nervous Nellie."

"But he was going through the logbook when—"

"Not in a million years could Purcell or his pals figure out Fitzpatrick's notes. He's not smart. But he is smart enough to realize the book's useless without me beside him to—"

"That's exactly why I'm worried. And he knows where we're staying, Leonard."

The girl seldom used his formal first name. Nickelby, seated, put his arms around her waist and pulled her closer. "How about this? Tonight, if the guy makes a decent offer, we'll sell the other silver coin and buy our own boat. Something big enough we can live on for a while. There's one at the marina I liked with a

----

broker's sign on it. We spend a week or two looking for ambergris and use that money to finance a bigger boat so—" He stopped, aware the girl had gone rigid. "What's wrong? Don't worry, I can handle Purcell. His friends, too, if it comes to that."

Lydia, from where she stood, could see beyond the patio to their private pool below. A man was there, white slacks, white guayabera shirt, his bearing confident like he was there for a reason. "Is that your coin dealer?"

Leonard got up. "Too early. He's probably some tourist who wandered away from the resort. If you want, I'll—" He started toward the door as the phone rang, their Bahamian BTC cell, prepaid a month in advance. "Get that, would you?"

She did, and heard a kindly male voice say, "My name's Tomlinson. Within sixty seconds you'll not only trust me, you'll thank me for—"

That's all she heard because two men wearing masks were waiting when Nickelby opened the door.

B
efore the feds confiscated it, Benthic Exploration had owned an ocean-going research vessel, the *Diamond Cutter*. It was outfitted in Norway with twin Storvik four-ton cranes, an instruments bridge right out of *Star Trek*, and accommodations for sleeping twelve.

A little cabin aft, portside, with a porthole view of the sea, had

----

been Lydia's home for a year. Sometimes, when the crew was off, it was just her and a maintenance guy or two anchored in a leeward cove where the water was clear and at least twenty feet deep since the vessel drew fifteen.

Spearfishing had become her passion. Few things were more satisfying than sitting down to a meal of fresh snapper she'd stalked and filleted herself an hour earlier.

When the men crashed into the kitchen and slammed Leonard to the floor, stalking fish was far from her mind. But when one yelled, "You got any guns? Better tell us now, lady!" that's what she thought about—the little pneumatic speargun she'd bought in Nassau. They brandished only a machete and an old scarred baseball bat. Big men, heavy-handed and barefooted, their pants wet up to the crotch, meaning they'd come by boat.

"Why would we?" she responded. "Just tell us what you want, you can have it—anything—but, for god's sakes, take your damn hands off him." Amazing how calmly the words came out despite the way she was shaking.

"Anything? That might be good if you was prettier," the man said. "Kick that damn phone toward me or I'll beat his head in." The phone was on the floor where she'd dropped it. Once he'd pocketed the thing, he turned his attention to Leonard. "So you the professor, huh? Mister, you better cooperate and stop your damn fighting. I ain't that marshmallow Sandman."

So that's why they were here.

Lydia said, "Easy, let's all calm down. Leo, goddamn it, do

----

what he says. We've got money. Lots of it. Cash. You can have it all as long as you promise not to hurt us."

"Leo's your name?" The men were smiling behind their masks. "Best listen to the lady, Leo. What we hear is, she's a witch. From her looks, sure enough could be true, aye?" More laughter.

They had Leonard facedown on the floor by then, arms behind his back. She cringed when he tried to kick free and one of the men responded by kicking him hard in the ribs. The whimpering sound he made was child-like. Heartbreaking. Two involuntary steps, she started to charge, then caught herself. "Do that again, I won't tell you where it is."

"Say what?" The man with the bat scanned the room and saw the logbook lying open on the desk. He flipped through a few pages. "'Pears to me this here's part of what we want. And even in a house this fancy, won't be no problem finding the rest. That big plastic case where y'all folks keep your dive gear, what I might need is the key." Then to his partner he said, "You got the tape? Find the damn tape while I see if the thing's too big to float out. Sandman says it's heavy."

"Our money's not in the case," Lydia said. "Look all you want, you won't find it. But I'll show you if you promise—" Leonard drowned her out with threats about his connections at the U.S. Embassy and the Bahamian police. Both men focused on him, but one turned long enough to say, "Yeah, all the money you got. And bring that key, while you're at it."

At a robotic pace, Lydia's raspberry high heels clip-clopped

----

across the lacquered floor into the master suite. From the kitchen, the sound of a thud and another child-like whimper finalized her decision. Sliding doors opened to a porch that circled the house. She kicked off the shoes and ran barefooted while Leonard hollered more threats from inside.

Beyond the railing was the sea and stars, a sizable boat anchored off the beach. No sign of the man dressed in white where tiki torches blazed by the pool. Piled near the outdoor shower was their snorkel gear. The pneumatic speargun was short, easy to maneuver. But it was difficult to load because of a high-pressure piston that powered the spear like a bullet.

The shaft loader was heavy plastic. She braced it between her feet. The spear was stainless steel, the point sharp as a stiletto. The head was attached by wire to a hinged barb that prevented a fish— or anything else—from pulling free once it had pierced flesh.

Click. A pneumatic metal sound confirmed the shaft was locked, powered, and ready. Safety off, she crept to the front of the house, where the door was still open. Light spilled out onto palm fronds. The shadow of a man dwarfed her own shadow as she approached, speargun up, shouldered like a rifle. She risked a quick look. One man was on his knees, facing inside. He was still battling to tape Leonard's hands, the machete on the floor within reach of the doorway. The man with the bat was standing with his back to the others. She listened to him call toward the master suite, "What the hell's taking you so long, witchy woman?"

That's when Lydia appeared in the opening close enough to

shoot him in the spine, which is what she hollered. "I'll shoot you in the goddamn spine if you turn around!" A nonsensical threat since it forced him to spin toward her. The other man turned, too, but not before she'd knelt and snatched the machete away, then lofted it overhead, ready to swing.

"Goddamn, girl, give me that. Hey, easy now . . . What you got there?"

"Speargun," the man on his knees said softly. He was trying to scoot out of range but was blocked by Leonard, who was on his belly, trying to get to his feet.

"Let him up. Get away from him," she hollered.

"Not 'til you give me my sword back, I won't."

That's what locals called machetes in the islands—swords—a holdover from pirate times.

Lydia aimed the speargun, the man's face only five feet away. Then lobbed the machete over the railing without looking to see where it landed. "Go find it if you want the damn thing and get out of here. Not you—" She aimed at the other man. "Not until you drop that damn bat."

"What if I don't? One little spear against two of us." Slowly, he began to move away from a spear that had a range of ten feet, max.

"You idiots, don't make me do this. I'm giving you a chance. Leave now, we won't call the police." She extended the gun at the man on his knees. "Tell him. Tell your buddy. Leave us in peace and—"

Leonard ended that possibility when he lunged, snatched the baseball bat, and tried to roll out of the reach of a man twice his size. It was so unexpected, Lydia froze long enough for the other one to charge from his knees and knock her backward. She clung to the speargun while he pried at her hands, then hit her with something—his fist, no doubt—and it felt like an exploding light in her head.

A hammering sound pierced the haze—pistons of a diesel engine that reminded her of being at sea except the cadence was random. Fleshy thuds were interspersed with yelps, wild profanities. Panicked bare feet thumped wood. More profanity, then Leonard's face parted the haze. He was above her, wonderful to see in the starlight.

"Lydia, babe . . . are you okay? Let me help you up."

She was on her feet, a little woozy but not too bad. It took a minute before she was lucid enough to piece together the chaos that had taken place. On the kitchen floor were splotches of red syrup—blood. Blood on Leonard's face, his hands, and on the bat he now offered her as a cane. "This might help. Can you walk? If that son of a bitch hurt you—"

In the dark yard, a man was crawling, stumbling toward the beach. Another was almost to the water, his bulk visible amid a stand of coconut palms.

"León," she said, a name she'd never used before. Gave it a regal pronunciation that slipped from her lips as Lee-ON.

It fit. He was pumped up enough to taunt their attackers. "There's more where that came, buster! Insult my lady again, I'll . . . I'll . . . You'll see. A witch, my ass."

The man dressed in white—where had he gone?

Lydia's gaze moved from the swimming pool area to the pools of blood in the kitchen, then to the thief outside, crawling to get away. "Oh dear god, Leo, he's hurt really bad. How many times did you . . . ? With the bat, I mean."

"Fuck him, I didn't have a choice. I hope he fucking dies." Leonard cupped his head in his hands, the reality of what had happened settling in. "Oh damn, maybe I did." He paced briefly, then from the railing hollered, "Hey buddy! Are you okay? If you need a doctor, I'm willing to help. No hard feelings, man. What do you say?"

The thief got to his feet, maybe looked back or maybe didn't—it was too dark to be sure—then stumbled toward the shadows, a glistening wedge of sea beyond.

"Oh Christ, now what do we do? Call the police, I guess. Report them before they—"

"No police," Lydia said, grabbing his arm. "You were in the right. They would've robbed us, maybe killed us, too. We've got to make a decision. We can't stay here."

"Yeah, could've killed us," Leonard reasoned, pulling away. "Then we have nothing to worry about from the police. Where's the goddamn phone?"

Only then did she remember a call from someone named Tomlinson. Next, an image of the phone on the floor came into her head. The robber had stuck it in his pocket.

"Thank god, that's all they took," she said.

"What, the logbook?" Leonard hurried into the main room. "No, it's still on the desk where I—"

"The phone. You can stop looking for the phone. Besides, we've registered under fake names at every place we stayed. How do you think that will go over if you call the police? Leo, think about the logbook and the coins—Fitzpatrick has had more than three weeks to report the theft, so they'll know about that, too."

Leonard wanted to inspect her forehead. He got her under the light, concerned, already close to an emotional meltdown. "You need an ice pack," he said. Then, in the kitchen, he put his hands on the counter and appeared to sag. "Shit, shit, shit. What if one of them dies?"

"If he dies, he dies," she responded. "We didn't ask them to break in with a baseball bat and a machete. The coin dealer you were supposed to meet, is he staying at the lodge or on a boat?" She was worried about the man in white. If he wasn't behind the attempted robbery, he might misrepresent what he'd witnessed to the police if they showed up.

There was a reason Lydia did not trust the guy.

Leonard was wringing his hands, pacing. "Okay, okay, here's what we do. I want you to fly back to Florida tomorrow. That's right, as soon as there's a flight. Yeah, that's what we'll do, then I'll turn myself in. None of this was your idea. I'll swear to it. Here"—he opened the fridge and packed a Ziploc with ice—"this will stop the swelling."

Lydia wanted to kiss the man. She did, had to get up on her tiptoes to do it. "That's a lie, Leo. This was all my idea," she said.

It was an admission that required a longer talk, but not now. A tequila and triple sec calmed him while she used a mop to clean the floor. "We need to leave tonight, so let's check out that boat you said's for sale. It's not even ten o'clock, and the music goes until midnight." Again, she asked about the coin dealer.

"What's it matter? I ran into the guy while you were napping. He owns a big-ass yacht, so I figured he might be interested. I never said he was a coin dealer . . . How's your head?"

The ice had helped. "Did you approach him or was it the other way around?"

"Yes . . . No . . . In fact, he came up to me and just sorta started talking. It didn't seem odd at the time, but now . . . You don't think—" A spark came into his eyes.

"We're on the run," Lydia said. "And, as of tonight, not just from the police. If the boat's not available, maybe rent a room at the resort and see what happens. No one will bother us with a lot of people around."

"I want to talk to that coin guy first. Pack your stuff. I mean it—no more discussion."

León had spoken.

It was the same León who waited until they were at the bar with a couple of rum punches to reflect with a hint of surprise, "You were right. No one seems to know or care what happened, or why I waited this late to ask to see the dock master. But the weirdest part about tonight, Lydia? I'm serious—I don't remember ever feeling more, you know, *alive.*"

8

- - - - - - - - - -

n the morning, Ford swam a quarter mile along the beach and jogged back to find a stranger seated on a stump outside his rental cottage. Human males do a visual appraisal automatically because their olfactory powers are weak. Caucasian, tanned, with some burning. Mid-thirties, six-two, one-eighty, delicate hands. A tourist fly fisherman, clothes a techno flag of expensive miracle fibers. Money, privileged class. A possible threat, but not the bust-your-head type.

This was not the ex-military cage fighter Tomlinson had warned him about. And nothing like the close call last night with Purcell.

He slowed to a walk. "If you're looking for bonefish, I saw a couple of schools on my run. Uhh . . . do you mind?"

The stump blocked a sandy path to the outdoor shower. The man got up, saying, "Dr. Ford? I pictured you younger—but looks like you're still in fairly good shape—considering. Want me to toss you a towel?"

This subtle barb was the first red flag. And one flag was enough. "Tell you what, come back and knock, then introduce yourself. That's how it's supposed to work. Half an hour ought to do."

"I already knocked."

"Try again, maybe your luck will change."

"It already has. She wouldn't answer, so I waited. That's how it works in my world."

Ford looked at the man, then past him, seeing a screened porch where a swimsuit—panties, a bra, too—hung drying on a line. The cottage was tiny, one room. Its roof of tin dented by coconuts from palms that shaded this stretch of beach. Inside, a woman's silhouette appeared near an open window, where she might be able to hear if they moved closer. Then it disappeared.

"Let's get out of the sun," Ford said, and walked to a pair of chairs near a hammock. "Why not start by telling me why you're acting like such an asshole?"

The man decided a staredown was unwise. "I get impatient. So, sue me. I've always been this way. I'm doing you a favor if you'll give me a chance."

"Impatient people can end up being patients."

It took a second. "Oh, I get it. Like in a hospital. A sense of humor. I didn't expect bad jokes either."

The man was working on a book, he claimed, about a modern pirate who was jailed for contempt after refusing to reveal where he'd stashed millions in gold bars and coins. His first book, the man said, and it might require a pen name because Jamie Middlebrook was too bland, plus, in stores, you had to get on your knees to see the *M* shelf. "What do you think of Sebastian Bunch?"

"One's as believable as the other," Ford replied. "What does this have to do with me?" He'd been warned about a journalist, too. But Middlebrook—whatever his name was—was more likely an Ivy League recruit hired by some federal agency. Over the years, he had dealt with enough to know. A plausible cover story, clothes too new, an ingratiating hard-on manner that suggested electronic intel and access to Black Hawk helicopters if necessary.

"I'm getting to that," Middlebrook said. He gave the cottage a look. "Why don't you ask her to come out? Might save us all some time."

"Think of me as a filtering device," Ford said. "It's a term biologists use. And time is something you're running low on. Start by explaining how you know my name and that I'd be gone long enough for you to case the place."

"I'm a thief, sure. That's why I chose your palatial rental cabin to rob. Now who's being an asshole?"

"I'm in sort of a rush. They don't teach social skills at Princeton or wherever it was you majored in—what?—political science, international law. Those used to be the favorites. I suppose it could be computers now."

The man's face went blank. "What's that supposed to mean?"

"Middlebrook," Ford shrugged. "Isn't that the name of a famous brokerage house or bank or something? New England, so I figured a family business."

"That explains it," the man said but wasn't convinced. "As I was saying, the guy I'm writing about started a company called Benthic Exploration. A really fascinating character. Then conned his investors out of a bundle—that's who took him to court first, his investors. Jimmy Jones. Does the name ring a bell?"

Ford, wearing just shorts, started to get up, a towel around his neck. "I'm going to shower and have breakfast. When you get to how this concerns me, wave."

"Dr. Leonard Nickelby. Does *that* name ring a bell?" The man smiled, pleased by the effect. "Finally, I have your attention."

"What about him?"

"Like I said, I'm trying to do you a favor. Don't take this the wrong way, Dr. Ford. You should stick to fish and give up playing amateur detective. Personally, I don't care about the old fool. Take him home to his nightmare of a wife. And your pal's logbook, while you're at it. Lydia Johnson is the one I want to find. Lydia

----

108

worked for Benthic as a low-rung gofer, or so the feds and everyone else believed at the time. I don't suppose you know where they're hiding?"

"*Nightmare* is a cruel way to describe the woman who's paying you," Ford countered. "Or is it just expenses and enough information to get you this far?"

Again, the sharp look of surprise. It faded. "You'd have to meet the woman to understand, but you're right. She wouldn't have told me a damn thing if I'd used any other approach. Like I'm actually going to write about her husband if he doesn't come home? Lydia is all I care about. I need to find her before someone else does. No shit. Jimmy ran off with four hundred million in gold, and she might be the only one who knows where he stashed it. Maybe you read about him being beaten to death in prison a few weeks ago."

"How much?"

"Almost half a billion reasons for you not to get involved. As a biologist, you might be unaware there are people who'd kill for a lot less."

Ford settled into his chair. Not meek but willing to listen. "I'm not naïve. That's why I think you're exaggerating."

"What if I'm not? Is it worth betting your life? Hers, too"— another nod toward the porch—"and anyone else who has information on that pair." Middlebrook saw the reaction he'd hoped for. "Good. You're a reasonable man—most are when it comes to that much money."

"When you say 'ran off,' how much would four hundred

----

million in gold weigh? You have to admit, what you're saying is hard to believe."

"Not really. Figure around sixteen thousand dollars a pound, but worth a lot more at auction. It would fill a space about the size of two refrigerators. Easy enough to move even with a fairly small boat."

"Up to a ton, maybe," Ford nodded. "It's a lot more manageable, you breaking it down like that. Even a recreational trawler could handle the load, sure."

Middlebrook liked that response, too. "Let me give you the backstory. The SS *Panama* went down during a boom period after the Civil War. It carried fifteen tons in gold ingots, for starters, a shipment ordered secretly by the U.S. Treasury. Add another two tons in gold bars, paid for in advance by the Spanish mint. You didn't read about this? I wouldn't waste my time looking for a logbook that belongs to some third-rate treasure hunter. No offense, I'm sure Mr. Fitzpatrick's a good guy and all, but get yourself killed in the process? You strike me as too smart for that."

"Obviously not." Ford smiled. "If I look up Benthic Exploration and the rest, the numbers won't change?"

"Worth more, according to some. As much as six hundred million. Spain wants its cut and so does the U.S. government. I've heard certain factions in El Salvador claim the gold is theirs, too, because that's where it was mined. Believe me, when news got out about Jimmy's death, the mercenary types started polishing their résumés. You really want to get caught in the middle of that?"

"Geezus, a perfect political storm."

"Afraid so."

"You came on like such a jerk I guess it's possible I overreacted."

"Don't worry about it. How'd you know I contacted Nickelby's wife?"

"Fitz is the old friend of a friend," Ford said.

"That's what I figured. Did he say anything about Lydia Johnson?"

"Not even her last name. And I certainly didn't know she was involved with—"

"I'm not the only one who thinks so. There's no hard evidence, but after eliminating almost everyone else it's what you might call a well-researched hunch. I know this much for certain—Nickelby's wife has a big mouth. If you and your pals know those two are in the Bahamas, how many others do you think are aware? I didn't have any trouble tracking you down, Dr. Ford. Think about it."

Ford appeared concerned. "The way it started was, I was here on a project anyway, so I thought why not poke around, ask a few questions, and help Fitz. Sorta fun, you know? But now . . . Geezus, I had no idea what I was walking into."

"The résumé thing—what I meant is, forget about common thieves and murderers. The behind-the-scenes power brokers will send in pros. Experts who'd torture to get information, then—" The man swiped a finger across his throat. "That's why I have to watch my ass every step of the way. Difference is, I knew the score, you didn't. So I thought a friendly warning was in order. I hope I can trust you not to blab this around."

"Not if it all checks out."

"I guess that'll have to do for now. There's someone else who wouldn't talk to me—Hubert Purcell. But he was very protective of you. He said don't mess with the biologist, like you were buddies. That you'd done him a big favor and he owed you. What did he mean by that?"

Ford shared a partial truth about fixing Purcell's GPS before getting back to Lydia Johnson. "I was an idiot not to do an Internet search before I left Andros Town. Instead, I researched Nickelby. Four hundred million, Jesus Christ, and I'm worried about Fitzpatrick's logbook."

"You wouldn't have found much on her. Lydia's not new to this game. She spent the last six years living under the radar. Fake IDs and a bunch of aliases. She and Nickelby will do the same thing until Lydia cuts him loose—and she will when she doesn't need a boyfriend and the logbook story as cover. But there's one thing those two can't fake. Any idea what that is?"

Yes—diver certification cards. Unless they were willing to lug scuba tanks and buy an air compressor, there was no getting around it. The Bahamian government monitored dive shops weekly. One screwup and the owner was out of business. But Ford replied, "The color of their skin, I suppose—no, that's wrong. There're thousands of native white Bahamians. I got it—their fingerprints."

Middlebrook got to his feet, smiling. "Obviously. Look, consider this an introduction. How about we get together this afternoon for drinks, then stroll over and have a chat with Purcell? I'm half a mile down the beach, the red house. You know the one? It sits off by itself."

That explained a lot. Half an hour ago, Ford had swam past the place. "I have a meeting this afternoon off island, so how about tonight? Around nine should be good."

"The sooner, the better. And bring her, now that you understand." He didn't bother to reference the cottage. "Just talking with those two has put her in danger, and, from what I heard, she's had enough tragedy for one life. I'll go easy with the questions."

Inside the cottage window, the blinds moved, while Ford asked, "What are you talking about?"

"Like you don't know. Her husband and kid drowned a couple years back. He was drunk." Middlebrook interpreted surprise as doubt. "Don't play dumb. I know she's in there. I would've found her last night if she hadn't gone back to using her maiden name. So tell her she can trust me, okay?"

"Tell who?"

"Jesus, you're a stubborn bastard. The dive shop owner. Tamarinda Constance is the name on the sign, but she took out the mortgage as Tamarinda Gatrell. That's what threw me."

- - - - - - - - - -

9

- - - - - - - - - -

text from Tomlinson: *When irony and lust collide, the detritus paints life as a hilarious absurdity. Don't fall for that nihil-
ist bullshit.*

A second text was meant to be funny: *At least she's your
second cousin, which is legal in border states and a few backward countries. Thank god, you-know-who is in Spain, far from the
TCT. Go and sin some more.*

You-know-who—Tucker Gatrell—was also Ford's cousin. *TCT*
stood for "The Coconut Telegraph." Which was sort of funny, but
only because Tomlinson had assumed the worst—or bawdiest
scenario—after learning that Tamara had spent the night at the
cottage.

Ford, smiling, pocketed the phone. He had tailed Middlebrook to a red beach rental just to prove he could, then flown his Maule amphib to a resort sixty miles east off Staniel Cay. Hubert Purcell's boat was anchored near the fuel dock, as prearranged.

That was two hours ago.

The name of the resort was Silver Reef. It was an island fantasy with beach estates, a casino, and yachts, on a wafer of sand dwarfed by the enormity of the sea. A call to Tomlinson from a hotel land-line was easily arranged. The staff was less cooperative when it came to questions about Nickelby and Lydia Johnson, who'd checked in four days earlier.

After Ford was done snooping, he joined Purcell aboard the *Sandman* to await something else that had been prearranged—a meeting with his Haitian drinking pals. That's where Ford was, near the helm with a view of the water, as Tomlinson's second text pinged in.

"Why you smiling, boss?"

Purcell's deference was irritating after almost coming to blows last night. The fight might have happened if Ford hadn't proved he could "fix" the boat's GPS. Interrogation skills and a bottle of Bacardi had played a role.

"Something a friend sent," Ford said amiably. "Call me Doc, okay? You're the captain, I'm just a client." Ford nodded toward the channel. "Is that who we're waiting on?" A dilapidated lobster boat had entered the basin and turned their way, a lone man at the wheel.

"One of 'em anyway." Purcell swiveled around in the captain's chair, got up, then decided he didn't need binoculars. "Yep, Quarrels is what he goes by. Too bad, I was expecting three other fellas, too. Let me talk to him private like, okay?"

So they could get their stories straight, Ford assumed, yet maintained an easygoing approach. "Whatever you say. When you're ready, give me a wave. I'd like to meet him."

"Not right off, man. I think he come here alone for a reason. The others are probably worried you're the po-lice after what your friend said happened."

Last night, Tomlinson's call to Nickelby had ended with a woman—probably Lydia—screaming before the phone went dead.

Purcell frowned at the lobster boat. "Lord, what's wrong with his face? Looks like Quarrels been beaten." Even from a distance, the facial swelling was noticeable. "Yeah, man, he all buggered up. I'm afraid whatever them Haitians did was bad—don't matter what the dock master told you. The group that fella runs with are the ones I warned you about. Same that laughed 'cause I was too cool, restrained myself, after the professor showed his foolishness."

Ford responded, "It takes a big man to walk away from a fight."

"There you go. But they like meanness. The staff here knows Quarrels, all them boys from Haiti, so they afraid to speak the truth. But don't you worry. Sandman gonna find out what you

----

need to know." The man, surprisingly nimble, went down the ladder and waited with a stern line ready.

There wasn't much Ford didn't know after his stroll around the resort.

He sat and waited, and kept an eye on Purcell and Quarrels below.

Nickelby and the girl weren't registered at the resort, according to a clerk he'd spoken with.

They'd checked out, in the words of the dock master, who'd accepted twenty dollars in exchange for information. The name Nickelby was unfamiliar, but he recognized Ford's description of a small bald American traveling with a much younger girl.

A talkative man, the dock master, when properly motivated.

"Oh, those two, yes, sir. León, is what he told me. She, I think he called her Lady Anne. Or Liddy Anne. Our scrape-n-rake band plays so loud, it was hard to hear."

"Leon or *León*?" Ford had asked.

"Like he was Spanish. Your friends had themselves quite a party last night up there at the Red Parrot. They was dancing to reggae and a bit drunk, you don't mind me saying. Rum punch, I believe, was their drink of choice, which is the dancingest drink

----

on this island. Only reason I met them was the bartender summoned me from my room at staff house. Mr. León was interested in a boat we got listed. See that little Grand Banks sitting over yonder?"

Nickelby didn't buy the boat, so Ford pushed the conversation along. Last night, the pair had booked a room in the hotel, possibly because the lady had fallen and hit her head. This made sense to the dock master. Why else move their luggage from the most beautiful house on the property? And the most private. The rum punches had fixed her up fine—no swelling around the temple unless the light was just right.

"Maybe they went back to the house when they checked out of the hotel."

"No, sir, they for sure gone. Can't sneeze on this island without folks noticing. Musta chartered a plane after Mr. León decided that Grand Banks needed too much work. That had to be before first light. My job starts early. I'd have seen a hired boat."

"They didn't leave without paying their bill, I hope."

"Doubt that, sir. The gentleman had plenty of money or the bartender wouldn't have summoned me last night. It was close to eleven by the time I was dressed proper to greet clients. By then, those two had the guests, and most the staff, too, on their feet, doing what we call the snake crawl but others call a conga line."

"Professor Leonard Nickelby," Ford mused, pleased with the incongruity.

"Mr. León and Lady Anne, is how the staff speaks of them,"

----

the dock master responded. "They a fun pair, those two. Oh, and there is something else I heard—well, I probably shouldn't say. Even with you being friends of theirs and all."

Another twenty changed hands.

Prior to taking the dance floor, Nickelby and the girl had been aboard a yacht. They'd returned to the bar with a satchel of cash. Blocks of hundreds—U.S., it looked like. The bartender had gotten a peek.

"Which boat?" The docks were a latticework of sports fishermen, sailboats, and blue-water cruisers, all large enough to be considered yachts.

"Man that rents it pulled out this morning," the dock master said. "They weren't aboard, if that's what you're wondering. I would've noticed when I loaded the gentleman's luggage."

"What kind of boat? Maybe I know him."

"I couldn't say, sir. What I was told was he come here a few years back and made a movie picture. Don't know the name of that either. Just that them Hollywood people do love their partying."

"The owner must be famous. Anyone else you could ask?"

"No, sir. A private plane, that was Mr. León's most likely choice. I suggest you wait. I'm sure he don't want a good friend like you to spend vacation alone . . . Is that all, sir?"

It was, as far as the dock master was concerned. He wouldn't discuss the movie person or describe the yacht. A fifty-dollar bill was refused.

"One more thing," Ford had pressed. "Are you sure there's not

----

another way they could've left? The landing strip here doesn't have lights."

The dock master hadn't considered that. "Dogged, if you ain't right. Couldn't have been a plane. Nope, unless . . . Wait—the mailboat. Today's Thursday, and Thursdays she pulls out early from the commercial quay north of here. Maybe they bought tickets."

"Bound for where?"

"Lots'a stops. Exumas, Sapphire Creek, Arthur's Town, maybe far as the Ragged Islands. I can grab you a schedule from the office. Mailboat's how all us islanders travel, sir. Always been that way, but I don't recommend it for guests. Too slow for folks in a hurry to have fun."

Ford had returned to the *Sandman*, schedule in hand. The same schedule he opened when Purcell climbed down from the bridge to greet the dilapidated lobster boat.

I t was almost six, nearly time to head back to Andros. He put the schedule away and walked to an aft window, where there was a view of mangroves and a swath of sand where his seaplane was anchored. The fuselage appeared darker than the Popsicle-blue water.

A window starboard side was a better place to observe Purcell. So far, the giant had not invited their visitor aboard. Quarrels, a muscular two hundred pounds, appeared slight by comparison. He wore baggy pants, a rope for a belt, no shirt. His face was grotesquely swollen like a plum grew from his ear. The fist of a powerful man might have caused the damage. Or a hammer . . .

Lydia Johnson had a head injury, too, according to the dock master. Maybe it was coincidence, maybe not. Last night, the GPS and a bottle of Bacardi had put Hubert Purcell in the mood to admit he was worried about something. It concerned his Haitian friends, Quarrels among them. That's all he would say—at first.

Ford had been through enough schools to know that empathy and liquor were the most effective tools of interrogation. Half a bottle had loosened the big man's tongue. It was possible, Purcell admitted, that he had bragged at too many bars that access to Nickelby's equipment case and a logbook were worth a punch in the face from a little fella like him. And he might have hinted the logbook was better at finding ambergris than treasure. A puffy little professor and a girl would be easy targets if handled correctly— something his friends could've figured out on their own.

Purcell had offered Ford the same deal he'd probably offered his drinking buddies.

"You and me should partner up before them Haitians take what's not theirs—and the book's not the only reason. You say it don't belong to the professor? Let me tell you about something else that don't belong to him—the fifty-fifty split of whatever we sell. That will be thanks enough. Plus, my normal charter fee, of course."

Purcell knew what was in the equipment case. He had palmed the keys while Nickelby was in the water—or so he believed at the time. Inside was a lot of expensive gear. There was also a small waterproof box.

"Two of the prettiest Spanish coins I've ever seen is in there. One was bright, shiny silver. The other, gold and shiny, but twice as big. Prof. Leo had carved out spaces in the foam. You know the kind of box I mean? A third space was empty, which explained why him and the girl had cash to charter my boat. Probably stolen, all three. Then they cheated me out of thirty thousand bucks by selling ambergris I found."

Ford had asked where they'd found the ambergris, and how it involved the logbook, before hearing the rest of it.

"Me looking in that box is what led to the misunderstanding I mentioned. Know why? Because I was too fair-minded even when that little fool hit me. Thieves, is what they are. Here, look at these pictures—" Purcell had pulled out his phone. "Tell me if it's worth going after what we both know don't belong to them."

There was a blurry photo of a silver coin, a Spanish real. In better focus, a larger coin, gold, ornate, a robust die. At the base, die marks read *Tricentennial 1714*. Ford had never seen a coin like it.

"At the bar, how many people saw these pictures as you passed the phone around?"

Many, judging from Purcell's indignant denial. More questions had produced more lies before Ford offered his own deal in a

----

friendly, empathetic way. "I hope your pals didn't do anything stupid. The police could get the wrong idea and arrest you, too."

"You think?"

"That's the way they'll see it, I'm afraid."

"Oh shit. Yeah . . . those boys too dumb to do anything that ain't stupid. You'll speak on my behalf, won't you, sir? I hear you got official papers from the Crown."

"If I can help," Ford had said. "Wouldn't it be better to give your friends a call, maybe arrange a meeting before something bad does happen? I'd hate to see you in jail. Tell you what. I'll charter your boat for a couple of days, then fly over and meet you at wherever it was you dropped Dr. Nickelby and the girl."

"Why there?"

"Because the police can't arrest you for preventing a crime. And Nickelby can't say much if we lay claim to what didn't belong to him in the first place. Just like you said."

The mix of larceny and reason had worked.

Now here they were, maybe a day too late, maybe not. Instead of four of Purcell's drinking buddies, it was only Quarrels, and he looked like he'd been beaten with a hammer. Ford, standing at the starboard window, took all this as a bad sign. If the other men were afraid to be seen in the area, it was possible that Nickelby and the girl hadn't left the resort by choice. Or even alive.

The portal glass was thick. He couldn't hear the men talking but could see that the exchange was becoming heated. The

- - - - - - - - - - -

mailboat schedule went into his pocket when Quarrels pointed at something—an obvious distraction. Ford was opening the door as the first punch was thrown. By the time he got down, Purcell was on his back, dazed, and the dilapidated boat was moving, Quarrels slunk behind the wheel as if scared.

"Hit me when I wasn't looking," the giant bawled. "Goddamn it, I warned them Haitian fools they was badass. Warned them all, but Quarrels faults me for sayin' it would be easy."

Ford had to leave for Andros soon. He wangled what there was to know about the Haitians before bothering to ask, "Warned them about who?"

10

ydia was the first to notice the seaplane, how low it was flying, and wondered in a distracted way if someone was tailing them.

"Probably a crew shooting a commercial," Leonard said.
"It's too rough to land out here. So, go ahead, wave like a
native. What are you afraid of? That they'll drop a bomb or
something?"

Aboard the 70-foot freighter *Fresh Moon*, dozens of Bahamians
lined the rail and waved wildly as the plane did a low pass. As it
circled back, Leonard accepted an invitation to dance from two
very large women. And why not? Everyone else was up moving to
the beat of steel pots. It was a spontaneous hello to the pilot, a man

alone in a cockpit way out here in a desert of blue that had consumed many freighters, many small planes.

"They were celebrating life," Leonard said, grinning, when the plane was gone. He plopped down on a box beside Lydia, a little out of breath. "Looked like the pilot might have turned toward Donner's place. He said his island's east of Arthur's Town."

She didn't want to discuss the man in white. Until last night, she'd never met him, but knew his name was Efren Donner. He was a Hollywood film producer who had invested millions in Benthic. That loss was followed by a sex scandal—physical abuse or porn, she wasn't sure—yet there was the yacht and an island he'd bragged about, and he'd paid cash for their Spanish reales. Coincidental? Not likely. Lydia stuck to the subject of the plane, saying, "I didn't see a camera. Why would the pilot pass so low?"

"Maybe the guy didn't want to celebrate by himself. Or"—a smile came into the professor's eyes—"he wanted a closer look at the most beautiful woman in the islands. Know what you should've done? Flashed him. Really! Give the poor bastard a nice long look. Share the bounty, I say, but not the salvage rights. Get it?"

God, sometimes the man was so damn cute it was hard to keep a straight face. "He wasn't flying that low, professor."

"That's not the way I remember those twin rapiers of yours, so time for another inspection. How about we stand watch in our cabin?"

They'd already "stood watch" in their cabin twice since departing the resort ten hours ago. It was a tiny metal closet, no sink or toilet, just bunks that folded out of the wall. Better—much better—up here on deck, despite an old tractor, and a couple of cars secured with chains, and mounds of cargo. The middle deck was to be avoided altogether. It smelled of livestock, chicken hutches, and caged pigs en route to market. Goats were tethered there, too. At the rear of the ship was the bridge. The structure was two stories tall, a tower of rusted steel that was the domain of the captain, a tiny man in his seventies with a big smile beneath a cap festooned with gold braid.

"Isn't this air wonderful?" Lydia said to change the subject.

It was León who responded by extending his hand. "The air will be just as nice after we finish inspection. Lady Anne?"

I n the months leading up to their escape, they'd plotted like kids building a secret tree house. Fake IDs required fake names, but not any name would do. The sound had to be similar or they might not respond when a stranger called to them.

Homophonic was the term Prof. Nickelby, who was still employed at the time, had used.

Lydia had become Lindy, or Linda Anne, and, when it felt right, Lady Anne. All a playful tribute to a real person, although Anne Dieu-le-Veut of France had been a pirate, not a lady. In the 1690s she was deported to the French Tortugas, now Haiti, where she threatened to shoot Captain Laurens de Graaf after an insult.

The famous buccaneer was so dazzled—or scared—when she pulled out a wheelhouse musket, he got down on one knee and proposed marriage.

"You invented that story," Lydia had laughed. This was at her apartment months ago.

Nope. Research confirmed that Anne Dieu-le-Veut had pillaged and robbed at her husband's side and had assumed command of their ship after de Graaf was struck by a cannonball off Jamaica.

Choosing names had been fun. Squabbling about how Lydia knew a forger who sold counterfeit IDs wasn't. The package deal—three sets of Florida driver's licenses (with holographs)—had cost a bundle. What troubled Leonard was her familiarity with the guy, a seedy canvas of tattoos who'd also offered to include passports at an astronomical price. A felony, yet no big deal as far those two were concerned.

Lydia's mysterious side. This is how he dismissed other troubling episodes, including her odd behavior last night at the resort. She'd refused to remain on a yacht that was as comfortable as the house the owner had described—this was after buying their last silver coin. What the hell? An interesting man, Efren Donner. A filmmaker with a list of credits who also knew a lot about marine archaeology. The man was a little too tall and good-looking for Leonard to feel immediately at ease, but a mojito and conversation had changed that.

If Lydia had stuck around, she might have been intrigued by the filmmaker's hospitality. Or the transparent duplicity of his

----

offer: Come to his private island, stay for a week or two, then travel by yacht anywhere in the Caribbean—as long as Donner could join their dive exploration.

"Maybe getting punched makes me overly cautious," she'd said afterward in the bar, loosening up with a drink and a satchel of cash at her feet. "But, prof, let's be honest. No one that rich and handsome is interested in me. And I doubt he's got the hots for you. So what's he really want?"

She was correct. On the other hand, why not find out what the filmmaker wanted? Aggressive curiosity was new to Leonard. It was testosterone-charged, fueled by recent triumphs yet mitigated by occasional self-doubt. In those moments, he had to wonder if he'd gotten lucky when he punched Purcell. No . . . the fear in the big bastard's eyes was real. And luck had nothing to do with getting so mad that he had lunged for a bat, outnumbered two to one by thieves.

Last night, almost killing a man had changed Leonard and his outlook on life.

If the thief died, he died.

Damn right. And good riddance.

The same with the job and bitchy wife he'd abandoned, and the stucco house he couldn't afford. All of it—that damn office, bills, bills, bills, a nervous sense of inadequacy, and a beat-up Volvo that personified failure—all gone.

The girl was his world now.

Sitting in their tiny cabin, he beheld Lydia. She lay naked, asleep,

----

within reach, the warmth of her hair soft on the lips. He dressed and closed the watertight door. Topside, the freighter was alive with folks packing to disembark and new arrivals. Stop and go, harbor to harbor. It had been like that all day. He did a spin around the deck, flirted with a previous dance partner, then walked aft for a lesson in piloting from his new friend, the captain.

A flock of boys caught his attention. Several had wild spiked hair and ashen skin. They were playing soccer near the railing, too close, it seemed, so he stopped for a while to shield the ball from the water.

Nice-looking kids. Good people nearby who were what they were, nothing more, nothing less, and granted that same freedom to others. Into his mind came the image of Lydia with child. Then another image: Lydia with a child in her arms on a safe, sandy island, water of clearest blue, and a boat of their own.

In that instant, Leonard knew what he'd sensed since arriving in the Bahamas—there was no going back to a life that was beyond repair. He had a new ride. This was his life to savor.

> Mailboat schedule, *Fresh Moon*, Thursday, 6 a.m. departure: Stanley Point, Warderick Wells, Exuma, Little San Salvador, Sapphire Creek, Arthur's Town (7 p.m. arrival +/-)

There'd been so many small harbors, piers, and villages of wattle-and-daub that Lydia didn't know where she was when she awoke to a booming impact. The shudder of reversing engines suggested they'd made the hardest landing of the day. But where?

It was nearly sunset, closer to eight than seven. What she saw through the porthole wasn't a village. And it certainly wasn't Arthur's Town. According to brochures, there should have been colorful restaurants, not cresting waves, a distant orb of palms, and a cement house atop a bluff as craggy as bone.

The schedule was consulted. If this was Sapphire Creek, the name was misleading. And why had they stopped so far from shore?

A scream . . . then several more pierced the bulkhead. Lydia threw on clothes and ran topside into chaos. Women huddled around a gaggle of weeping boys while men gestured at something in the freighter's wake. Engines clunked into gear. Black exhaust screened whatever was back there as the boat turned into the sun's glare. She struggled to stay on her feet and found a woman she recognized. Twice she had to shout "What happened?" and finally took the woman by the shoulders. "Did we hit something?"

"They gone," the woman cried, pointing to a section of broken railing. "They was there one minute, now they gone. Don't know how many boys."

"Oh my god, can they swim?"

"Sea took 'em, they drowned by now. Been too long in water this dark . . . unless Mr. León—" A look of recognition came into the woman's eyes. "My lord, you're his wife."

"What about Leo? Tell me." Lydia realized she was shaking

----

the woman, so she pulled her close and forced a smile. "I'm sorry, but I need to know. Where is he?"

"He gone, too, sugar. First one boy, then another—they was kicking at some ball and the railing broke. Mr. León was the first to notice and he almost fell himself—I saw the whole thing. That sweet man, he yelled something and jumped. Didn't wait for the boat to stop, no he didn't, just jumped into water so black, makes me faint. That's the last anybody seen of 'em. I know, yes I do, the sea don't give back what she takes because—" The woman, in shock, continued babbling.

Lydia pushed away and ran toward the bridge. The captain was up there with binoculars, braced against a stanchion outside the wheelhouse. He waved directions to someone inside while battling to see through the glare. Nothing in their wake but seagulls and an oil slick, miles long, made by the ship's propellers. Men had organized a sort of bucket brigade, passing life jackets, not water, and throwing them over the side.

"Do you see them?" she yelled. "Stop wasting those PFDs until you're sure. Do you hear me?"

No response. She kept running. The stairs to the bridge were a series of switchbacks. Elevation magnified the impact of waves and the torque of an old steel hull in a tight turn. She didn't intend on grabbing the captain's arm but did when the bridge suddenly rolled as she stumbled onto the promenade.

"Ms. Lydia, what you doing up here, girl?"

"I thought you could use another set of eyes," she said. "Where are they?"

The captain, in his braided cap, elfin-sized and cheery, wasn't smiling when he lowered the binoculars. "What I hope didn't happen was we'd run 'em over with the props. Don't know, but so far don't see no sign." He resumed his search, adding, "Two fine boys, I was told, and—hate to say this, ma'am—your husband, too. I saw him go overboard myself . . . You ain't gonna faint on me, are you?"

Lydia felt a dizzying sense of unreality but maintained control. "He's not my husband," she said. "We're just traveling together."

"That a fact? So it was worry for a friend that brought you running clear up here?"

"Yes . . . no. See, I worked on a commercial vessel for more than a year, and we did a lot of man-overboard drills. If I can help, I want to."

"A cruise ship?"

"A special service vessel named *Diamond Cutter*. I wasn't skipper but went ahead and got my mate's license anyway. But if you don't want me on the bridge—"

"Stay put, girl. My eyes aren't what they used to be." Again, a quick glance. He didn't know what to think of this small, boney woman with her cool, detached tone, a little out of breath but otherwise calm. "Did you see what happened? Reason I ask is, I didn't. Maybe you got a better idea of where them boys went in."

"I was asleep. I thought we'd hit something. You weren't on the bridge?"

The little man waved and hollered a change of course to a pane of glass, then spoke normally. "Your . . . friend, I guess, Mr. León, he was at the wheel as they went over—and I'll probably lose my ticket for it. Doing a fine job, too, I don't give a damn what the maritime board's gonna say. If he hadn't kept an eye on those boys, jamming us into reverse like he did, they might have been long gone before anyone noticed."

"Wait . . . Leonard was up here? A woman just told me an entirely different story. That he was—"

"Here on the bridge, yes, ma'am, at my invitation. If there's a hundred souls aboard, you'll get a hundred different stories if something bad happens at sea. It's always that way. That's why ships have a log. What happened is, I was in the head—the facilities, so to speak—and when the engines rang into reverse, I come out just as your gentleman friend went over the railing. Lost his balance, I thought, but I know better now."

"He jumped?"

"Mate saw him do it. Don't you worry, Ms. Lydia, a man that brave deserves to be found. Them fine boys, too. Here"—he looped the binoculars around her neck—"you look while I get back on the radio. I raised the yacht club at Little San Sal and a private vessel of some kind nearby. They supposed to send more boats and a helicopter."

Lydia, dazed, peered over the railing and had to step back.

- - - - - - - - - - -

Thirty feet below, a river of water peeled along the hull churning sargasso weed and froth. "Jesus Christ," she whispered. "*Leonard.* The fall alone could've killed him."

"Went after them boys, yes he did. I'm gonna give him my cap once they're all safe aboard. A medal, too, if I had one. You sure you're okay?"

She had to pretend she was. When the captain returned a few minutes later, she had the binoculars focused and managed to say, "Off the bow, about two hundred yards, at one o'clock, I see what could be a plastic bag, a log maybe. Something floating, not swimming. Oh, and there's a hell of a big shark in the area. I got a glimpse of its fin."

"The big deacons are always along this ledge," the old man said, and banged on the glass to get the mate's attention. "Point to what you see," he said. She did, and the freighter swung a few degrees to the right. "Think it could be . . . something else?"

Lydia thought, *Yes, a body,* but said, "There's a vessel approaching from the west, maybe the one you mentioned. I think I recognize it from last night at the resort. A private yacht, at least the lines are similar. Want a look?"

"You point, I'll go back inside and steer," the captain replied. "The hand signs are something you seem to know just fine."

She waited until the captain was gone to remind herself that parting with Leonard would've happened anyway.

11

- - - - - - - - - - -

Tamara was in Ford's cottage showering when a van with black-tinted windows drove past for the second time that afternoon. The shower window was small, the outdoor pump loud. Water off, she heard the van accelerate, but it turned out to be a plane approaching from the east.

Thank god, the biologist was finally back from his meeting with Purcell. It was nearly sunset.

A towel and sandals were handy. From the porch, she watched the plane angle low toward the beach, wings like crystal in the harsh light. Then it unexpectedly banked south along the coast, shrinking smaller and smaller, until trees blocked it from view.

That was odd. It was Ford's plane—a blue-and-white fuselage

with big torpedo floats. She'd never flown but knew that a float-plane needed daylight to land on water. The biologist had told her so. Where was he headed? There was nothing south but a dead-end road, then thirty miles of mangroves linked by bays and unin-habited islands. After that, open sea clear to Cuba.

Maybe the van had something to do with it. She knotted the towel and walked to the beach for a better angle. No plane, but the sound of its engine was audible over the slow wash of waves.

Crazy fool's lost, she thought, but knew it couldn't be true. The man was too studious and aware. She had similar doubts about something else on her mind—the claim they were cousins, albeit a second cousin. So what if the biologist had an uncle named Ga-trell who had fathered children in the Bahamas? That didn't prove a damn thing. It was Tamara's way of dealing with what might have happened last night if she'd acted on emotions that were still fresh in her mind today. Her alone in the double bed, Ford on the other side of a door that didn't lock, in a cabin so small she could feel his heat through the wall. Sleeping there was his idea. A safety precaution because of Purcell, supposedly, but she believed it had more to do with the man who'd come around asking about the bald little American, Dr. Nickelby.

All because of a stolen logbook? Tamara wasn't convinced this was true either. Not that the biologist would lie to her. He was a rarity—a gentleman. Quiet, solid in his behavior, but had a fun side, despite a wall that blocked what was going behind his eyes.

The biologist. That's the way she thought of him, although she managed to call him Doc, and a few times Marion, which had a nice, familiar feel rolling off the tongue.

Like last night. She'd stepped out, wearing the oversized shirt he'd provided, and used his name in a scolding way, saying most decent folks were asleep by midnight and it was almost 2 a.m. Meaning come to bed, which she didn't add because of his startled reaction. It scared her—a cold, cold stare—when he glanced up from a book. Then the coldness was gone, tucked away behind the glare of his glasses. Only then did she notice bedsheets on the couch. And felt like a fool. Her, standing there naked, save for his shirt; the biologist, indifferent to an invitation that was obvious even without being said. As a gentleman, he'd tried to spare her feelings, which only irritated her.

"You look great in that Tigers jersey. Too good for me to wear, so it's yours." He motioned to a chair as he got up. "How about we split the last beer? There's something you can maybe help with."

Tamara was unaware the difference between a baggy shirt and a baseball jersey was the name Lamont and the number 22 on the back. "If I can," she said while he crossed into the little kitchenette. "But first, all I meant was, it's late. I didn't mean sleep in the same bed together."

That got a smile, at least, before he responded, "Don't I wish."

The biologist had a kindness about him. His request for help, she believed, was a contrivance to avoid further embarrassment—

----

even more irritating. He sat her down and explained that he'd proposed to a woman prior to leaving Florida and suspected she might say no. One way or another, the news would come in the form of a letter, the woman in question being the old-fashioned type and a stickler when it came to etiquette.

"Did she send you a thank-you card after you got her pregnant?" Tamara asked—a saucy guess, but her instincts were right as usual. The biologist admitted he wasn't sure who the father was, which caused her to say something she regretted. "I'd like to see the etiquette book where that situation's covered."

The man was bulletproof, thank goodness. Didn't appear to notice the slight. Nor did he bring up the subject of her late husband and the child she'd lost, so she took it upon herself as penance for the mean remark.

"It's easier pretending it never happened," she explained. "And tourists don't want that sadness anyway. I shouldn't have used Dixon as an excuse not to meet you for dinner. That was wrong."

"Your son?"

"He was five. The guilt of pretending he's still alive never bothered me before. It was a way of dodging certain situations—men drunk, on vacation usually. But you're different. I knew it before we found the wreck, and the way you handled Purcell proved it's true. That should make you feel a little better." Perplexed, she stared as the man put his face in his book and pretended to read. "Are you . . . You're not laughing?"

He was. Couldn't seem to hide it. "Not at you. Me. The whole

----

damn human comedy. What you don't know is . . . Well, listen. The woman I told you about, that's all true, she is pregnant, and she'll probably say no. That's why I was out here waiting for you to fall asleep—so *I* can sleep. Don't you get it?"

"Being faithful," Tamara nodded.

"No. It's a perfect excuse to climb in bed with someone else— not that you'd have allowed it—but what a crappy thing to do. Use someone like you, a woman I respect, for what? An ego boost? I asked you to hide out here for a few days so you'd be safe. Not to abuse the situation."

If it was all a lie, it was the sweetest lie she'd ever heard. That made it difficult to sleep. Images of Marion Ford occupied her mind. The width of his shoulders. His forearms, nicely veined. Hands that might gently explore, should she allow him to take liberties.

And she would allow it—a decision made that morning before the biologist went out for a swim. And before the stranger in his fancy sportsman clothes had revealed her maiden name.

Tamara returned to the present as she walked to the water's edge. Where in the world was that pretty little plane? The sound of its engine seemed louder yet varied with the wind. She waded out a ways and strained to see down the beach. Driftwood, plastic debris from freighters, lined a ridge of high-tide sand. A potcake dog, curly-tailed, trotted out from the palms, hiked a leg, and sniffed for crabs or turtle eggs.

Offshore was a spine of iron rock that could cut a man to pieces if the sea was up. More rock to the south, where the island curved along a portion of beach and the roof of a red beach house was visible. The stranger in the sporty clothes had claimed he was renting the place. She'd eavesdropped earlier and planned to accompany the biologist there for drinks after he landed.

If he landed.

Above a canopy of palms was the most likely spot for the plane to reappear. Pigeons, white-crowned, exploded like leaves into the sunset, spooked by something near the road. Curious, Tamara turned and saw two men coming toward her from the cottage. Official-looking, not tourists but young and hard—ball caps, slacks, collared shirts, and carrying bags that didn't belong on a beach. That was a first impression, her standing there in only a towel, until she realized they wore their caps low as protection from a sun that had already set. Something else: one carried a baton too large to conceal, although he tried.

"We have been looking for you and your friend Dr. Ford," the man hollered in a strangely formal way. A few steps later, he said, "How'd you like to help the Bahamian government and make some money?"

His accent wasn't Bahamian, and he wasn't the Cuban-looking guy who'd asked about Dr. Nickelby.

"Wait in your car while I change," she replied. "Or come back

- - - - - - - - - - -

in half an hour." There was a landline phone in the cottage. Her plan was to lock the doors and call the local constable.

The men kept coming, separating in a nonchalant way that was intended to put her at ease—or cut off her escape if she fled north up the beach.

"We won't take up much of your time," the man with the baton said. The baton, out in the open now, an electronic-looking device that might have been a cattle prod.

Tamara was trying to decide—run or swim? Either way, she'd have to drop the towel. The indignity this guaranteed would be worse if they caught her, a terrifying prospect. In that moment of indecision, a gust of wind brought the sound of a plane landing, baffled exhausts, its engine revving mightily for several seconds, then silence.

The man with the cattle prod stopped, looked from his partner to Tamara in mock surprise. "Oh . . . I didn't realize you are not dressed for visitors. Like you said, we'll come back later."

His partner responded, "Yes. Let us go find him." Foreigners with strange accents.

Tamara bolted the doors when they were gone and tried to call the constable stationed at Fresh Creek, twenty miles away.

The house phone was dead. Perhaps the men had cut the wire.

Because of the tin roof, she had to go outside to use her cell and was told by a woman, "Unless it's an emergency, missy, constable will have to wait 'til morning."

The Maule amphib was designed to make long hauls and land in tight spaces. Fully fueled, the six-cylinder turbo cruised at 130 knots with a range of six hundred–plus miles. But it wasn't quiet. Engine decibels rivaled an old Huey chopper, which is why Ford banked south to avoid alerting Jamie Middlebrook or anyone else in houses scattered along the beach.

Three miles of pine flats and mangroves was enough before circling back. He put down in a lagoon south of Mars Bay, killed the engine, and sailed the plane across a mile of shallows until the tide made the tail rudder useless. He waded ashore, rigged lines, and was on the beach in the last tangerine rays of sunlight. Deserted, a curving ribbon of sand. Shorebirds, rocks, and litter. In the far, far distance, an animal—a dog gone feral, curly-tailed, had found a turtle nest. Nearby, birds exploded from the palms. Pigeons, spooky on an island where they were baked in pies.

Ford adjusted his bag and walked. Middlebrook's rental was along the way, a red box on stilts, closer to the road than the water. He decided to stop, say hello, and make sure their time wouldn't be wasted later tonight.

The house was a typical pre-code beach construct built to be rebuilt, not to last. The yard was sand, a path outlined with conch shells. Requisite vacation equipage included a pair of cheap kayaks,

----

a grill, and a dented beach bike that lay rusting beneath palms. Out front, a small white Toyota also showed wear. Thousands of the used sedans were imported annually from Japan to augment the Bahamian rental fleet. A few hundred yards down the beach, the same model was parked outside Ford's cottage—if Tamara wasn't using it.

Social protocols were in order after butting heads with Middlebrook earlier in the day. He banged politely on the banister and called, "Hello, the house," then started up the steps but stopped. The door was open. Not wide, but enough to invite a cloud of sand flies swarming from the shade. The oversight would've been noticed by someone inside.

An internal warning bell began to chime.

He backed away for an overview. To the right of the entrance, a window bristled with broken glass, and a section of porch railing was gone. No . . . it lay in the weeds near the steps. Closer inspection showed a smear of what could be dried blood.

Someone might have taken a bad fall.

The rental car was worth a look. Keys were in the ignition. On the passenger seat, a bag of groceries—a six-pack of beer, a tub of butter, visible—sat in the late-afternoon heat. It was seven miles of bad road to the nearest store yet Middlebrook hadn't bothered to refrigerate his perishables—or was interrupted before he could.

Cerebral chimes signaled full alert. Social niceties were dismissed.

Ford opened his bag and removed what he needed. Wearing

----

gloves, he went up the steps, nudged the door open, and inspected the kitchen over the sights of his 9mm Sig Sauer pistol. The pocket version, a P938. Small enough to conceal in one hand if Middlebrook appeared from the bathroom or awoke after sleeping off a drunk.

"It's your neighbor," he called through the doorway. "You in there?"

Hopefully not. The main room opened seaward to a porch, where the rail was missing. The window had been broken from the outside. Glass and a busted screen littered the counter. Furniture was bamboo—one chair was overturned, and a couch had been positioned against the wall as a temporary incline—two freshly drilled holes in the wall suggested this was so. Remnants of duct tape and a water-sopped floor confirmed it. Cushions would be soaked, too, no need to touch. Ford knew what had happened. The other rooms appeared undisturbed but there wasn't time for a thorough search.

If the people who'd done this hadn't broken into his cottage, they soon would. Tamara was there alone.

The Toyota was tempting, creating more evidence for police wasn't. And a bicycle would be quieter. He pedaled north on Queen's Highway, a regal name for a lane of limestone that tunneled through scrub along the beach. Lots of potholes, and sand adrift like snow. Ahead was a blind turn. He slowed at the sound of a car coming fast from the other direction. A van, not a car, with its headlights on in the failing light. The van swerved, skidded toward him on a patch of sand. Ford dumped the bike and

----

looked back. Sat there on his butt and watched the driver's door fly open. When he saw who got out, he grabbed his bag and disappeared into a tangle of vines.

"Are you okay, mister? Jesus Christ, that was close."

"My leg," Ford hollered in response.

"Ah! Then you are injured?"

"My leg, goddamn it. Hurry up."

The driver continued calling out apologies as he approached the bicycle. Distinctive, the Germanic accent. Ford synced his movements with the voice while he circled toward the van. Through an opening in the scrub was the road. A man with a flashlight had joined the driver. No need for the light yet but there soon would be. He was dressed similarly: cargo slacks, a generic ball cap. Both were young, skinny, but soft around the middle, and they wore XL shirts, shirttails out, over Polos, to conceal the weapons they carried.

Tactical types, from the look of them, on some kind of job. Maybe badasses, maybe not. But if they hadn't left someone to guard the van, they certainly weren't well trained.

Twilight brought the misty weight of fog. Ford used it as cover. He ducked out from the brush with pistol drawn and slid through the open door into the van's driver's seat. He confirmed what was in the back before checking the ignition.

The keys were there.

Nope, they weren't pros. It meant there was a chance he could scare them into talking and maybe cut a deal.

12

- - - - - - - - - - -

At 9 p.m. Tamara made another call to the constable in Fresh Creek. To her, the disappearance of a biologist with government papers was an emergency. But not to the woman who answered—the constable's wife, most likely.

Ten minutes later, Tamara had finished a note to Ford, explaining her absence, and was going out the door when headlights chased her back inside.

It was the van. She slammed the dead bolt shut and retrieved the knife she'd kept nearby ever since her first dealings with the two. The blinds were drawn. On her knees, she crawled to a floor lamp, pulled the plug, and was about to peek outside when a familiar voice called her name. Blinds parted. The van was parked beneath the palms, and the biologist was almost to the porch.

"Turn on some lights," he said. "Bugs about ate me alive out there, and I need to use the head. Come on, we don't have much time."

Tamara ignored the urge to throw her arms around the man and followed him inside. "Where are they?"

"Who?"

"The ones belonging to that van. Why're you driving it?"

"So you met them. Is one of them the guy who asked about Nickelby? Their accents aren't Spanish, but I understand how you could've—"

"No. How do you know them? Those two acted more like big shots, mean, their eyes."

Ford noted the fear in her voice. "What did they say?"

"It's what they almost did. They would've chased me down if they hadn't heard your plane land. Are they outside waiting? They're not friends of yours. Can't be, thugs like that."

The biologist placed his bag on the table, not angry but almost. "Threatened you, in other words."

"I believe so, yes."

"They're fools. I had a talk with them. They left out the part about terrorizing you, but, trust me, the subject will come up again. Did they touch you?"

"Threatened me, that's all. Sort of spread out so I couldn't get away. I was on the beach wearing—well, doesn't matter. One

----

carried a thing, looked like a cattle prod. You know, an electric stick farmers use."

"A Taser—yeah, I saw it." He started toward the bathroom. "If you don't mind, start packing my stuff. Just as a precaution. We'll stop at your place on the way if it turns out you're not safe here. Depends on whether they're willing to come to an agreement."

"Those men? I can't leave. I've got a shop to run. Besides, go where this time of night?"

His voice answered through the bathroom door. "I'll let you know after I untie those two. I gave them a choice, now it's up to them."

They were in the van when she learned the biologist had left the men in the mangroves after saying, "Think about it."

W hat kind of man tied up thugs rather than go to the police? Tamara fretted while she waited in the van. Was it smarter to get out and run rather than involve herself in bad business like this?

It was after ten—late on an island where people matched their waking hours to the sun. And much too late to be alone here, parked far from the main road, which wasn't much of a road to begin with. Ford had left her with the doors locked, and waded into the scrub. On a headband he wore the scope he'd used earlier, the one that glowed and allowed him to see at night.

- - - - - - - - - - -

Fifteen minutes listening to screaming frogs had seemed like an hour.

On the drive, he'd explained that the men had been hired by someone—he didn't know who—to find Dr. Nickelby and the young woman he was traveling with.

"They're mall cops with some training, but they don't know when to stop. Jamie Middlebrook, the guy we were supposed to have drinks with tonight? They broke into his cottage and water-boarded him, I think. They swear they didn't, but . . . Anyway, it's an interrogation technique, if done right. Done wrong, it's murder. I have no idea where he is, and you and I were next on their list. They admitted that much."

"That they killed him?"

"They claim he was gone when they got there, but they damn near killed me. I'd just left his place and they tried to run me over. Somehow, I got lucky. They left the keys in the ignition when they came looking for me—I'd crawled into the brush to hide. The door was open, so I climbed in and found a gun in the console. The rest you're better off not knowing."

What Tamara knew was the biologist had lied just as convincingly about his lack of water skills.

"You shot them," she'd said, her tone flat to suggest that, either way, she wouldn't judge.

No. He told her he'd left them in the mangroves near where his plane was anchored. Dilly Creek, the area was called, a place

----

where old-timers claimed you could swing a pint jar and catch a gallon of mosquitoes.

"I don't know which is worse," she'd replied, "a bullet or an hour tied up in that swamp. What I'm wondering is, why a man who studies sharks and coral disease wouldn't call the police right off? And other stuff—waterboarding—how do you know about such things? I don't expect an answer, but if you were a teacher, it's not biology I think you'd be teaching."

"You might be onto something" was not the reply she expected. He had parked the van and looked at her in a thoughtful way. "A lesson, I guess that is what I'm trying to do. Like Purcell, there are other ways to turn people around. I promise you this, though, if those punks killed Middlebrook, we'll call the police as soon as—"

Tamara had cut him off, saying, "It wasn't no teenager that came after me with a cattle prod, or whatever you called it—"

"Half my age is close enough. So why not give them a chance and maybe get something in return? Like adults tell kids sure, games are fun, until someone gets hurt. That's the lesson for today. I'm not being nice. I want to use what I find out as leverage to make them leave you the hell alone."

Earlier, the men had been too cocky to answer questions—even at gunpoint.

"They knew you wouldn't shoot," Tamara had suggested.

Hearing that, the biologist had cleared his throat. "They got

----

more talkative when I used duct tape from their own bag. I suspect they took a course or two in security, now they're so-called private contractors. They probably see it in their heads like a movie. Big screen, fake blood. Violence isn't real until it happens to them, which is when the director is supposed to call cut. That's not the way it works. And they'll keep playing the role until they do something really stupid—even stupider than threatening you. Middlebrook, I'm still not sure what happened to him, so I gave them a choice."

Like before, Tamara didn't expect an answer but got an idea of what the choice was when the biologist reappeared from the darkness carrying a flashlight. He motioned for her to lower the window and used the light to herd the men onto the road.

It was pitiful the way they stumbled along, their skin and clothes caked in mud. The cockiness had been drained out of them. Probably a few pints of blood, too. Mosquitoes hovered like steam as one of the men looked at her without making eye contact and mumbled, "Sorry. We won't bother you again," then asked Ford in a surly-accented way, *"Ess daht goood enuf?"*

"As long as the rest checks out," he replied. "I'll leave your vehicle where you can find it. Sound fair? I don't expect to see you two again."

"Like we have a choice. What about our phones and equipment? We have much money invested."

"Enjoy your walk" was the reply.

That was it.

On the way back, he said, "They're from the Netherlands. Security guards, until they paid an agency to book them as ex–military contractors. No background check, obviously. The dumb-asses don't even know who hired them, but their fake bios must have been impressive—a decent chunk of expense money was waiting when they arrived in Nassau. Sloppy work all around. Ever hear of White Torch Limited? That's the company that cut their first check."

"What about that man, Mr. Middlebrook?" Tamara asked. Abducting thugs was bad enough. Murder, she'd have nothing to do with. Then said, "Thank you," as they turned down a lane where Middlebrook's cottage looked black in the headlights, sea and sky blacker in the distance.

The biologist parked. Rolled down the window, sniffed the air, and said, "His rental car's gone. No police. That's a good sign, I guess." He opened his bag and got out, wearing gloves, a flashlight in his left hand and something concealed in his right. "I won't be long. Keep the doors locked."

Tamara got out, too, saying, "Waiting gives me the spooks. Besides, I want to see for myself." She trailed him up the steps, careful not to touch anything because he warned it might be used as evidence. The cottage had a Halloween feel, the creaky darkness of it. Room to room they went, guided by the flashlight.

"Someone cleaned up—Middlebrook, I hope. His things are gone, even the sort of stuff most burglars would leave behind—shaving kit, like that. Let's check the bathroom again."

They were in the van when Ford opened up a little. "If I was sure he was dead, we'd be in my plane, headed for an airport with lights, and those two would still be tied up, waiting for the police. I think either Middlebrook left in a hurry or a fourth party is involved."

"I never saw him before he showed up this morning," Tamara said.

"Middlebrook?"

"None of those men."

The biologist was silent for a while. "The Cuban-looking guy you mentioned—do you remember anything else? Some Cubans have a lot of Indian blood."

"Same with most of us islanders. We didn't talk for long. There was something, a coldness in the way he acted. It's hard to describe."

"I was thinking more like an Aztec Indian. A guy who might be called that because of his looks."

"I don't understand."

"Or could be there are five or six or ten wannabe badasses all looking for the same thing. If it's not safe here, I'd like to take you along. Ever flown in a seaplane?"

She replied, "Being second cousins doesn't mean you owe me anything—even if it's true."

The man's glasses glinted in the lights of the dashboard. He was smiling. "Oh?"

"Not to me. There're a lot of Gatrells in the Bahamas."

"I'm beginning to believe it. The one I knew was a con artist. People liked him anyway." Ford talked about that, how the behavior of people sometimes confused him—no, mystified him, is the way he put it—adding, "Especially women. They loved the old crook. It still doesn't make any sense."

"The acorn," she murmured. That reference, and the scrub along the road, brought to mind the question he'd posed about White Torch: "It's the name of some of those trees along the road."

"What is?"

"The company you asked about. White Torch. There's black torch trees, too. I can't tell the difference. That's what they were used for back in the day: torches. And there's a shoal bridge off Little San Salvador called that—bits of land that poke up out of the sea—but I've never heard of the company. Isn't there an island in Florida named Torch Key?"

"Probably because of the same tree. What's it like?"

"Never set foot there."

"I mean the islands off Little San Sal, not Florida."

"That's what I'm saying. White Torch is a long stretch of shoals with only one island that's big enough to chart. It's private. Boats wouldn't stop—not local boats anyway—because the people there don't like outsiders. And they're . . . different."

"How so?"

"I see them on the mailboat. It's partly the way they look. Not

----

big, but great big hands and spiky hair—red hair sometimes. They're nice enough, unless you try to set foot on their island. What some say happens I don't believe because I'm a Christian."

"Really?" He asked a few more questions, before saying, "Maybe they spread the rumors to scare people off."

"Doubt it. They scary-looking, too. Families there only have two or three last names between them. The Marl people, is what they're called. Been that way for hundreds of years, I was told. Ever hear of 'em?"

Ford asked more questions before saying, "Maybe . . . in a way."

There was a sociological term, *castaway microcultures*. He wondered if it applied. In a previous century, he wasn't certain how far back—pirate times, most likely—survivors of shipwrecks had settled on the same remote islands that had saved them. After generations of isolation, living off the land and sea, inhabitants had bonded in unique subcultures, tribes with their own customs and religions. The Maroons of Jamaica were an example. The blue-eyed, copper-haired progeny of the Pinder family on Spanish Wells, Eleuthera, was another.

He said, "I suppose Marl is the most common family name."

"I doubt if that's the reason. You know that gray color of clay? Might be why they're called that. Inbred, is what some say, came here in back times from Scotland. A boat carrying witches that Scotland wanted to hang or burn is another rumor. Oh, there're all kinds of stories about White Torch."

"I never noticed it on a chart."

Tamara replied, "Most don't show a name. It's Marl Landing to lobstermen—that's all those people do, fish and catch lobster. No tourists. No beach neither, 'cause it's all rock and drops off like a mountain. Others, the old folks—I don't know why—they call the northern point of the island Deacons. The rest of the shoals, what bits of land that're high enough, must be named for the torch trees."

The biologist was interested. "Stay at my place again tonight. I've got stuff for sandwiches, and you can show me on the chart."

Tamara was dealing with those feelings again, in bed alone, in a space so tiny she could feel Ford's presence through the wall, when a distant scream took it all away. A second scream followed, the extended howl of an animal in pain.

"Lock up," he hollered from the other room. "Turn out the lights and stay away from windows until I get back."

She got a glimpse of the biologist going out the door: shorts, no shirt, boots untied, a gun in his hand. It was a little after midnight. His reading light was still on and he had yet to put the chart away. What she heard next was so chilling that closing a simple dead bolt became a complex task. A voice, a man's voice, far away. It shrieked fragmented notes of pain from somewhere inland. Then a single, distinct word—"*Mama?*"—and went silent.

After that, no more. Fear the man might scream again tainted

----

the possibility. On the counter was a knife, a folding knife, black carbon. The biologist had left it for her as protection. Despite what she'd been told, Tamara carried it from window to window, peering out after re-checking each lock, then to the bedroom, which had no lock. After twenty minutes, she remembered the constable at Fresh Creek.

The landline didn't work. There was no cell reception inside the cottage because of the tin roof. She would have to turn the lights bright and walk outside to make a call.

This time, Tamara decided, I'll get dressed first.

One of the security guards from the Netherlands was dead. A segment of his body hung from a tree near the van where Ford had left it, doors unlocked, key in the ignition. As a tether, the killer (or killers) had used a shark hook crimped to a long wire leader.

It was tackle commonly found on the island.

This man hadn't had time to scream.

Ford had grabbed only his pistol and a flashlight before running out to do a loop around the cottage. The van's dome light had lured him several hundred yards farther down the road. Too far to leave Tamara unguarded but too close not to look inside. It didn't take long to conclude the second man had been the source of the screams. Not here, somewhere nearby, and the abrupt silence suggested he was already dead.

With the flashlight, Ford searched from the bushes to the tree. What he saw was a ceremonial tableau. Body parts had been posed around a rib cage pendulum. Centered beneath were conch shells—also common on the island. They encircled a mound of viscera that cradled a human heart. Bark from one side of the tree had been slashed—out of rage or as the killer's territorial mark. Ford would have moved closer, but the area had been swept smooth with a palmetto frond that now lay at the edge of the road.

Instead, the flashlight probed incremental pools of sand. A triangular wedge of shell was within reach. He held it for inspection—a shark's tooth, not a shell. The angle and serrated edge suggested the genus *Carcharhinus* but were not conclusive. There were sixty species of requiem sharks and many genera.

Ford pocketed the tooth. The surest way to protect Tamara was to intercept the killer. He had to move fast. Sand and limestone were poor archivists when it came to footprints, so he searched for a blood trail.

If one existed, it, too, had been swept away.

He returned to the cottage at a run. A siren haze of mosquitoes kept pace. Lights were on, and the front door was wide open. He called her name, going up the porch stairs. Inside, no sign of a struggle. The backdoor handle came off in his hand because it

----

was locked. Carrying the night vision lens, he went out the front and ran to the beach.

"Tamara?"

Over and over, he called her name.

A sea wind rustled the palms. Waves thundered over a distant reef of iron rock. Focusing the monocular was no different than adjusting a camera lens. Close focus showed mushy sand along the tide line. Shoes larger than Ford's size 13s had exited the water and cleaved a path that trailed north and vanished in the drier sand of a dune ridge.

A twist of an optic ring brought a mile of lucent-green beach into focus. Staring back from the distance was a man. Tall, big shoulders, too far away for details except for the sheen of his rain-coat. No . . . possibly a biohazard suit that blood would not stain. And something else: a device the man wore on a headband. It emitted infrared light—invisible to the human eye. But not fourth-generation night optics.

A cyclops, one single glowing eye, was the impression—a thermal lens, possibly a camera. In the man's hand was a long-bladed knife. He lofted it overhead, yelled something, and charged. Ford walked toward him at a steady pace, the pistol concealed but ready. It was a strategic error. Killers expect victims to flee, not engage. The man slowed, hesitated, and finally stopped to reconsider.

Damn it.

Ford noted the hundred yards that separated them. Risk a foot-race or try to lure the guy within range? He turned and went the other way to invite pursuit—which is when he finally heard Tamara calling from the water. Indistinguishable, her words, but she was in distress, possibly hurt. It took another focus adjustment to locate her head bobbing midway between the beach and the reef.

"I'm coming," he yelled. Maybe the killer heard this as a threat. Ford watched him escape inland and abandoned any hope of pursuit. He holstered the pistol and waded out. Tamara was fully dressed, shivering but okay. "Wait until we're inside," he told her.

She was sitting with a cup of hot tea, a blanket around her, while the biologist alternately checked windows and listened. Tamara had left the porch to call the constable and had surprised the man as he crossed the yard toward the road.

"I don't think he was looking for me—it was the way he reacted—but I was so scared I ran. Get to the water, like this morning with those other two. That's all I could think about. Good thing because when I looked back, he was on the beach, wading in after me. He had a knife, a sword we call them. So I kept swimming. Even after he was gone I stayed out there, waiting for you. Who is he?"

"Did you get a close look?"

"It was dark, and I was so scared. I knew it wasn't you. I hadn't dialed the constable yet."

Ford said, "I think someone's killing off the competition. Hang on a sec."

What did that mean?

He went out and returned a few minutes later, saying, "We're

----

good. Whoever the guy is, pathology's involved. Or religion—it's hard to hang a tag on manic behavior. Middlebrook warned me that anyone looking for Nickelby is in danger. I should have listened. Now we have no choice. We have to get the police involved."

"Middlebrook . . . that's who was—"

"No. The two guys I left in the mangroves—one of them, that's who we heard." A warning hand discouraged questions. "You don't want to know what happened to him. Probably the other one, too. Shit." The biologist clubbed a fist against his thigh.

"You're not blaming yourself?"

"Not as the cause, but for the results. If I hadn't tried to teach them a lesson, they wouldn't have been on foot, unarmed, when he ambushed them. Yeah, one's dead. The other, I can't just go off and leave until I'm sure, so while I search you'll stay in the car. The rest can wait until we're on the plane."

Tamara wanted to fly out with him but didn't want to appear too anxious. "Like I said, you don't owe me anything, and I have a business to run."

"It's the slowest time of year for tourists," the biologist reminded her, "so why not? I'm meeting a friend in a couple of days on Cat Island—Tomlinson, the guy I said wrote a best seller? You'll like him."

- - - - - - - - - - -

13

Tomlinson caught the *Lady D* out of Nassau, a fourteen-hour mailboat fest to a casino resort near Spanish Wells. He appreciated art. The pool was resplendent with sculpted silicone breasts, but rich husbands gave him the willies.

Time to move on.

Governor's Harbour. He attended a drum circle at Bamboo Point. Feral cattle abandoned by conquistadors grazed with indifference as Rum Cay locals led him into a cave adorned with Lucayan petroglyphs a thousand years old.

No one had seen a short, bald American traveling with a woman who might be using the name Lydia Johnson.

Several stops and two days later, he was on the docks north of Arthur's Town, Cat Island, when a familiar seaplane flew over.

Wings wagged hello. The amphib banked east toward Little San Salvador, a speck on the horizon twelve miles away.

"That there's the deacon coming to collect," said a man cleaning fish. His words were a melody of percussive notes: *Dat dare's dah dee-CON cummin' tah CO-lect.*

"The pilot?" Tomlinson replied. "Uh-uh, he's a pal of mine. To get him in church, there'd have to be an aquarium behind the pulpit. Or a commie. Back to what I was saying—Dr. Nickelby's kind of a small, uptight dude. Bald. Probably wears—"

"No," the man interrupted. "Out yonder . . . That there's the deacons I mean. See 'em?"

The cleaning table was built over a creek that pushed a stream of indigo through shoals of copper and jade. An outgoing tide flushed seaward where water blackened hundreds of feet deep. A shadow appeared. It resembled a torpedo, snaking up from the depths. Several shadows followed—a slow, serpentine parade.

"Holy Begeezus," Tomlinson said. "Sharks. I was swimming here not an hour ago. Had to wash my hair."

"Looks nice, too," the man replied. "I like the bandana. Red's okay. Me? I'd select green if you regular in your bathing habits. The deacons come calling, they less likely to eat a man who resembles a bush."

He was cleaning snapper and one big bull dolphin—mahi mahi—that lay glistening in the sunlight. The knife freed skin from vertebrae, the head was severed. He flung the carcass, a cloud of gulls trailing it down as it smacked the water.

Shadows turned. The surface erupted. A scythe tail stirred a sustained explosion while the shadows tumbled in a glassine gel. The gel's clarity showed sharks large enough to snap off a man's leg. Beyond the shoals, a semicircle of fins sprouted. Fins converged beneath seabirds that hovered and dived for tidbits, quarrelsome as hyenas, while the water boiled.

"Deacon, he collect tithes for the gods of deep salty," the man explained. "As the Book says, *Every man give a tenth of his wealth and blessed he shall be.* I wouldn't expect a modern person such as yourself to understand."

Tomlinson replied, "Here's another one: *Each according to his heart give ye not grudgingly for God loveth a cheerful giver.* That's Corinthians 9:7 . . . Shit-oh-dear, look—I've never seen so many big goddamn sharks this close to shore."

"You know Scripture!" The man's eyes were rheumy as peeled grapes when he smiled. "That there's a rare quality in modern folk. Proud to meet a Bible-reading brothah, sir, yes I am."

"Doesn't mean I understand it. You've got to love a book where the hero dies in the middle but just keeps trucking on toward the Apocalypse. The Four Horsemen . . . Geezus"—his attention returned to the sharks—"that big bastard could swallow a saddle. How many people they eat annually?"

The smile broadened. "You're the first I met, sir, righteous enough to put cleanliness above losing a leg. As it's written, *Ye shall laugh at violence and famine, and will not be afraid of wild beasts.* Book of Job. Got any more? I love hearing Scripture while I work."

- - - - - - - - - - -

"I don't remember many laughs in Job. Cain and Abel were the Marx Brothers compared to that poor mullock."

"Oh, true, true. There's nothing funny about an ash heap with bugs crawling on your face, that much I can say from experience. Ever do any preaching?" Another carcass spiraled into the water's cauldron of froth.

"Not on purpose."

"Shoulda. The light of the Lord is in your eyes, sir."

"Fake it until you make it, I guess. I sent off fifty bucks for a divinity degree, so most of what I learned was out of guilt. Look at that sonuvabitch—a tiger shark, you think? It's hard to tell when they get a certain size."

"You ordained in a legal manner as well. That's smart."

"Sure, paid for with thirty pieces of silver."

"Thought you said fifty? Got my reverendship in a similar manner, but it weren't so expensive." The man leaned in to squint at a small gold Masonic ring on Tomlinson's finger. "Oh my," he said, and put down the knife.

"What's wrong, preacher?"

"The light of your ring is blinding to these old eyes. May I ask you something?" His question, a benign reference to travel, was, in fact, a Masonic test.

Tomlinson said, "Preacher, this is too cool," and provided the correct response.

After two more questions, the old man asked, "From whence do you hail, sir?"

- - - - - - - - - -

Tomlinson repositioned his feet and referenced a compass. Then said, "Tropical Lodge 56 in Florida, and Logia Soles de Martí, Havana. What about you?"

The old man, grinning, shook his hand in a peculiar way. "We Masonic brothahs in blood and the Gospel as well. This sure 'nuff is my lucky day. I am Josiah Bodden at your service, Brothah Tomlinson."

They talked about that for a while, Masonic lodges throughout the Caribbean, where, since the late 1700s, men of all colors and social standing had met in secret but on common ground. Finally, the old man returned to his fish and the subject of preaching.

"What matters is the fire you feel. Had my own church for a while, too. Out there"—the knife became a pointer—"on a little island, deep water all around. Like a plate the way it drops off, so that's how it's known. The sharks you see here ain't nothing compared to what feeds in them shoals on Deacons. You get seasick?"

Tomlinson, shaking his head, asked, "Why'd you give up your church?"

"Not because of the Marl people, that's for true. They ain't bad, just different, that's all. I can't abide a person who thinks that way. It's against our Masonic teachings. You got anything against thems that's different?"

"Padre, are you kidding? Look at how I'm dressed. I'm crazy about the Marls and I've never even heard of them. *Different* is what I'm about."

"What about naked womens?"

"Whoa! . . . Is this a trick question?"

"Amen, tricky is what they can be. But can you resist temptation when your eyes behold a feast?"

"Oh, I get it. *Whosoever looketh upon a woman with lust hath committed adultery in his heart.* Book of Matthew. Is that what you're after?"

"Just looking at womens ain't my problem, sir. Can't take you along if naked bothers you."

"Where? I might be willing to give it a try."

Again the knife became a pointer. "What I've been talking about. Some say a rich man bought the place, and his wife's always strutting around—or so they tell foreigners."

"Bought your church?"

"The island, brothah, is what some claim," the man said, "but now I deliver fish, not sermons. Come, avert your eyes if you want—that's up to you. She is one Jezebel-looking blonde. We can talk Scripture on the way."

The woman wasn't naked, but might've been stoned, when she stepped from behind a shed and beckoned in a secretive way. "You don't belong here," she whispered. "Do you work for the creep who's supposedly my husband?"

Her countenance was Surf City, not Portuguese. Even so, the song "The Girl from Ipanema" was suddenly so loud in his head

----

that answering became a challenge. "Uhh . . . no. But I could, sure. I mean, I will work for the creep if you want me to apply. Just—"

"I've seen you somewhere. What's your name?"

"It's, uhh . . ." That took a while, too.

"Tomlinson . . . ?" Her expression brightened. "Your first name, it's unusual. Sea-GARD . . . ?"

"Pronounced SAYG-ert, but the spelling's Norse, so don't even try."

"Hmm. That's familiar, too. Films maybe? I know I've seen the name somewhere, but it doesn't matter. Not as long as you have a boat and—" She paused. A slow-dawning look of recognition came over her. "Wait . . . can't be. You're not the writer, the Zen guy who was, like, a druggie genius way, way back and wrote—"

"That was so long ago, I don't even remember writing the damn thing," Tomlinson said, "but, yeah, okay. Now you can tell me why you're afraid of your husband the creep, or whatever he is. And why you're afraid of something else, too. I can't quite nail it to the wall. Is there a place we can talk?"

"Oh my god, this is so weird."

"I tell myself that umpteen times a day. Like now, this sort of shit—I couldn't dream up if I tried."

"Then it's true."

"Depends on the definition. What's your name?"

"Oh wow. I sort of remember the picture on the dust jacket—" She stepped back for a full-length view. "My god, you look enough

----

alike him, even if you're not. The title was . . . It'll come to me in a minute . . . That book saved my life when I was in rehab."

"I should probably read it again," Tomlinson replied.

"Seriously. And for you to show up here, it's just too freaky to be a coincidence, you know? Uh-oh, quiet." The woman watched the old preacher hiking up the hill, her eyes smoky green like a cat in moonlight.

"What's wrong?"

"We can't be seen together. Wait until Josiah goes in the house to do whatever it is he does. Through those trees there's a little cabana. I'll meet you there. Hurry."

The song trailed her toward the watery wedge of the sand— *Tall and tan and young and lovely*—a beach girl Amazon in a sarong and white bikini top that darkened her skin. Hips swaying, a tangle of cobalt hair swept the small of her back. The pleasure it caused was like a knife in the ribs, and Tomlinson sighed. "Holy moly."

"I got a Bible verse for you, too," Josiah called from the pathway. "Goes, *Get thee behind me, Satan.* I'd settle for your ass behind me once you fetch that other box of fish. Cover 'em good with ice, hear?"

Tomlinson did it, and caught up. "Who owns this place?"

"The man who's gonna cut your pecker off, you mess with that girl," the old preacher replied. "You think I'm lying? Some say he's done it. I told you to avert your damn eyes. What'd she say to you?"

"Baloney. That's what the owner wants you to believe. Basic fear tactics, man. What's his name?"

"Because it's true," Josiah countered, "ask around. No . . . wait 'til I show you what we come to see before they run our asses out of here. That building up yonder? Some claim the man's got pieces of people in jars and shit. Ain't been in there lately myself and don't wanna. Man owns that place, he's not a person to cross— that much, sir, is true. She invited you to her cabana, I suppose."

"What a prick," Tomlinson responded, looking up at the villa, which was coral pink with a red tile roof. On the bluff above was a block structure, slabs of concrete or rock with two small windows deep-set like the eyes of a pit bull. "I'd bet you the owner spreads those rumors to keep the locals in their place. His taste in architecture sucks, too. Does he own a string of Internet media companies? That would make sense."

"What you talking about?" Josiah said, offended. "That house been there forever."

"I mean the bunker up there on the bluff, the one with the pickled body parts. Like it was designed by twenty punch-drunk Nazis, and the owner probably treats his wife the same way. That girl's afraid of something, Rev. She needs help."

"Brothah Tomlinson, that there building is what used to be my church. You never been through a hurricane? Built it with my own hands."

"Oh . . . and a beautiful job you did, preacher," Tomlinson

----

amended. *"Closer to Heaven is a step closer to God,* like the Book says."

They were making a second trip as he asked, "Don't suppose you still have a key?"

On the rare days Josiah delivered fish, he also enjoyed a leisurely lunch with the cook. Tomlinson suspected romance was involved when the man warned, "A quiet, prayerful sorta lunch, so don't bother me. Be on the footbridge in thirty minutes, then we go."

"Why not the dock?"

"Never you mind, you'll find the bridge. And don't leave your pecker where it don't belong. I offer that as brotherly advice."

This gave Tomlinson permission to roam before angling back to the cabana. The island was a geology of pancaked rock, layer upon layer stacked high above the sea. Descending ledges were like steps for a race of giants. A tangle of yellow hibiscus framed a voyeur's view of the beach. He stopped and lingered to confirm she was alone—a rationalization. But what wasn't?

The cabana was thatch-roofed, opened-walled, with curtains that caught the breeze. The woman, a staged presence within. She stood, lit a cigarette . . . no, a joint—the savoring mechanics were unmistakable—then turned in profile to fan smoke from her face.

Her blue sarong was worn low on the hips. Outside, her white bikini top lay abandoned on a towel.

Whew! A vision to behold on an island that was more like a fortress out of Dante. Limestone peaks and blowholes like the inside of a cavern. Stone stairs that led to the bridge Josiah had referenced. And a lagoon with no dockage or beach but with a few old pangas pulled ashore.

Along the way were shadow people, yes, the color of marl, with wild hair. They worked from their haunches until approached, then skulked away or pretended not to hear Tomlinson's cheery greeting, "Hey, man, got a minute?"

None did except for her, the stunning female below. But the vibe was no longer hypnotic. It was troubling. She knew she was being watched. He sensed it, a telepathic awareness. The woman— a girl in her twenties, really—was in trouble: broken or afraid or desperate. The energy patterns were similar. So why not zigzag down the hill and lighten the mood?

He did, sidled close enough to say, "Does your husband really cut off body parts and put them in jars?"

"What took you so long?" she said, spinning around. "Josiah believes those crazy stories for the same reason I'm supposed to pretend I'm married. Come on, I'll have to get dressed if we stand out there." She parted the curtain just enough to allow him to slip past, then offered the joint. "You wouldn't like that, would you?"

Her wearing clothes, is what she meant, but he took a hit and

----

exhaled, saying, "Depends on the quality of the weed. There's no shame in marrying an asshole. My ex did it twice, and the first one was me."

"Don't say such things. I'm glad you're here . . . We don't have much time." Then she came into his arms a little too eagerly, but the trembling was real. "Are you really the writer? I don't need any more proof that I'm an idiot who makes shitty decisions. Two weeks I've spent on this shithole of a rock and I don't want to die here because of another lie."

Tomlinson held her at arm's length. "I don't accept payment for doing what's right. Just talk to me—your name, for starters."

"Not until you swear it's true. What I told you, I said I was in rehab when I read your book, but it wasn't rehab, it was a sort of hospital. If you are the writer, us meeting is no coincidence. You must know that if—" Her expression changed and she stepped back. "What's . . . Why are you doing that?"

Two wise blue eyes, unblinking, probed her forehead, then her face.

"Stop staring. I'm not trying to buy sympathy—just your help."

"I know."

"Then quit it. We're here, we're alone, and you're the first man—the first one he doesn't own anyway—so why not enjoy . . . Oh, I get it." She began to back away. "You think I'm crazy. Well, I'm not. And I'm not dumb enough to believe you're anything but—"

"The shock treatments," Tomlinson said gently. "For me, that wasn't the worst part. It was the humiliation. Like a lab rat in a

- - - - - - - - - - -

cage. Do they still use saline gel and a piece of rubber so you don't swallow your tongue?"

The woman gulped, weakening, then was suddenly suspicious. "How do you know that?"

"You asked for proof."

"That doesn't prove anything. Go—" She slapped the curtain open. "I've changed my mind. For all I know, this is one of his freaky games. I want you to leave."

"No you don't," Tomlinson countered, his voice soft. "You were hooked on something. Coke, probably. Your family has money. Or—" He paused, aware of their connection. "Christ, it was synthetic flake, wasn't it? That hellish shit. No wonder. But your family didn't send you here. Someone tricked you into believing . . . what? What happened three weeks ago?"

"There's no way you could know about that."

"Something happened, and I want to help you."

Her face contorted into a sob that was quickly contained when she fell into his arms. "Then it is true. It wouldn't have mattered. I'd about given up hope. Do you have a boat on Cat Island? Please say you do."

"You want to leave now?"

"Hell yes. Why do you think I stand out here like a whore at a bus stop, showing my tits, hoping a strange boat comes by? You could rent a boat—I'll pay you back, but it's got to be big enough and fast. Cat Island, that's too close. Nassau would be better. And don't tell anyone or word might get back to him."

"Fuck him," Tomlinson said. "Josiah won't mind giving you a ride. And I'll talk to—what the hell's the name of your husband, or whoever he is, the guy who owns this madhouse?"

"He doesn't own it, he leased the house for a month—a god-damn producer who said he'd get me into the movies. And forget Josiah. None of them will help. I think they're using me as bait because he left me and they know . . . Oh shit, hear that?"

She spun away. The thrumming approach of a helicopter had been masked by waves on the windward side. Her manner transitioned from fear to panic. "You've got to leave. Hurry"—she pushed him from behind—"but promise you'll come back. When? There's no way for me to contact you."

Tomlinson was going up the hill, screened by palms, as the chopper roared past. It tilted crab-like over the cabana as if to batter the woman hiding inside, then levitated over the bunker that had once been a church.

"Tomorrow or the next night," he had told the woman. "I'll signal with a flashlight."

"The Lord smiles on crazy people and fools," Josiah remarked later, "but not a dumbass peckerwood with shit for brains. Using her for bait 'til the man what brung her returns, is what she said? Could be she's smarter than you know."

"You're honor-bound to tell me the truth," Tomlinson said after repeating the story.

"Within the length of certain cable," the old man reminded him. "And I will. What I'm saying now is, you a fool to come back

----

here in a boat. Brother, you don't know nothin' 'bout piloting this stretch of bottom 'cause there ain't no bottom for a mile down. Here, watch."

They were on a footbridge above a creek, the sea—a black ledge—on one side, mangroves on the other. Josiah stomped several times and hefted a bucket of fish heads. "Don't need bait. The deacons, they know the sound a man makes. Like dancing." He stomped some more. "Go ahead, dance. You'll see."

Tomlinson, staring seaward, muttered, "Think I'll sit this one out, Rev." He glanced up to confirm a plane wasn't overhead. No clouds either to justify the size of shadows arising from the depths. The shadows took form, massive compared to the sharks he'd seen earlier. Pectoral fins like wings, their bodies slow, languid missiles accompanied by a flight of remoras.

There were three of them, ocean-going white tips, eighteen to twenty feet long.

"Those aren't sharks, man. Those are deep-space voyagers and they're returning to Earth. Doc's gotta see this."

"Maybe you crazy after all," Josiah replied and dumped the fish heads out in a slurry of blood. "Stand back . . . watch yourself. Some folks get dizzy, like they're too close to a fire. Now you understand?"

The island was a plate on a spindle, he explained as they motored away from the dock. Come by boat, there was only the lagoon with enough water to navigate, and the commercial dock they'd just left.

"Years ago," Josiah continued, "some foreigner stuck a bunch of mooring buoys off here like he was doing us poor natives a favor. Guess how long they lasted before them lines was cut? No sir, Brothah Tomlinson, to fetch that girl from the beach, you'd have to ground a vessel and wade ashore. Either that or swim."

14

T he story Leonard was learning to embrace did not mesh
with his memory of what transpired after the boys were
swept overboard.

A lot had happened in forty-eight hours. The details—
some anyway—were still fresh. He'd been at the helm of
Fresh Moon, high above the deck watching boys play soccer. Even
a lumbering old freighter was easy to steer, which allowed his eyes
to keep track of the score. Ahead were miles of golden-sunset
water. In the cabinet overhead were a few simple gauges and a
radar screen that showed a vessel of some type closing fast from
behind. The captain, a likable old guy in a braided cap, had

explained it all, and traded a few stories, before saying, "S'cuse me, gotta walk the dog."

The old Leonard Nickelby might have winced at this crude euphemism for a visit to the urinal, but not now. After battling thugs and winning a fistfight, he was able to appreciate the manly fellowship the remark shared. It was a humorous metaphor. Animals weren't even allowed on the bridge. Darn right, it was funny, and he'd made a mental note to use the expression himself—see how Lydia reacted.

Variations were playing through his head—*S'cuse me, Lady Anne, I gotta unleash the hound*—when it happened: A crush of boys went after the ball. A wave jolted the deck, the railing gave way, and the ocean swept the boys in—at least two, possibly three.

Oh my god. Stunned, he'd grabbed for something to steady himself—the gearshift, apparently—and slammed the engines into reverse while the wheel spun out of control. It was like hitting a wall. There were screams, mass panic among the passengers, as the freighter tilted in an impossible turn that flung open the wheelhouse door. Leonard was suddenly stumbling downhill.

After that, details became fuzzy. Only a few facts meshed with what eyewitnesses would later swear was true. What was real, what was fiction?

At first, Leonard tried to be honest with himself. What he remembered was that inertia, not bravery, had tumbled him outside onto the catwalk. It was possible his concern for the boys had sped

----

him faster toward the railing—too fast. The first mate claimed he had looked back to holler orders, then jumped. What Leonard remembered was the rail, waist-high, somersaulting him into space. Horrific long seconds of free fall ended with an impact that had jetted water up his shorts and almost ripped his arms off.

The rest he remembered clearly. He wasn't proud of how he had screamed for help while watching the freighter steam away. Then he had seen the boys in the water. Their heads had resembled twin coconuts bobbing in the wake, the sun low behind them. They'd found a wooden pallet to cling to. Odd-looking kids he recognized, with wild spiked hair, and both in hysterics, until they saw him wave and swim toward them.

For Leonard, everything changed after that. All decisions were simple because he had no choice. If he surrendered to panic, the boys would die, too.

A cascade of life jackets had flowered from the ship and were left behind. He'd gathered several and got the boys buckled in. For thirty minutes they'd drifted, watching the freighter circle the wrong goddamn area. A black-hulled yacht had joined the search, both vessels visible only when their heads crested a wave.

The tide, he realized, was pulling them toward an island maybe half a mile away. On the highest bluff was what looked like a bunker made of cement. No signs of life, no welcoming lights, and it would be dark soon.

"We're going to swim for it," he had told the boys. "Don't worry, it'll be fun. With these things"—the life jackets, he meant—"we could stay out here forever, but I'm getting a little hungry. How about you?"

In his previous life, children were noxious creatures best ignored. These two kids were different, which one proved when he replied, "Don't mind me sayin', sir, it's 'bout goddamn time you come up with a plan. Mudder be cookin' supper 'bout now."

"Your mother isn't on the boat?"

"The mailboat? Yes, sir. But not the same mama stays home and cooks."

Humorous, the boy's matter-of-fact manner. Like it was no big deal to be adrift as long as there was an adult along to supervise. They had kicked and splashed to within a hundred yards of land, pushing extra life jackets along as floats. A quarter moon had sprouted from the bluff and faced the sunset's last bronze rays. Leonard remembered smiling, listening to the boys chatter back and forth. Their accents were as different as their looks—Bahamian with a Scottish brogue. Lots of slang he didn't understand.

"Almost there," he'd said, then had to laugh. "I'll be damned, finally there's a boat—and I think those are people coming down the hill. They must've seen us. Wave . . . Keep waving . . ."

A small inflatable was speeding their way. That's when the other kid had cried, "We be so jumbey-fucked now!" which didn't make sense until he screamed and pointed to a pair of massive dorsal fins. Like periscopes, they cleaved a track straight for them.

"Don't move," Leonard remembered saying. And he might have said, "Pretend like you're a piece of wood. They don't give a damn about wood." But this was another blurry patch. What he knew for certain was, fear had caused his bowels to jettison all the water his shorts had ingested during the fall.

From shore, a woman's voice had shouted a warning. Men joined, yelling and waving directions to the boat. What Leonard remembered with absolute clarity was tucking a boy under each arm, the oily sheen of dorsal fins as they closed, and the lie he had whispered, which was, "Stay close. I won't let those bastards hurt you."

A woman, perhaps the boys' mother—that was unclear—had provided a hut on a rocky shoreline, where, two days later, Lydia sat and tried to concentrate on a diagram she'd found in the logbook.

She'd been at it a while. Her Spanish wasn't good, but she knew triangulation. And, although pleased to have Leonard back at her side, she was getting impatient with the newly anointed hero. "Stumbled or jumped, who cares? Lighten up and take a look at this." She indicated the diagram, then pointed. "Fitzpatrick could've been anchored out there. See? A rock pinnacle to the south, the way the shoreline curves—a lot of the elements match."

"Here and a hundred other islands," Leonard said, dismissing it as unimportant compared to recent events. "I don't care if the first mate changes his story. Maybe I did yell an order before I jumped. Yeah . . . it's possible. All I know is, I was the only one aboard who had the balls to save those kids."

"Yes, dear. Now please pay attention. Here, written in Spanish—*choza de esclavos*—a slave hut. It could be the place we're staying—you said yourself the walls, wattle with lime cement daub, are really old. These stick figures aren't much of a code. You know better than anyone what these upside-down *V*s represent."

The man thought for a moment. "Dorsal fins—Christ Almighty, don't remind me. It was hard enough to sleep the last two nights. Have you noticed the people here follow me around like . . . not like they're scared of me, exactly, more like I have some weird power, you know, magic, that drove those sharks away. You're the only one who knows the truth—I shit my pants, I was so scared. Capt. León's mysterious shark repellent—yuck! But it's probably better not to disappoint them, you think?"

"Leonard, the captain gave you his cap, not a cape with an *S* on it. Yes, you saved the boys. Be a gracious hero and let them have fun thanking you. While we're at it"—her eyes moved from the whitewashed hut to the water, then a spire of rock to the south—"we can use this as a base of operations."

"Those boys adore me, I think."

"Yes, Leonard."

"They need a role model, and I'd hate to . . . Okay, let's say at

----

the pig roast—the ceremony, whatever you want to call it—the men get drunk and order me to prove my powers by getting in the water at feeding time. How do I handle the situation? Me against two or three islanders, not a problem. But a whole drunken pack? You have to admit they're a scary-looking bunch. Inbred—and that's not a judgment, it's textbook. The crooked jaws and dwarfism, the hands twice the size of—"

"For god's sakes, do you hear yourself? You talk the way people probably talked about us before—"

"Okay, okay," Leonard cut in. "God, I hate it when you're right." He smiled and extended his hand. "Come on, I want to show you something."

Lydia found this so charming, she kissed his bald head and told him, "Lead on, Capitán."

He'd found a cache of shell tools near the water. A sharpened clam axe and a pick fashioned from the spire of a whelk. There were several conch shells that had been drilled and fitted with handles long ago.

"Pre-Columbian war clubs," he said, finally not so serious. "Some variety of the Taino people lived here, maybe fought a battle on this very spot six, seven hundred years ago. Look around. You're the one with the gift for ancient places."

"It's nice to see you back at work."

"Archaeology? Yeah, the timeless thread." He rinsed sand from another clam axe head. "The last person to touch this might have been the first to spot three strange-looking ships. And

----

stranger-looking men who wore armor. It's possible. But instead of using this"—he hacked the air with the clam—"they welcomed Columbus and his men as gods. Lydee, I'm not going to blow it like the Spaniards did."

The good vibe vanished. Lydia said, "Of course not—my Lord. Let's split up and see what we find."

It was one of those crystalline tropical mornings, sea and sky fused by a soundless ringing of aquamarine notes. White-crowned pigeons fled the low harsh light while the sun orbited on a meridian of deeper and timeless blue. A good day to ply the shallows for evidence of previous lives. Lydia waded, stooped, and inspected a bone that resembled a fish gorge, aware that Leonard was trying to make a point that had yet to gel.

The logbook was on her mind. A more pressing concern was the owner of the yacht that had joined in the rescue two nights ago—Efren Donner, the man dressed in white. He had caught her alone last night and insisted they talk privately. A boat would come for her in the afternoon. She hadn't shared this with Leonard.

"Are you listening?" he asked. The man was in teacher mode.

"You were discussing the indigenous Taino, professor," she replied.

"Or the Arawak, the Caribs—all considered tribal divisions of a single people. It was accepted as academic scripture that they migrated from Siberia to the Americas about thirteen thousand years ago. The theory began to change in the last decade, largely

----

based on archaeologies—artifacts, human bones—found in Argentina. Some date back—arguably, of course—fifteen, some claim sixteen, thousand years, which is before the Siberian land bridge existed. Isn't that wild?"

"Just crazy wild," Lydia said with a gentle sarcasm that he, of course, missed.

"Yep. Near-simultaneous dual migration. That's the new theory, meaning the Taino and others traveled by boat from Polynesia to South America. Later, filtered north to the Bahamas, possibly even Florida. When I was teaching, I refused to grant the theory more than a mention. The evidence is so flimsy." He shrugged to indicate something, she wasn't sure what, but was interested when he said, "Let's keep walking. There are some unusual petroglyphs on a stone I want you to see—and it's not the only thing that doesn't make sense about this island."

The main village was up a footpath, across a ridge, and down a sandy road. On both sides, rock crevices had been burned to expose the only fertile soil around—potholes planted with corn, gourds, pumpkins, beans. Gardens in a trash heap, is what they resembled. Most were marked with bits of rag or straw figurines.

"On any other island," Leonard said, "I would think they're Santería totems. To invite good luck or ward off evil. Voodoo, you know? But here, it's probably a mix of Gaelic and African."

"How do you know?"

Again, the secretive shrug.

From atop the ridge was a view of the sea and the village. A

----

scattering of houses embraced the shoreline. They were tiny, whitewashed, and thatched like the house where they'd slept after getting a little drunk the night before with the islanders.

"The water, the varieties of jade, it's so incredibly clear," she said.

"The more coral, the fewer the nutrients to murk it up," Leonard said, an expert on that, too.

Built out from the shoreline was a commercial pier. A crane linked the pier to a warehouse. It was a barn-sized building where lobster and fish were weighed, iced, and transported to populated areas such as Nassau. A sign on the building was too far away to read

MARL LANDING FISHERMAN'S CO-OP
NO VISITORS, NO WHOLESALE, NO TRESPASSING

"Buyers can't dock here," Leonard said. "Outsiders aren't welcome. No foreigners—it's the way they refer to all outsiders, Bahamians included. Last night, one of the boys' uncles confided in me. He said I was sent here for a reason, they believe. That I can be trusted. And, by god, they might be right."

Lydia thought, *I've created a monster,* but asked, "What else did he say?"

"Others took me aside after the uncle gave his okay. I've been accepted as one of them, you know. That's what yesterday's ceremony was all about."

"I believe you've mentioned it a time or two," she replied.

"Sarcasm," he said. "It's quite an honor, okay? This place is a real study in sociology. They told me stories they've inherited to keep foreigners away. Ghosts, blood rituals, typical voodoo stuff. The most interesting is that a rich man owns the island and lets them live here in return for taking care of a house he built years ago—you can see it only from the water. The place is actually on a chunk of rock that's connected to this island by a bridge." He paused, made eye contact. "Sound familiar? I learned a lot after you went to bed last night, dear."

Lydia sensed a trap that had to do with Efren Donner. "Are you saying it's the same house that what's-his-name bragged about owning? I warned you, didn't I?"

"Not just him. They've told the same story for decades. The house—a villa, they call it—isn't for rent unless the right person comes along. I'm not sure of the criteria. Could be someone they want to keep an eye on. Over the years, they've become experts at protecting themselves from outsiders. Keep that in mind," he added, then swept a hand along the coast. "Tell me what else doesn't make sense in a village inhabited by poor fishermen."

Lydia felt her stomach tense. She did a quick scan, seeing rickety buildings, a truck parked in the shade, a couple of tractors, a backhoe, no cars, no paved roads. Bicycles were common property, abandoned wherever the previous rider had gotten off. The island was not postcard idyllic. Trees on the ridge were wind-sheared, the landscape knobbed with limestone bluffs. No welcoming

----

189

beach among the coconut palms below. Just rock . . . except for a cove in the far, far distance, where there was a splotch of golden sand. A person was there—a woman, possibly.

When Lydia moved to get a better angle, the woman was gone. "What am I supposed to see?"

According to Leonard, what she hadn't noticed was the village medical clinic with air-conditioning. There was a dirt landing strip, a general store. The most incongruous was a small desalinization plant. Nearby was a building roofed with solar panels.

"A generator," he said, "that powers the entire island. The Bahamian government didn't build it. The police, public officials, they're not welcome either—and don't press the issue. I didn't. They appreciated that, I could tell."

"How does it feel to be so popular?" she asked, an affectionate jab with an edge.

"You still don't get it," he replied. "Everything here is different, the way people look, the language. But think about it. It took more than wild stories to stop the big-money syndicates from bribing officials and turning this island into a theme park like over there."

Twelve miles away, Little San Salvador was a misty knoll on the horizon. A few miles farther was another landmass. It resembled a bank of clouds girded to a single low peak.

"They haven't spoiled Cat Island, either, from what I've read, but only because the economy's doing okay. There's tourism, the

----

healthy sort, and commerce with other islands, but not enough to tell the government and everyone else to stay the heck away."

Lydia reacted as if a light had snapped on. "Ambergris," she said. "How else could a fisherman's co-op afford solar power and the rest of it? That airstrip—on an island that doesn't have a road? Or drugs. Or both."

"No," Leonard said. "It took me a while, too. What I think is, these people are rich."

Lydia took that as a metaphor for happiness, then realized. "You can't be serious."

"How else do you explain it? I think they have more money than God. They own the island and everything on it."

"Someone told you this?"

"Not in so many words. The people know they don't fit in with the outside world and they don't give a darn. So they bribe the right officials and spread rumors to protect what they don't want anyone to know. Whatever they need, they build or buy themselves. What else makes sense? I don't know where the money comes from, but there's been enough to keep them isolated for generations. It's only a theory, but . . . Come on."

She followed him uphill. The structure she'd seen from the mailboat materialized from a tangle of brush, but it wasn't concrete. The walls were rough-hewn rock covered with faded lime cement. Windows were as small as gun ports. The door was heavy planking bound with brass that had turned green.

"Don't bother, it's locked," Leonard said. "It used to be a church. Last night, she took me inside and showed me the stone. Symbols, some of them she knew I would recognize. The trust that shows, do you have any idea what it means?"

"It means we walked a hell of a long way for nothing," Lydia said, then softened up. "Look, I know she's an important person and all, but only here, nowhere else. I'm starting to wonder if she slipped something in your drink."

She was the woman who had looked too old to be the boys' mother yet had taken charge of them and every detail since their rescue. Then later, when a fire was built, had wrung Leonard's hand and addressed the villagers in a language that sounded foreign because of her accent and wording.

A passage recorded on Lydia's phone had taken them both time to decipher. A lilting voice with a brogue saying, "Dis gentl'man be sent us by Heaven, peoples, and dis be where he stay. Cap'n León, the man who gobsmacked dem shark. Jumbied 'em bad, he did, so us owes him two lives. Understand you me?" A dwarf of a woman, she and Leonard encircled by islanders, a hundred ashen faces suspended above a fire.

Mudder, the children called her—"Mother." The confusing part was the word was also used to address other females of child-bearing age. To adults, she was Kalik, also confusing. It was the name of a Bahamian beer.

Lydia, in weeds near the building, referenced the recording and

----

said, "Don't get carried away with all this, Leo. You weren't sent by Heaven. We flew coach out of West Palm Beach, remember?"

"Anthropomorphic signs of godly powers," he replied patiently. "It's common in isolated cultures. You probably learned about it in my class. On the other hand, a culture that has survived this long has to have something going for it. Right?"

"Oh come on."

"No. Think about the timing. Every person on that boat was in the right place at the right time. But only one of us had the courage to jump overboard and save Kalik's grandsons."

"You didn't jump, you fell," Lydia reminded him. "Why'd you really bring me here if you knew the place was locked? Did she tell you to do that, too?"

"In a way," he said, and motioned to the east. "Turns out, it's the perfect spot to ask about him."

Far below, on the island's windward side, was a black-hulled yacht Lydia had been trying hard to ignore.

"Oh," she said. That's all, putting it together—the old woman and other inhabitants on an island where nothing went unseen.

"Efren Donner," Leonard continued. "Last night was the second time you refused to set foot on his boat. Efren felt slighted. I got the impression he's more interested in you than me."

"That's just plain weird."

"Is it?"

"Of course it is. I said from the start he wants something. For all we know, he sent those gangsters to rob us. The gold Tricentennial is probably what he's after."

"You really believe that?"

Lydia surprised herself by replying softly, "No, Leo, that's not what I believe."

Leonard seemed equally surprised. "Thanks for admitting it, darling. Whatever the truth is, you can trust me."

"I do. The coin's part of it, maybe, but I think he wants to get me alone and pump me for information on Benthic."

"Ahh," he said. "So that's it. Something to do with the great Jimmy Jones. How long have you and Donner known each other?"

"We don't. I recognized him, that's all. He was an investor, not part of the crew. I know, I should've told you, but—"

Leonard's fingers found her hand. "It doesn't matter. You and me, we're a team, right?" A gentle squeeze communicated a bond. "I wish you would've come aboard last night. It's quite a boat. The guest suite is huge, nice shower, and there's satellite TV. And it's all ours for a week or so if you want. Donner made the same offer he made at the resort."

"I don't want anything to do with the man. Why didn't you just ask me before hiking all the way up here?"

Leonard had something else on his mind. "I've never pried into your personal life because I don't give a damn about your past. After those sharks, knowing I was going to die, the only thing in this world that scares me is the thought of losing you."

Lydia felt her tension fade, until he added, "That's why I need to ask you about last night."

How much honesty could her new love handle? "I don't want to lose you either, Leo," she said carefully. "Maybe I wasn't as sure as I should've been, but I am now. So why risk it?"

"Because it's how these people survive," he said. "She notices everything."

What did you and Donner talk about when you snuck off alone? is the question Leonard finally asked.

15

ord said, "Why is it I don't believe you left my mail on the
mailboat accidentally?"

"Ha-ha, you've got to appreciate the irony," Tomlinson
replied, a little nervous about what wasn't a lie, exactly, but
more a Freudian intermission. He knew what it was like to
travel with a bummed-out biologist. The linear chill of the man,
an emotional bottle rocket who, by god, refused to emote, let alone
count down from ten.

"Guess so," Ford said like it was no big deal. "On the bright
side, I see you didn't go off and leave your stash."

Tomlinson's hand leaped to his breast pocket. The biologist had
the nose of a goddamn bloodhound. "I'm just helping the local

economy, *hermano*. It was part of the deal I made for the boat—plus information we'll need tonight. We don't want the islanders to think we're both pinhead screws, now do we?"

"I didn't commit to tonight," his pal countered. "Right now I'm more concerned with someone stealing my mail."

Tomlinson assured him it would be okay. The clerk at Arthur's Town had agreed to lock the letters away in return for another ten-dollar bill. "We'll talk while you drive," he said, and started toward the little Toyota he'd rented. "You'll like the hotel. No TV, but there's a bar."

Not so fast, Ford said with a look. More time was needed to obsess about getting his seaplane situated in Joe Sound Creek on Cat Island's leeward side. And more questions about the truant mail—had Tomlinson opened the letters?

"I don't like what you're implying. And the answer is no. Sorta."

"I thought so," Ford said. "Toss me a line when I'm ready. While you're at it, tell me what was in the letters you didn't read." They were hip-deep in water, the bottom rough sand, with mangroves all around.

"Your son's turning out to be a carbon copy of you—but otherwise doing fine. He got out of some scrape in Granada. The envelope was too thick to decipher details. Something to do with a girl and a guitar player."

"Granada, as in Nicaragua?"

"Geezus, the island Reagan's storm troopers invaded. No wonder you two don't get along. Communication is key to everything,

----

man. Let's see . . . your daughter likes the Shimano racing bike. She flunked algebra but loved the class trip to Amsterdam, and both mothers still think you're a bumbling nerd and an asshole. No surprises there. That's a quick summary gleaned with the help of a magnifying glass and a light."

Ford responded, "I want to meet the old guy, the preacher— Josiah Bodden, you said? Some of what he told you doesn't make sense. I'm reluctant to kidnap a woman, whoever she is, until I know more."

"What's to make sense of?"

"Maybe I got the story wrong. The preacher sells fish on an island where people make their living catching fish? A fisherman's co-op. That strikes me as odd."

"He delivers to a private party who's in the film business, supposedly. Nothing strange about that. I'm not clear whether the guy owns or rents. He's a manipulative prick, that much I guarantee, and the woman is definitely in trouble." The hipster paused for effect. "You didn't ask about Hannah's letters."

Ford replied, "Is the guy's name Efren Donner?"

"Who?"

"You heard me."

"Efren, as in the movie producer? Where did you come up with that?"

"I have sources in Nassau who're interested."

"Then why ask me—unless it's to avoid talking about Hannah?"

- - - - - - - - - - -

"Geezus, just answer the question, okay? They seem sure it's him, but it would be nice to hear it firsthand."

"Efren . . . hmm. I don't know, I hope not. Wait, maybe I do. He hasn't made a picture in years, but the name's coming back to me. Yeah, Efren Donner. The biggest sleazeball in Hollywood. Or was. This could be a chance to stick his casting couch where it belongs—behind bars." Tomlinson followed the Hollywood tangent a while before getting back on track. "You're not curious about Hannah's letter?"

"No need. You'll tell me anyway."

"That's what you think, pal."

They were in the rental, driving north, before Tomlinson finally caved. "I didn't snoop. I was tempted, sure, then decided, don't get in the middle of something that's none of my business. Also, Hannah would be pissed if she knew. I'd lose her respect. A woman like her? No thanks. Doc, my advice is bang on her door and loop a ring on that finger like you never saw the letter. Which, thanks to my little oversight, happens to be the truth."

"Did me a favor, in other words?" Ford smiled. "This from a man whose expertise on monogamy ranks with hamsters and love-bugs." He laughed for the first time since finding a second mutilated corpse in a grove of what might be white torch trees.

It was a guess, still not confirmed.

Two nights ago, Tamara had accompanied him to the Consulate on West Hill Road in Nassau, where local police had deferred to a trio of national agency types. Now the woman was safely

----

tucked away at an undisclosed hotel—Ford didn't want to know—and he'd acquired a memory stick with information that allowed him to offer some advice of his own. "This isn't about Fitzpatrick's logbook anymore. It's about you getting home while you're still in one piece. Literally."

"Because of Efren the film creep?"

"I didn't say that. At least two men have been murdered in the last few days. More likely, three. Why? Because they were asking questions about Nickelby and Lydia Johnson. So I suggest we have a quiet beer, then you fly back to Florida tomorrow."

"Can't, man. The woman we're liberating said my book saved her life. I promised I'd be there last night or tonight—you'll understand when you see her. Karma involves all sorts of implicit debt. And what about Fitz?"

"Getting yourself killed won't help either one. Fitzpatrick sent you into the cross fire of something a lot bigger than you realize. When I say murdered, I mean butchered. I found the bodies."

"Like a revenge deal? I haven't pissed anyone off."

"I seriously doubt that," Ford said. "A cross fire—three or more factions all after the same thing. And it's not a logbook and a few stolen coins. Did you find out anything new about Nickelby?"

"That's why I'm not worried. Between Nassau and here, I must've spoken to a hundred people. Nada, is what I have to report. Well, except that a few days ago an American dived off the tower of a ship and rescued a couple of local boys. A hell of a swimmer, apparently. Doesn't sound like a government dweeb to me."

"Just asking questions about those two puts you in their sights. This is business to the people I'm talking about. They won't sympathize with your tales of friendship and woe when they grab you some dark night."

"If Fitz has nothing to do with it, why would they give a damn about me?"

"I just told you and you need to pay attention. There's a fourth player who doesn't fit the business template. That's who you need to worry about. Night before last on Andros, I got a look at him after I'd found a guy who'd been hacked to death like in some satanic ritual. He would've tried the same thing with me if I hadn't . . . That part can wait. You know those biohazard suits? He came dressed to kill, so he's either a psychopath or wants police to believe he's part of a cult. If that doesn't scare you, I've got pictures. So why not book a flight as a favor to me?"

Nope. Tomlinson only shrugged and said, "Maybe later when we get to the hotel. Josiah's waiting, so take the next left. The boat's all fueled and ready."

Ford continued straight. "Forget the damn boat and listen to reason."

"Right, man, like I'm gonna start now." Said it in a cheery way, as if to say, *You've got to be kidding.*

They went back and forth. Finally, Ford got frustrated. "Okay.

But I'm not going anywhere until I meet the preacher who sells fish to an island that's already ass-deep in fish. You don't think I asked the cops when I was in Nassau? They'd never heard of a minister named Josiah Bodden. But the island? Oh yeah. And their advice was stay the hell away because—"

"Because cops are xenophobic assholes," Tomlinson cut in, "judging people by the way they look. It's what they do, man."

"Wrong. I spoke with the regional commander. The island is under something called IPA jurisdiction, not his. He got pissy when I asked if he meant India Pale Ale, so I looked it up. Indigenous Protected Area—it's a designation similar to the Australian model created in the 1990s to preserve aboriginal culture. In other words, don't expect help from the Bahamian police."

"That'll be the day." Tomlinson chuckled. He had his arm out the window, steering the wind into his hair. "Indigenous—very cool, man. The Marl people—that's what they're called. They wouldn't talk to me, just went about their business like I was invisible. You're gonna love them. I still can't believe I haven't seen an article or something."

Ford caught himself before embarking on a discussion of the Taino Indios, not the Marls, and DNA evidence that suggested the Caribbean tribes were long gone. "There's nothing to read because IPA policy prohibits exploitation of any kind," he said. "No journalists, no Efren Donner types, and no sightseers, which includes us. Modern charts don't show the island's name because that's the way they want it. The islanders *are* the IPA. Are you following me here?"

"Marl Landing, is what I was told," Tomlinson replied, unimpressed. "They're a lovely agrarian people. We'll pop over, grab the girl, and be gone—with enough evidence to put Donner, or whoever the schmuck is, in jail. It'll make a good story down the road"—he grinned—"to help convince the grandkids you're not a nerd-slash-asshole."

"It's going to take more than sarcasm to convince me," Ford said. "White Torch is the actual name, if you're interested."

"Whatever, man. How about sharks?"

"What about them?"

"The day I was with Josiah, I saw the biggest sharks I've ever seen—ocean-going white tips twenty feet long. Aren't you working on some kind of repellent based on how sharks respond to sound?"

Ford didn't buy it. "Oceanic white tips don't get that big."

"They do around Marl Landing." Tomlinson watched wire-rimmed glasses tilt with interest before continuing, "The island's like a plate on a spindle—that's the way Brother Josiah described it to me. We're both thirty-second-degree Freemasons, by the way, so he wouldn't lie. We took the same oath about certain obligations, so your cop buddies got it all wrong."

This was a rare opportunity for Ford to respond, "Whatever."

"You'll like Josiah. Interesting guy, and he'd be a good source for your research project. Big-assed ocean-going white tips the size of canoes, they zoom up out of the blue within a few yards of shore."

- - - - - - - - - - -

The rental car slowed. "How close? Oceanic white tips are rarely found in water less than forty meters deep."

Tomlinson tried not to smile. His pal was like a security camera, clicking away without emotion until something pissed him off or interested him. "Close, man. I saw them with my own two baby blues. Josiah didn't even need to chum. Just stomped his feet like he was dancing. A Pavlov's dog sort of deal."

Ford, of course, wanted more details, before he conceded, "They're conditioned to respond to sound—I'll be damned. A wooden footbridge . . . makes sense. Wood conducts sound in the low-frequency ranges that sharks can hear, humans can't. To them, two octaves below the lowest note on a piano is the equivalent of a siren."

"Dude, you should've seen them. But if you've made up your mind, no worries, I'll go it alone."

The biologist didn't hear the last part. He was somewhere in his head for a while, then decided, "Guess it wouldn't hurt to take a ride out there—but now, not tonight."

Walking toward the old preacher, he added, "You didn't talk me into this. If I get a boat, you're booking a flight out tomorrow. That's the deal."

- - - - - - - - - - -

16

ord wasn't interested in dueling Bible verses, so he wandered off to inspect the boat Tomlinson had rented. It was a beat-up 28-foot Mako with outriggers and twin Chryslers that pre-dated four-stroke dependability. A second concern was that most boats over 26 feet sink when flooded because manufacturers aren't required to add flotation to the inner hull.

This small-print detail had drowned more than a few novice mariners.

Even so, a nice rig in its day. Tomlinson had provisioned the cooler. Twin bilge pumps worked, running lights did not. The VHF radio was passable. Safety equipment included a plastic whistle and life jackets, two of which were leaking kapok. A flashlight was used to inspect the inner hull. The stringers were mushy despite a fiberglass veneer.

Strike three.

Ford returned to the wharf, where the Reverend Josiah Bodden sat mending a net, and said, "I think we need a smaller boat."

"A minimalist"—Tomlinson chuckled—"who, I swear to god, never even saw the movie." He was addressing the old man, who was tall and sinewy, with big hands that had memorized the weave of the net he was patching. "There's been a development," the hipster added, looking at Ford. "Listen to this."

"We been talking," Josiah said, "and, fact is, the lady in question don't need your help, 'cause I carried her to Arthur's Town yesterday. Claimed to me she ain't married to the gentleman says he rented that house. Hope I did right, sir. I got no power when womens seek me out in tears."

"Don't we know it." Tomlinson smiled. "Helped the lady despite the schmuck, whoever he is, that claims he owns the island, too."

"Oh, there's no doubt Mr. Cailleach's the one owns the place and he is a bad man to cross. Whole family been that way for years."

Tomlinson heard the name as Kalik. "Like the beer?"

"Similar. Spelled different, I think. I'd have to see it on paper. I never believed she was his wife, a gentleman that old, but a man rich enough to rent that house?"—Josiah shrugged and tied another knot—"could have me jumbey-dicked, nobody'd lift an eye.

- - - - - - - - - - -

But as the Book says, *The name of the Lord is a strong tower that guideth the righteous.* Proverbs 18:10."

"Damn right, you're righteous," Tomlinson said, then explained, "Josiah drove her to a house near Fernandez Bay, so we'll probably see her at the bar tonight. That should be interesting. I booked a couple of rooms there."

Ford was dubious. "Could you be talking about an American named Efren Donner?"

"Him? Might be he's the gentleman rented the main house for a bit. The owner allows that sometimes, I've heard."

Ford said, "I don't know what jumbey-dicked means, Reverend, but it doesn't sound good. So why take the risk? You could've made an anonymous call to the police or some other agency if you thought she was in danger."

"The po-lice ain't welcome at Marl Landing," Josiah replied. "Reckon I ain't welcome there myself no more. Yes, sir, what I did gonna hit me in the pocketbook. And another spot more dear than money. The cook out there, her and me are what you'd call special friends." A locker-room smile came as naturally to his lips as the quotation that followed. "*Even though the spirit be willing, the flesh of a lonely man is weak.* Book of Matthew."

Tomlinson sensed his pal's skepticism. "All men of God have a raven pecking at their heart. Dude, it's called being human. I know what's on your mind. Go ahead, ask the man."

"You do it," Ford said. "Maybe I'll learn something about myself."

"He's the suspicious type, Rev. He's concerned you made up a story about the girl to stop us from interfering. Left out details, who knows? Or so we wouldn't piss off the people by going ashore."

The old man looked up at Ford. "I hear you're a scientist, sir, that studies sharks. You're a smart one, and you're right. The part I left out is, folks there wanted that woman gone. The rest is true. She 'bout cried for happiness when I told her to pack her things. Just doing my godly duty at the same time."

"Why would the owner rent the place to Donner, or anyone, then get rid of a woman who was with him?"

"Mr. Cailleach musta wanted his privacy," Josiah said, pronouncing the name as Ka-LEEK-ah. "Maybe because of what happened two nights ago. A tourist jumped off the mailboat and rescued some island boys who woulda drowned if not for him. Some say he killed a big shark, too, and the Marl people, they very superstitious."

"What kind of shark?" Ford asked.

"Dunno. It's possible, sir, they didn't want the lady to view a certain ceremony held for the tourist gentleman as thanks for his bravery. As the Scripture says, *Suffer not the Prophetess Jezebel for she seduces and fornicates, and despoils all that her eyes behold.*"

"Book of Revelation," Tomlinson said.

"Ain't he something." Josiah cackled, then looked from Ford to the 28-foot Mako, floating bow-out from the dock. "Sir, where you're wrong is, if I wanted to stop you, why would I rent you my own boat?"

"That's yours, huh? Guess I owe you an apology," Ford said. "Don't suppose you'd be willing to come along as our guide?"

The man considering the question was up in years but not old; still demonstrated a physical swagger in the easygoing way he moved. Like now, getting to his feet, saying, "You want to study sharks, sir, don't even need a boat. Just chum, and I got a big block in the freezer. Your friend there will tell you." Josiah motioned to the cleaning table.

"He already did," Ford said. "I want to go to the island, the place you stomped your feet and—"

"Same as here," Josiah said. "I dance and the deacons, they come. You'll see." He was walking toward a building where there was a gas pump, and conch shells piled high at the water's edge.

When they were alone, Tomlinson opened the trunk of the rental car, a tad dispirited. "If he wasn't a fellow Mason, I'd wonder about the guy myself, *hermano*. You don't think he backed out as our guide because he futzed with those engines somehow, do you?"

"Kill us or leave us adrift, maybe," Ford said, "but I've yet to meet a fisherman who'd damage his own boat. Besides, I've got an electronic device I want to test. Better here than in deep water with oceanic white tips."

J osiah Bodden did it, stomped his feet, until he noticed the biologist looking at his watch. "You got some place you gotta be?"

"I'm timing the process in case they show."

"The deacons? It's a little early in the day, sir, but, yeah, man, they gonna show." He stomped and banged a pail of ground fish offal that had been frozen. A chumsicle, as it was known in the small—and misguided, in Ford's opinion—circle of operators who specialized in shark diving trips.

Baiting sharks for entertainment was a pet peeve. In 2001, Florida banned the practice, chasing operators to the Bahamas, where "experts on human–shark interaction" could still make a profit.

It was the way they promoted trips that was irksome. Instead of an honest we-bait-sharks-and-sell-tickets approach, they advertised themselves as saviors of a misunderstood species. The only way to appreciate the benign nature of sharks was to observe them underwater, within stroking distance, as they fed. Some even spoke of communicating with their saltwater kindred on a deeper level—a pun entirely missed, which, in Ford's experience, was typical.

The first casualty of the self-righteous was humor.

"I'd prefer you didn't chum," he said to Josiah.

"Man, why not? This where we clean fish."

"If you had fish to clean, fine. But what interests me is, do they associate the sound of your feet with food? The connection is, have they learned to associate human activity with feeding? Or is it the chum that attracts them?"

"Oh, fish got brains, sir. They quick to learn. Don't you doubt that."

"I don't," Ford said, aware that his personal bias was a threat to his own objectivity. Previous studies on the cognitive abilities of fish also had to be ignored. A long list:

> Common channel catfish recognized the voice of a specific human up to five years after last being called to eat.

> Rainbow trout had been trained to press a bar to get food and remembered the process three months after the bar had been removed.

> A study on carp provided evidence of what many Florida anglers already know—fish remember stress associated with capture and become more difficult to catch. Snook and tarpon were particularly frustrating examples.

Spatial and social learning skills had also been documented:

> Groupers solicited joint hunts with moray eels by shaking their heads near the morays' coral hideout. The morays

----

flushed prey from the coral and were rewarded with scraps
from the frenzy that followed.

Fish could return to a specific foraging area in an acre of
coral by geometric integration. They employed a wide range
of techniques to navigate, using the sun, magnetic fields, and
landmarks as cognitive maps.

The aquaria in Ford's lab provided daily anecdotal examples.
Snapper dozing in the dark became excited when he opened a
cabinet where brine shrimp were stored. Sea horses and crabs responded to the sound of his footsteps. Flick on a certain light, the
whole room came alive because it was feeding time.

Years of observation had cemented his belief that fish, crustaceans, even filtering bivalves, learned cognitively. For this reason,
Ford employed a maxim to keep himself on track: *Belief is not
science. Belief is subjective.* It is an opinion—often a well-researched
and considered opinion, yet accurately applied only to politics and
religion and one's own canted view of the world.

Science was a process. It was ongoing, a discipline always to be
challenged and open to review—particularly data collected by a
field-worker with beliefs as deeply rooted as his own.

Which is why when Tomlinson pointed, yelling, "Here comes
a bull shark," Ford replied, "I believe you're right," as a warning to
himself. What he observed today, although part of the process,
would prove nothing.

The cleaning table was built over a creek, mangroves on the opposite side. The current had plowed a clear-water swath through the shallows and branched seaward in ribbons of indigo. Coming toward them was a shark, a six-footer, wide-bodied, with a head as blunt as a sledge.

"Yeah, bull shark," Ford said. "It's one of the few there's not much doubt about. I'm going in the water if it's okay, Reverend."

"Wouldn't recommend it, sir. No one swims here but fools— 'cept for your friend who the Lord smiled upon once. Wouldn't count on it twice."

Ford opened a small waterproof case. "I'm testing something that's supposed to repel sharks. Take a look."

The old man stopped clomping long enough to examine a coil of coaxial cable connected to an ankle strap. The strap housed a battery with a red switch. He eyed the device, oddly interested, as the biologist explained that the cable emitted a continuous electronic field. Fish were not fazed, but sharks, if they came too close, received a shock because their noses were dotted with supersensitive pores.

"A sort of gelatin in each tiny pore," Ford said, "called the ampullae of—well, the name doesn't matter. This is a prototype based on a concept developed in Australia. Shark Zapper, is how the designer wants to market the technology."

"My lord . . . Shark Zapper." Josiah was fascinated. "Does it work? Reason I ask is, I know people who'd pay a lot of money for something that does." He sounded serious, like a man who had

- - - - - - - - - - -

unexpected connections. Then added, "But they'd want to know if it works in a chum slick. Want me to chum or just keep dancing?"

"Just the sound of your feet for now," Ford replied.

He was walking away when Tomlinson pointed again. "Holy Begeezus, Doc, three more."

Another bull shark and two cinnamon-colored nurse sharks.

The dock extended into the creek. It was sided by mounds of conch shells butchered over the years. Ford followed a path through rubble to a ledge below the cleaning table. He wore shorts, gloves, rubber booties, and had a dive mask around his neck. Josiah, looking down, watched him strap the cable to his ankle. "Don't you got to flip that switch, sir?"

"Not until the sharks have made a couple of passes," Ford said, and stepped off the ledge into the water.

Tomlinson was already shooting video with his phone. "And here comes a freakin' big one," he said.

The advantage of diving beneath a dock is that pilings and cross struts provide protection. An open cage, of sorts. Razor barnacles were the drawback. They coated the pilings, so small cuts and blood were an accepted part of the process.

Ford held himself against the tide, breathing through a snorkel. A bull shark glided toward him with an escort of remoras. A scattering of sergeant major fish, yellow-striped, blocked his vision for an instant. The shark became a shadow that banked away. A brace of two-by-fours shielded his back—not completely, but enough for him to concentrate on the nurse sharks that followed. Buckskin tan in color, they hugged the sand similar to stingrays. Bottom-feeders with flat teeth that didn't cut, thus the name nurse.

The bull shark reappeared. Its pectoral fins were angled low like a jet ready for combat—a feeding display. Smell, sound, and turbulence detection lured it toward Ford, a bleeding primate. "Eddy chemotaxis," the combination of attractants was called. A larger bull shark materialized from a veil of blue. Then a tiger shark, thick-bodied, young enough that its denticle stripes throbbed with color—another sign of feeding mode.

Overhead, Josiah had ceased stomping. Ford lifted his head and called, "Drop some chum in. Downtide. Let's see what happens."

The feeding response was immediate. Sharks tangled like snakes, following a cloud of viscera away from the dock. A frenzy of smaller fish—jacks, barracuda, and snapper—joined in.

Again, he pushed the snorkel from his mouth. "Now uptide. And keep chumming. When they're close enough, I'll hit the switch. Tomlinson, you getting all this?"

"Yeah, video. Dude, you've got an out, right?"

Ford wouldn't have risked it otherwise. With three short strokes he could be out of the water. Or he could grab an overhead strut and hang like a monkey. "Keep chumming. I'll wave just before I zap them."

From the opposite side of the dock, fish heads rained down and swept past in a bloody murk of scales. For a nervous few seconds, visibility was zero, but a shock wave of displaced water indicated the sharks were coming at him en masse. He clung to a piling, freed a hand long enough to signal the men above, then twisted the switch on his ankle.

Six feet of cable began to pulse with low-amperage current. It was harmless to humans and sharks. Twin electrode plates completed the circuit only when immersed in saltwater. Like now.

The chum veil parted. Bull sharks rushed toward him, then ricocheted away like they'd been shot in the ass with a BB gun. The tiger shark made two passes before it had had enough. The nurse sharks, wherever they were, didn't bother.

"Switch off," Ford called. "Try it again."

They kept at it until there was no more chum. The only hitch was when the business end of the cable drifted into contact with Ford's leg—a hell of a shock, but harmless.

Josiah, the old preacher—if he was a preacher—greeted the biologist on the dock, saying, "Sure 'nuff did zap them deacons, sir! Say, I've been talking with Brothah Tomlinson and there's some things I didn't lie about, exactly, but . . . Anyway, after what I just saw, I've decided to trust you, too—even though you be a man outside our craft."

17

hile working for Benthic, Lydia had seen too many yachts not to equate bad taste with ego. Sometimes, not always, it was also the measure of the owner's capacity for cruelty. So it was no surprise that Efren Donner had embarrassed her last night by making a show of his secret invitation.

Less surprising was what he said now that she was aboard, just the two of them. "Leave it to Jimmy to choose a woman no one else would screw, let alone suspect. Brilliant, on your part. That's a compliment, Lydia. You'd understand, babe, if you knew anything about me or the film industry."

Lydia had to play along by saying, "I've always been interested in how creative people think."

That opened the door. He expounded on his "blockbuster" HBO series and awards, which came after he, a kid with a diploma and an attitude, had founded an addiction clinic that catered to the stars.

"Tough love," he said. "I was the first to take the cognitive-morality-is-bullshit approach and it worked. I admit it got me into the movie business, but I never used some actor's sick little secrets as leverage. Well, not much. Ha-ha-hah."

His laugh was three sharp notes, teeth clenched, in a face where chin, nose, and eyes formed a sunburned triangle.

This was while she toured the "yacht." It was an oversized speedboat, black hull, black trim, of a type rented by honeymooners or an executive who wanted to impress a mistress. The bar was adjacent to a hot tub, the interior fitted with ebony-and-purple accents. The air was fresher on the flybridge, at least, built forward of the entertainment deck. There, a view from the captain's chair had provided enough of a segue for Donner to admit who he was and that he knew a few things about her.

There had been plenty of hints along the way. Topside, cradled aft, was the inflatable boat that had participated in the search. This had given him an excuse to say, "Sorry your new boyfriend survived. That has to be a hell of a disappointment. How are you going to handle it now that your father fixation has become a native hero?"

The snag regarding her ego theory was that Donner didn't own the yacht. She'd used the restroom as an excuse to sneak a look at the registry papers posted, as required, near the helm. The boat was out of Caracas but titled to a company in Shanghai, as *Island Time*, the most generic name possible.

Strange.

Why would a Chinese company entrust the boat to a shrink turned film producer who'd been blacklisted, supposedly, after a scandal? Porn or pedophilia, she hadn't had a chance to look it up, but a sex scandal in Hollywood? It had been a while since the worst of them had been booted out of the business.

Strange indeed, yet interesting. Lydia was no longer intimidated by men. Twenty-two years of cowering had been enough. She knew Donner's motives for inviting her aboard. He was convinced she could lead him to the gold Jimmy Jones had stashed before going to prison. But was Donner working alone? An answer was worth tolerating his verbal abuse—for now.

"Do you hire a crew based on location or do you have a permanent staff?" she asked. It was a mild dig at the absence of crewmen on a boat so pretentious. They had settled aft, main deck, beneath a canopy that could be shuttered in or out depending on the sun. The settee couch was plush. The bar teak, but no one around to serve drinks.

"Small talk from a woman who likes big boats. Fabulous," Donner said. He smiled and opened a humidor. "Locals, if I need them. Usually by the day, then I boot their asses home . . . Cigar?"

"Instead of breathing yours, I think I'll move to a windward chair." She did, wineglass in hand.

"Windward. I like that. You sure know the salty dialogue. Might hire you as a consultant one day." The lighter he used whistled like a blowtorch. He puffed and puffed, lit the cigar again, and sat back. "Funny you should mention location. That's how I met Jimmy. Right here, in fact, seven, no, it was eight years ago. I'd just finished a project in Mexico and was under the gun to scope out the Bahamas. That's the first time I leased that place over there on the hill." He motioned to a small villa he had previously claimed to own. "Recognize it?"

"I saw it from the mailboat two days back," Lydia said without bothering to look. The architecture was Madrid Gothic, old, with columns and a red tile roof, built on a chunk of rock separate from the island where, that morning, Leonard had led her on a hike. "What I don't understand is, you're obviously wealthy. So why lie about owning something you don't?"

"Did I?"

"That's what you told Leonard the night you bought the coin. You don't remember?"

"Got me," he chuckled. "In a way, I do own the place, because I used it in a picture. A setup shot. *Broke its cherry*, in Hollywood-ese, which means no one else can use it again." He blew smoke and considered the coral colors of the house, the way it was built on an islet, across a wedge of water spanned by a rickety bridge. "Still looks great from a distance, huh? Back then, it really was

----

great. I mean, damn near perfect. But the plumbing, a bunch of stuff, has gone to hell over the last eight years. A big disappointment when I flew in three weeks ago. Bahamian fucks. If I hadn't brought along a protégée and paid the owner in advance—well, any port in a storm."

"You're not staying there?"

"I was until my little protégée got pissy about all the cobwebs and spiders. Why put up with that shit when I've got this?" The yacht, he meant. "Anyway, we were here doing a James Bond sort of thing and needed to grease some officials in private. That's why I rented the place. Babe, it's all about connections and tax breaks. Like Florida, the rubes dumped their film incentives program, which is why . . . Did you see *Pirates of the Caribbean*? The fifth episode was shot in Queensland-fucking-Australia. Not for the setting but because the Aussie government paid Disney a bundle. That's why. Hell, Georgia looks more like the goddamn Caribbean than Queensland. And no kangaroos to screw up your takes."

That set him off for a while, then he circled back to, "Don't believe the shit about artistic integrity and standards, the whole activist crap. It's pure fluff. Name any actress, I'll tell you where she started and I guarantee it was on her knees. Guys, too, for that matter. It's all about the money, babe. Fame seekers invented the bottom line."

Donner, a good-looking man for a fifty-year-old jerk, tilted his head and laughed, exhaling a stream of smoke. Then attempted an expression of concern after a glance at the island. On a hill

----

above the village, a fire burned, and people with wild hair prepared food. "Seriously, how're you going to lose the doofus professor? Jumps off a moving ship, my ass. The yokels might believe it
but I don't. What really happened?"

Lydia started to answer, but he cut her off. "What you don't
want is publicity—even from one of the Nassau rags. Understand
why? Then I'll tell you. A crazy-assed killer is looking for you and
your boyfriend. And I've got the video to prove it."

He opened a laptop, Lydia saying, "A man who makes films,
sure, I'm going to believe whatever it is you spliced together? There
won't be any publicity. The mailboat captain wanted a big ceremony until I spoke to him. So they're roasting a pig in Leonard's
honor, that's all. He promised."

"Oh, he promised." Donner chuckled. "In that case, sure, go
ahead, get yourselves killed. When you see this"—the laptop
again—"you'll understand. Does the professor know about you
and Jimmy?"

"Drop it, Efren. There's nothing to tell. What do you want
from me?"

Donner said back, pleased by her reaction, "Enough with the
jokes. What I want is to save your ass, but first let me finish about
Jimmy. Jimmy, he came on like a wunderkind. Met him at the
Atlantis in Nassau with couple of my regular backers. We listened
to his spiel—the underwater robot, tons of gold, yada yada yada—
and, goddamn, if that redneck cowboy wasn't right. Plus, it
sounded fun—a big production with a big payoff, like a script

----

from a movie only for real. I even had a couple of our writers do a treatment—*Caribbean Rim* was the working a title. What do you think?"

"You'd have to cast Leonard as the lead, is what I think."

"More jokes."

"Because he's bald and I'm not pretty enough? Fine, I couldn't stomach bargaining from my knees anyway. I don't know where Jimmy hid whatever it is you're looking for."

Donner's smile melted. "Don't play innocent. You and Jimmy screwed me over big-time. After he ran off, my backers blamed yours truly, which is why I haven't made a film since—no matter what the goddamn newspapers say. Me—one of the biggest names at HBO for nearly three years. So I visited the asshole in prison. The same prison where you signed the visitor sheet at least six times—but only once used your real name." He stared at her. "You must know a pro to get credentials that good."

Lydia didn't respond.

Donner viewed this as a victory. He said, "Hang on, I got something to show you." From a leather satchel, he produced a miniature baseball bat . . . no, a club with the handle taped, a single rusty nail protruding from the fat end. He placed it next to the humidor. "That Jimmy, huh? A redneck charmer with a degree from MIT. He gave me this during the shoot. A fishbilly, he called it—we'd been marlin fishing. Spoke to me like I was a city boob who didn't know jack about livin' off the land, swillin' moonshine, all that other country-boy crap."

He abandoned the good ol' boy accent and plunked the table with the club, the nail pointed upward. "Not long ago, I reminded Jimmy of this little present. You know, to illustrate what might happen. Then I gave *him* something—one last chance to draw a map for me and the other investors. In return, we'd drop the charges. Well, you know how that worked out. It's been almost a month, hasn't it"—the cigar provided a smoky pause—"since a con used Jimmy's head as a piñata? A thousand bucks. I guess it's a lot of money for a psycho doing life-times-two. Think I should've lowballed the job?"

"If that's a confession," Lydia said, "I didn't hear it, so don't get any ideas."

"I'm explaining how badly I was hurt, you know, *emotionally*. The banger who arranged it all had done a stretch there. As an actor, he stunk, but I know how to get the best out of the very worst actors you can imagine." Donner let her process that. "Did you happen to catch Jimmy's snuff scene before they pulled the clip from the Internet?"

Lydia swallowed, sipped her wine, and thought about throwing it in the face of a man whose eyes had never been impressed by anything larger than a mirror. But then what? Leave without knowing if the other investors were involved?

Donner leaned close enough to share the odor of his cologne. "Let me ask you something—the shrink in me is interested. When you saw poor Jimmy bleeding to death on YouTube, did you spend a few minutes in mourning? Or did you pack your bags and look for a stooge to mule your dive gear to the Bahamas?"

Enough. Half a glass of wine blinded Donner as she pushed out of her chair, but he grabbed her and pulled her back. "A little too close to the truth, sweetie?" he asked. The same glare, but brighter, like something behind his eyes had snapped.

She didn't try to wrestle her arm free. Told him calmly, "Efren, you might think Leonard's a fool, but the people on that island don't. All I have to do is wave and a boat will come. Good luck impressing them with your film credits."

The effect was startling. Donner took a deep breath and released her arm. "Inbred freaks," he muttered.

The man was afraid, she realized. It gave her confidence. "Then why did you come back?"

"Nostalgia, better days, I guess—and a card the realtor sent offering me the place for next to nothing if I'd book the whole month. But I'd forgotten just how nasty those people are. Didn't allow them on my side of the bridge after dark—that was in the first contract, too. The locals got pissed when they caught me shooting some drum ceremony. Me, what I'm thinking is a documentary for Sundance. A serious piece of art. They're thinking roast my head on a spit. I'm not shitting you."

Lydia, interested, offered him a towel. "Recently?"

"Eight years ago, after we'd wrapped. Personally, I think they intentionally fucked up everything we did on that shoot. Or tried

----

to. Third World magic, fear, blood offerings. But they don't scare me. People like them are easy to control if you know which buttons to push. Sort of like actors. Ha-ha-hah." That laugh again, while he used a towel and regained his composure.

Folding the towel, he said, "The Chablis's not too bad, huh? A joke, babe, loosen up. Look, I've got a proposition for you. But first"—the laptop had to be repositioned—"if this doesn't convince you we should work together, I'll take you to shore myself."

The video was rough-cut, shot at night with infrared, and time-stamped. A man—his hands were too big to be a female—wearing a GoPro camera had documented his voyeur-like pursuit of two people she recognized, one she did not. No audio. Just ghostly images like overexposed negatives in black-and-white.

"What they have in common is you," Donner explained. "One way or another, you and Leonard must've come into contact, spoken to them—I don't know, you tell me." He was nervous, wanted her full and friendly attention.

Lydia found it hard to breathe despite a breeze that would have pushed the yacht ashore were it not for automated thrusters and a GPS. "Who is he?"

"The shooter?"

"The one sneaking around with the camera."

"Same thing. I hope it's the shitty actor I mentioned. He stunk in a B flick about cage fighting, so I hired him as security on some legitimate shoots. Ex-military from El Salvador, which, by the way, is a gorgeous country. He knew about Jimmy, so it makes sense he's on your trail. If not"—Donner looked shoreward—"then maybe it's one of them."

On a hillside above the village, half a mile away, smoke filtered up through he trees. Lydia noted that a boat she'd seen earlier was no longer docked at the warehouse pier.

"Can you zoom in?" she asked.

Donner's attention returned to the computer. "You recognize the woman, right? I can tell. I know how to read my audience."

"It's been almost two weeks," Lydia said.

"I can read a time stamp, too, for Christ's sake. That's not what I asked."

"Yes, a large woman, sorta pretty. We talked for maybe ten minutes. Her name's Tamara-something. She runs a little dive shop on Andros."

"Tamarinda Constance," Donner said. "And the big guy with the pumpkin head, he's captain of the boat you and Leo chartered. The three of you sold a chunk of ambergris in Nassau."

"How do you know all this?"

"I know a hell of a lot more than you realize. What about him?" His finger tapped a frozen-frame shot of a man at night wearing glasses.

Lydia folded her arms in a way that meant *Not another word until you explain.*

"Stubborn, okay. It's part of the deal I'm offering you. Ask yourself who really owns the gold Jimmy salvaged? Not according to the courts—screw maritime law. The feds say it belongs to the U.S. government. Spain claims it belongs to the Spanish mint. But who really owns it? I'll tell you—the country it was stolen from in the first place."

She was confused. "I don't know what . . . You're working with the Mexican government?"

"Think Central America. Where the gold was mined, taken from the ground by poor native bastards who still live like slaves, a lot of them." He allowed his indignation to register. "Yeah, and the same mines that produced the coin your boy Leo has been flashing around—a gold Tricentennial Royal, isn't it? My people know about that, too. There's an island down there I'd give my left nut to own."

"Your people from where?"

"It's a small country that's tired of being shit on. The most beautiful beaches you've ever seen. And the head honchos aren't afraid to play hardball. They want what belongs to them. Is that so wrong? In return, I'm back in the movie business, and a legal citizen of a country that appreciates talent. Doesn't give a damn about headlines and my sex life. Satisfied?"

"Some banana republic intelligence agency," Lydia said, not a question, just wondering if it could be true.

Again, Donner indicated the shot of a man wearing wire-rims. A good jaw, and an intensity that reached through the camera lens. The skin of his face glowed against a dark backdrop. "Supposedly, he's a marine biologist from the States. But I wonder."

"A biologist—no, never seen him before. Did the same country send the guy with the camera?"

"That's what I'm trying to figure out. Watch it again."

She did. Watched the man remove a shoulder bag, open it, then pivot like he sensed he wasn't alone, searching through glasses that glittered with infrared light. In the bag was a tube, a scope of some type. It emitted an eerie glow. The man knelt, put it to his eye, and, suddenly, the camera was bouncing toward shadows that were trees.

"The cameraman's running away," she said. "I get the message, Efren. You're working with a badass and you're trying to scare me into cutting a deal."

"No idea who the biologist is?"

"I just told you."

"Okay, I saved the best for last. Actually, the worst. All trimmed to hell—don't blame me for the hack job. The shooter, whoever sent these, he sucks as bad with the lens as he does the cutting tools. Speaking of that—" He started to get up, then decided, "I'll grab it in a sec," and hit play.

Three nightmare minutes was all she could take. "Why is he torturing that man? I don't know him either—stop trying to guilt me into thinking I'm the cause."

"Waterboarding, is what it's called. He's a Treasury Department agent named Middlebrook. Or was. He questioned me a couple of years back about my connection to Benthic. You missed another snuff scene, only a lot bloodier than Jimmy's. Too bad there's no sound."

"You're sick."

Donner gave her a tolerant look. "The sound of pain is a diagnostic tool, sweetie. What did our shooter find out? Does he enjoy killing? The freak's either been lobotomized or enjoys gore—that would've been my assessment as an outsider. But it doesn't fit with what I know about Phil."

"Who?"

"Phillipé—Phil—the guy who did security for me. He's Salvadoran, so he fought under a couple of names because Phil sucks. I don't know . . . all those concussions, and a head full of meth. And he's ex–special forces from there, so—" The former shrink had to consider it. "Maybe, I guess. There's a clip of what he did to two mercenary types—talk about bloody, Jesus. They weren't worth whatever some fool paid them. Like a warning to me, I guess is why the video was sent. You sure you don't want to watch—"

"No."

"In a way, I'm glad. Christ, even made me sick. He used a machete with teeth—you know, like a savage who's gone back to analog. In that way, yeah, maybe it is Phil. Around the set, we called him Aztec because it's the only name he ever won a fight with."

- - - - - - - - - - -

Again, he reached for the space bar. "There is one more short clip you need to see. A woman in Florida, I think. One of those stucco slums you might recognize." Donner wanted to savor her reaction so gave it a beat before asking, "Did you know Leonard's wife?"

Lydia shot up from her seat. "What the hell is that supposed to mean?"

"Sweetheart, I'm as confused as you. Fine, we'll save it for later." He pushed the computer aside. "The deal is, you do for me what you did for Jimmy. Don't give me that look—as if I'd want to see you naked. This is strictly business. As of now, you're with me. You'll be safe from that freak—whoever he is."

Lydia was still staring at the computer. "You had Leonard's wife murdered?"

"No, but it could happen. You're not listening. Babe"—he clamped a hand around her wrist—"you need to focus. I've got a compressor aboard and all the gear. Tanks are full, and there's enough catered food for an army. It's simple. Show me where Jimmy unloaded the gold and we'll do a percentage deal—of the gross, of course. Under one condition—"

Beneath their feet, the deck jolted. Donner paused, aware a boat had bumped the hull, possibly someone tying up.

No . . . When the producer turned, Leonard was already aboard, looking down from the flybridge, red-faced at what he'd just witnessed. His arrival had been planned. What Lydia didn't expect was the Spanish-looking sword in Leonard's hand, or one

- - - - - - - - - - -

of the boys he'd rescued to be beside him, a machete strapped to his shoulder like a bandolier.

"Take your goddamn hands off her," Leonard called down. His voice shook.

The producer, wide-eyed, saw only the boy. "Don't trust that goddamn kid. I'm serious," he yelled. "Do you know who he is?" Then said to Lydia, "Talk to him, Jesus Christ. You'll get us all—" Leonard was at the ladder, coming down. "Fuck, that does it." Donner grabbed the fishbilly, strode to the ladder, and waited.

The man's look of surprise—totally shocked when the boy vaulted the railing and landed feather light to face him—the boy barefooted, waist-high to the movie producer, the machete still strapped to his back but ready.

Donner swung the club without thinking. Not hard, more of a get-away-from-me response. That was Lydia's impression until the boy collapsed as if a plug had been pulled. Lights out. Blood streamed from a hole in his head no wider than a rusty nail. But it was intentional because Donner straddled the boy, ready to swing again, until Leonard ran toward him, screaming, "Stop, stop, stop . . . You can have it all."

Donner froze. Turned his wild eyes to the short, bald man, who looked ridiculous in shorts, white socks, a scabbard belted to his waist. "Jesus Christ, you're both nuts. See what you and your stupid bitch made me do?"

Leonard advanced slowly. "Don't hit him again. Stay calm. Whatever you want, Efren, okay?"

Donner looked from the boy, fetal-positioned, feet twitching, to the little man in horn-rimmed glasses. Pathetic . . . hilarious. "Jesus, Leo, Indiana Jones you're not. So drop the sword, already, and back off."

In Lydia's mind, it was the bravest thing Capt. León had ever done. He let his weapon clatter to the deck, then stood tall, saying, "I don't give a damn what you do to me, but we can't let that boy die."

Leonard was on his knees, considering CPR, when Efren Donner used the club again.

18

When the old preacher entered the bar, hours after most islanders were asleep, Tomlinson knew something was wrong.

Ford read it differently. He noted the staff's deference, their imperceptible nods of respect, eyes averted, and said, "Josiah's more than just a fisherman. He's a local honcho. Does your sacred Masonic oath obligate you to lie to a pal about things he told you?"

"Can't tell you," Tomlinson said, getting up. "Wait here."

They were at Fernandez Bay, a small hotel on a cusp of beach, nothing but stars out there on an empty, lightless sea. A breeze rustled thatching above the bar. Ceiling fans spun in lazy sync.

The house they were in was a quarter mile down a shell lane. No Internet there, unlike the bar. Ford used the interruption to search variations of words that sounded like Kalik, the local beer, but were spelled differently.

The *Oxford English Dictionary, Unabridged,* was an unimpeachable source:

Cailleach (ḳal-əḳ) Scots-Gaelic: old sorceress, orig. "nun," female witch. A divine hag, a creator deity applied to mythological figures in Scotland and the Isle of Man.

Tomlinson returned from the beach and motioned, *Come on, hurry.*

Ford did. Read a second definition in a rush: *1783. Applied to women burned as witches or banished for witchcraft on a slave ship renamed* Ketch Cailleach.

He copied and saved, and said as they walked toward the rental car, "Now what?"

"Something really bad happened, man. Josiah didn't give me all the details. He's waiting for us at the dock. Are you up for a boat ride?"

It was late on an island fifty miles long, two miles wide, population fifteen hundred, where generators often kicked off before ten. "I'm not sure I trust your new buddy, and I sure as hell don't trust his boat. Carrie's not part of this, I hope."

Carrie was the Jezebel blonde, as described by the preacher, who turned out to be a nervous wannabe actress from Cincinnati. She had a room at the hotel, pending the next flight out, and had refused to talk about Efren Donner. "I expect you to be on the same plane," Ford added.

"It involves Lydia Johnson and Nickelby," Tomlinson countered like their deal had been trumped.

"What about them?"

"Josiah found Fitz's logbook, maybe the coins, too. That's where we're headed."

"Where, White Torch? You don't think it's odd he makes the big discovery a few hours after seeing how those sharks reacted?"

"Marl Landing, is what they call it," Tomlinson replied. "In return—well, apparently Nickelby and the girl split and left their gear behind but stole something valuable. Valuable to the islanders anyway. I don't know, but seriously bad kimchi is involved. Now he has to find them."

"Use us to find them," Ford said, not surprised. "You just figured that out?"

U p a path on a limestone crest, the wind crossed four thousand miles of water out of Africa. With it, a fecal-edged odor caromed up the hillside from the fish co-op and village below.

"Ambergris is profitable," Josiah explained, referencing the Shark Zapper, "but it ain't enough lately. That's all I'll say for now. This is what I'm willing to let you see." He motioned to a hulking structure anchored among the scrub. "I still hold services occasionally, but not the kind you think."

"Church is church," Tomlinson said. *"Where two or more are gathered,* like the Book says. I should've told Doc about the jars full of pickled peckers."

Josiah laughed, because the biologist heard it as "pickled peppers," and warned them both, "The logbook and coins better be in there, too, after hiking way the heck up here."

"I want you to see what was taken from us," Josiah said. "You brought a torch, might as well use it."

Ford switched on a flashlight the old man claimed they wouldn't need once their eyes adjusted to the stars and the wafer of fresh moon. It was a church. The walls were stone covered with faded lime cement. Small windows, a door of black *madera—lignum vitae,* Spaniards had named the strange tree that was too dense to float but cured diseases. Above the door was a Gaelic cross. It had been etched with a stick long ago while the cement was still wet.

"You're not old enough to have built this place," Tomlinson said.

"We are flesh yet our days be a hundred and twenty years," Josiah replied. "Genesis 6:3." Keys jingled beneath an ancient brass padlock, and the door swung wide. "Wait until I get a lamp lit," he said. Went in, came out, and looked at the biologist. "Brother Tomlinson done vouched for you, sir. These days, to most a promise don't mean much, so I must ask you to swear what you see will go no further."

Ford said, "Are you kidding? You should've mentioned that on the boat."

"What's inside is private, sir."

"Fine, I understand, but I can't." He offered Tomlinson the flashlight, saying, "I'll wait out here."

Tomlinson refused it. "Rev, he's a stickler for nuance, which I think I mentioned. What he means is—"

"What I mean," Ford said, "is it's unfair to promise anything in advance. Some don't take it seriously, but I do when it comes to keeping my word." Then took a chance by adding, "Up to you . . . Cailleach."

Cail-LEECH, he pronounced the word, right out of the *Oxford Unabridged*.

Josiah said softly, "Caill-EK-ay," a subtle correction. Then asked Tomlinson, "You told 'em?"

"No, but down the road I would've dropped a few hints if he hadn't figured it out. He's usually pretty quick."

"There's the honesty of the craft," Josiah said, still observing the biologist. "A man takes matters of honor serious-like, that ain't bad either. Reckon I'll vouch for you myself, sir, even though you're wrong in how you addressed me. I ain't the sovereign of this island, she is." He looked down on the village, where a line of torches had formed and appeared to be marching uphill on the path to the church.

"Uh-oh, Rev." Tomlinson was tugging at a strand of hair. "I love the whole Illuminati thing, but just wondering. She's not pissed off, is she?"

"Aren't they always, brothah? But you wouldn't be here if her

----

wisdom had not allowed it. Three hundred years, women of her blood have ruled this island. Done just fine, too, with no outside help except a few times—like now."

Ford didn't care for the odds. "Let's get this over with. If you have the logbook, Dr. Nickelby and the girl must be somewhere on the island. Or were. You want the Shark Zapper in return for—"

"They be gone," Josiah said, "that's what we're trading. Find them and the man they ran off with. A bad man. He took a fine little boy as well. And something else *she* values. That's what I come up here to explain."

"Why would Nickelby take off with a kidnapper?"

"Doubt if Capt. León did, sir. The glory of God is to conceal, the honor of man is to search. Speaking of that, I hear you got you a fine seaplane as well. It would be part of the deal."

"Something else you could've mentioned on the boat," Ford said. "My advice is, call the police."

"They can't. It's the way things are here," Tomlinson said. "Tell Doc the rest."

Josiah levered a kerosene lamp open, matches ready. "Could be even you don't know the rest, brother. We make it our business to learn about those interested in us before they *know* about us. Eight years she's conjured that man to return but she sure didn't expect what happened today."

"Efren Donner," Tomlinson explained to Ford, as the old preacher lit the lamp and held it high.

"She wants his head, sir," Josiah said agreeably. "The boy that moviemaking sonuvabitch took is our grandson. And another item of importance—a sword. You'll have to step inside to understand."

Ford was in bed, going over notes, comparing symbols he'd seen inside the church with his diagram of the ceremonial murder, when a delicate tap-tap-tap at the door told him it wasn't Tomlinson.

Strangers seldom enter a two-bedroom beach rental at midnight with peaceful intentions.

Ford switched off the lamp, already on the move.

Protocol on the road was different than at home. Under the pillow, to his right, was the pistol. An LED tactical light lay on the nightstand to his left. Finding his underwear in the dark had not been as carefully planned.

Tap-tap-tap. "You in there?" A woman's voice.

"Give me a second, it's locked," Ford said, hopping on one foot.

He was buckling his fishing shorts when the doorknob turned and confirmed the occupant was a liar.

"I saw your light, then it went out," said Carrie, the wannabe actress. Her silhouette filled the doorway but wasn't posed for attention. "I need someone to talk to. Hey, do you mind?" She reached for the wall switch.

- - - - - - - - - - -

Ford was shirtless, holding a towel, when the light came on. "Tomlinson was at the bar last time I saw him. How'd you get in?"

"I was scared," she said, and started to say something else but was distracted by a scar on his shoulder and another that bisected his sternum. "Geez, what happened to you?"

"Scared of what?"

"Oh. Uhh . . . maybe it was my imagination. It's so damn dark out there, the beach, and this was the closest place, so I—"

"Check the fridge if you're thirsty," Ford said. "I'll be right out."

Carrie's peasant blouse and gauzy pantaloons reminded him of Cambodia, the way tribal women dressed. A hint of hemp smoke, the way she sat cross-legged in a chair, added to the illusion. He had spent time in the jungle along the Mekong, one of a few sent to confirm that a genocidal leader, Pol Pot, was dead. It caused him to think back.

It also caused her to say, "Sorry to bore you. I was hoping you'd walk me to the hotel. Oh well . . ." She placed her bottle on a coaster. "What I imagined was that weirdo, Efren, was following me."

Ford's attention shifted. "Maybe he was. Or it was someone else. Why didn't you want to talk about him this morning?"

"You think it could've been that weirdo?"

"Depends. Are you sure it was a man? How far from here?"

"Close enough," she said, "but more likely just a worker from the hotel. Don't worry about it. Seagard said come to you if I was scared, so . . ."

- - - - - - - - - - -

Ford, getting up, said, "Who? Oh, Tomlinson. I'm glad. When your instincts tell you something's wrong, you're almost always right. Let's find him first."

The outdoor bar was empty, lights off, no music. "Check your room," Ford said. A series of stone cottages, two suites in each, faced the sea. She balked at the door, so he slid it open and went in. A light was on, the bed unmade, but otherwise the place was neatly kept. "What didn't you want me to see?"

"We smoked, that's all. He told me you don't approve."

"Meth?"

"Oh please. When Seagard fell asleep, I went for a walk. At first, I thought it might be him following me, so I stopped, you know? But it wasn't. I could tell by the creepy way the guy tried to hide behind a palm tree." She pointed vaguely to the water. "That's where we should've started. Where do you think he is?"

"Hopefully, meditating in one of those beach chairs."

"Not Seagard, that weirdo Efren," the woman said. "Cat Island's one of the few places he's not afraid to drive his boat. He told me."

"Which marina did he use?"

Carrie's facial response: *Duh, like I would know.* "He scares the hell out of me," she said. "Mind if we lock that?"

Ford, standing in the open doorway, said, "Good idea, but first—" He checked the bathroom and a closet, then picked up his bag. "Don't open the door unless it's Tomlinson. I won't be long."

"Are you some kind of cop?" She sounded guarded. "Efren

----

warned me about that, sorta paranoid. He thought he was being followed."

"It's not paranoia when there's a reason—wanted for sexual assault in his case," Ford said.

"That wasn't what worried him. You'd know what I mean, I guess, if you really are a cop."

"Does it have something to do with a guy named Jimmy Jones?" Ford asked. "Or about how rich you'd be if you kept your mouth shut?" It was a small gamble that paid off. Yes, she knew— a little bit anyway. It was in her expression and quick denial.

"When I get back, I'd like to hear what else Efren warned you about," he said, and went out carrying his bag.

If Tomlinson was meditating, it wasn't nearby. He circled the hotel, peeked in at Carrie, and walked to the water. Night vision showed a mile of empty beach, palms shadowed by starlight, a wading bird. Far to the north, a white four-second flasher marked the entrance to Smith Bay Harbour.

What was the depth of the channel? Josiah had said Donner's yacht was a rental out of Nassau, black hull, probably drew five feet. *Island Time*—one of thousands of boats with the same name. Estimated distance to Smith Bay: two miles, much of it rugged bush and limestone. Tough to negotiate on foot.

Where the hell was Tomlinson?

Ford walked south past the cottages toward a shoal inlet, Fernandez Creek, and the rocky point where windows of their rental house glimmered among palms. It was the same stretch where

----

Carrie had seen someone. Or something. Or was she so stoned that this was all a waste of time?

Once again, he put the NV monoc to his eye. A meteorite streaked toward a silent woof of lightning . . . cloud shadows on a silent, iridescent sea . . . then, to the east, hillocks along the road bristled with manufactured light. Random beams of white among the low trees that suggested not one flashlight but several carried by a ragtag line of people.

Ford understood when he was close enough to identify a tall scarecrow shape among a group of locals. They carried lights and burlap sacks. Tomlinson, an observer, watched his colleagues beat among the bushes with sticks.

Ford laughed, wanted to join the fun, but . . .

Oh well.

At the hotel, Carrie had lit another joint and was pacing behind a door that was locked and barricaded with a chair.

Whatever the woman had seen was real.

Probably a man hunting giant land crabs" was not the explanation a woman, stoned and afraid, was equipped to deal with. "Oh my god, are they dangerous?"

"Depends on the man," Ford said, trying to be lighthearted. Make her laugh at the situation, was his objective.

The humor was lost on Carrie. "Fucking giant crabs, man. That's the sort of crap Efren would lay on me. Like the sharks. And a bloodsucking—I forget the name, this savage dude who would track me down if I tried to leave the island." Near meltdown, she asked, "Why are you doing this to me?"

Ford said, "Sorry. Geezus, I'm an idiot. All I meant was . . . you're safe, do you hear me? Nothing to worry about."

"Then why tell that stupid goddamn lie about giant crabs?"

"I was talking about edible crabs, that's all. The locals hunt them at night. Have a seat. It's sort of interesting, really." He extended his hand. "Please?"

On the couch, her crying jag was a mix of fury and chagrined relief. Tea was refused. Beer over ice provided a mild sedative. The transition from anger to embarrassment is often circular. The needle has to spin itself to a stop.

It took a while.

When she was calmer, he said, "I found Tomlinson. He's hunting crabs with some locals. Giant land crabs—that really is what they're called." He spread his fingers wide. "A little bigger than this, some of them. The crabs migrate at night during the rainy season. And they're a favorite food. Locals pen them up, feed them until the market's good, then sell them to make a little extra cash. Understand? All I meant was, the person you saw was probably hunting crabs, not you."

Carrie grimaced and wiped her eyes. "Bullshit. Are you sure?"

Ford decided she was strong enough to hear the truth. "Nope. It could've been Donner. Tell me about him. He scares you, that's obvious. How did you meet? I assume you didn't show up in the Bahamas blind after answering a classified ad."

"Don't be sarcastic," she said. "I need to pee and freshen up."

On a folding valet was her suitcase. When the bathroom door closed, Ford went through her things while her voice echoed off the tiles. "I'm not naïve. I knew what was expected in return for my airfare and a month on 'his' island—or thought I did. Mostly, I was alone, but the first three nights, my God, the dress-up games. Truly sickening. My role was to act like his . . . Just a minute."

The toilet flushed, a sound sanitized by water in the sink, before she continued. "My role was to play his virginal wife. I mean, like really his wife, and he had a thing for horror flicks—George Romero. You ever see *Night of the Living Dead*? Efren claimed he could get me a part in the zombie series. He's an authority on substance abuse counseling, too, which was part of his sales pitch. That's true. Check the Internet—Efren Donner, the movie star shrink. See, I'm not stupid. Just too damn trusting."

A cabinet opened, a toothbrush tapped the sink, the water stopped. Ford was seated when she exited. Watched her plop down on the bed, not playing a role, just being herself and tired. "I must look like hell. Sorry."

Her cobalt hair was pulled back, eyes puffy in a hollow,

angular face that a camera might love but did not interest Ford, who pretended otherwise. "Why are beautiful women always so tough on themselves?"

"That's sweet," she said, and looked at him differently, maybe seeing him for the first time. "Seagard said you're a good guy and all. And funny, because you're so straight. Sorry I asked if you were a cop."

"She might take it as a compliment. Carrie, you had to have read about the sexual assault charges. So Donner's offer, the thing about making you rich, must've—"

"Efren said it was all fake news bullshit. And seriously, who believes anything anymore? That's not why he's worried about cops. The reason is, he carries a special goodie bag and he's not licensed in the Bahamas. Do you know what I'm talking about?"

"Pharmaceuticals," Ford said.

"Drugs," she said. "Grass. Glass and mollies—that's speed."

"Isn't glass a type of—"

"Meth," she said, impatiently. "Psychotropic candy. He knew I had a history, but alone on an island, in that stinking old house? Things really got freaky, so I was glad when he split after a few nights. I was the virginal wife who had a psycho stalker or I was a tough biker chick out for revenge—Efren's directing me the whole time, understand. Like there's actually a camera. Him in this weird wooden mask. Or wearing—"

"What kind of mask?" Ford was thinking of the church, what he'd seen inside. Artifacts that predated a shipwreck, in 1784, and survivors who had intermingled with Indios and slaves three hundred years ago.

"I don't know, scary, with teeth, and straw for hair. He brought all kinds of masks, props—we're talking Broadway-quality. I went along with it until he really freaked out. That was on the third night. He told me to wait inside for twenty minutes, then cross a little bridge and try to find him. Like hide-and-seek, you know? When he screamed, I thought it was part of the act. But he kept screaming, and ran right past me to the house. And, guess what? The asshole locked me out. There was blood on the door—real blood, not the red syrup he liked to use. Then he got in his boat and split, not a word, and left me there alone on that fucking island, day after day until I thought I had gone . . ." She stopped, a moment of revelation that caused her to sag. A familiar wave of panic flooded in. "Oh my god. I didn't realize how sick this all was until now telling you. Could I have . . . Tell me the truth. Do you think I imagined it all? Or that I'm . . . that I've gone insane?"

Of all the emotions Ford had witnessed in life, fear expressed by a hapless victim touched him on a level he could not dismiss intellectually or dismiss with a calming lie.

"I think you need sleep, Carrie," he said. "Come on. You're staying with Tomlinson and me tonight."

The plane's emergency kit included mosquito netting and a coil of quarter-inch nylon. Their rental house fronted a tidal creek, on a rocky point with a breeze, where a hammock was strung beneath a glowering of palms.

Ford rigged mosquito netting on a nylon bar while Tomlinson talked about the fun he'd had hunting crabs. The elders had carried torches, not flashlights, and their tickle sticks were hand-carved, dating back to the days of hunting whales under sail with harpoons.

"The passage of time here, man, is in slo-mo. Every day is as new as that sunrise three hundred years ago."

He was referencing what they'd seen inside the church, not Cat Island, although the mismatched simile might have applied.

Ford was preoccupied and a tad pissed off. He chose to listen rather than inquire about a shipwreck and symbols his pal had yet to discuss.

Back to crab hunting. The technique hadn't varied much over the centuries. Giant white or black land crabs, which were actually bluish gray, dug burrows deep in the coppice, an island term for low wooded bush areas. Tickle sticks were used to breach their holes, and, by god, watch out for those big-assed pincers. And the small ones were even worse. They were sharp enough to snip buttonwood and coco plum—carrion morsels, too—which is why the locals penned the crabs and fattened them with rice, grits, and coconut for a few weeks before eating.

"It's more of a psychological thing," Tomlinson, a vegetarian, reasoned, "which I totally get. They told me the best time is August, three days before the full moon, because the females have to—"

"It's part of the cycle," Ford interrupted. "Land crustaceans migrate to saltwater to lay eggs. You think I don't know this? The females molt while their eggs become part of the plankton chain. A high mortality rate for all involved, particularly because of fish. And car traffic. And people like you." He knotted the mosquito net securely over the hammock. "Can you guess what I'd rather talk about?"

Tomlinson cleared his throat and looked toward the house, where Carrie's bedroom light was on. "Sorry, man, I shouldn't have left her alone. But I figured with you so close by . . . And where the hell is there a place safer than this?" Arms spread, he included all of Fernandez Bay.

"I wouldn't sleep out here if I didn't have my doubts," Ford said.

"You're pissed."

"Darn right—well, not mad, just irritated. She's your responsibility, but Josiah is what I meant. And the church. A lot of your supposed secrets are as common as the back of a dollar bill. So why wouldn't he talk about the shipwreck of 1784? Or you, for that matter?"

"Fair question," Tomlinson said softly. "Guess it does seem a little silly. Secret handshakes, passwords—kid stuff, in a way. But remember, the Brotherhood dates back to a time when the Church, and other sects as well, ruled the known world, monarchies included. Popes and bishops and ministers and preachers decided what people could think, what they could say and do. Back then, science was considered the Devil's craft. *Craft*, man, is the key word. How about this, Doc—tell me what you know and we'll go from there."

What Ford had seen in the church was a sad little makeshift shrine created by survivors of a shipwreck. Some of the men, presumably, had been Freemasons. It was possible that castaway societies viewed the random luck that had saved them as God's work, so divine importance was assigned to items that had washed ashore after the wreck.

It was a theory, nothing more, based on what he'd seen.

The church's eastern wall was a shrine of seafaring detritus: a ship's bell, a captain's chest wormy with age. In the chest, a tankard still used for sipping Communion wine. Marlinspikes, remnants of clothing, and a collection of swords with one missing—a saber gifted to Leonard Nickelby.

Josiah had refused to provide a reason for giving it to an outsider, or why it was held in higher esteem than the other swords. Ford was working on a theory about that, too.

Centered forward of the shrine was a brace of wooden chairs, a podium, and, on it, a dusty old gilt-edged Bible. Each was em-

----

blazoned with a pyramid and the omniscient eye of God, similar to images on the dollar bill.

Masonic symbols all. They decorated the church walls like points of a compass. They had been chiseled into rock and wood. But side by side with them, sometimes intertwined, were carved totems—a jaguar, an owl and a frog, motifs that were familiar to a biologist who'd traveled Mesoamerica. These were indigenous symbols created by a lost race. On a slab of rock near the altar were petroglyphs that could still be found in Guatemala's Maya Mountains and the jungle ruins of Tikal.

Ford said, "An interesting combination, but it doesn't explain all the secrecy. Something else might." He referenced a tattered flag, frail as tissue paper, that had been stored—or hidden—out of sight. Impossible to hide was a carving on a lintel above the church pulpit.

"Since when is the skull and crossbones a Masonic symbol?" he asked.

Tomlinson responded, "Dude, I told Josiah you'd ask. Since the thirteen hundreds, but not in a Jolly Roger kinda way. Although, you've got to wonder. The Brotherhood had to survive somehow. And the churches of England and Spain weren't exactly shy about burning heretics at the stake."

"A pirate ship." Ford nodded.

"Privateers, more likely. I'm guessing, same as you."

"Okay. But why keep it secret for three hundred years unless they're hiding something else?"

"Don't forget the witches," Tomlinson said like that meant something. "Freemason Scots and Jews had a thing for robbing their enemies and rescuing heretics."

"What about rescuing kidnapped children? You might've promised Josiah not to call in the cavalry, but I didn't. An antique sword is one thing, but go after a little boy to protect some . . . whatever it is the old guy's protecting . . . that's bullshit and you know it."

"Cavalry, as in cops? Well . . . never thought I'd see the day, but you're right, man. We've got to pull out the stops on this one. Let me powwow with Brother Bodden and I'll explain to him how you're—"

He let his friend talk. Tomorrow, Tomlinson and the girl would be on a plane home, or sequestered in a hotel with Tamara, because that's the way it had to be.

Ford had his secrets, too.

19

L ydia recognized the seaplane that passed low as if interested—white fuselage, blue trim, with big torpedo floats. The same plane that had buzzed the mailboat.

"Don't even think about waving," Efren said, standing at the helm of his rented yacht. "I told you what would happen if you do something stupid."

There was a list of what would happen should she try to summon help. The boy, who was comatose, would not be put ashore at a place where someone might call an ambulance. And Leonard, now that he was conscious, would remain padlocked in the engine hold. The temperature in that tiny space rivaled an oven.

Right. Like she believed a coked-up Hollywood has-been who planned to kill them anyway once he got what he wanted. He'd almost done it yesterday, and would have, had she not soothed him like a spooked horse, using flattery and promises to talk that goddamn club out of his hand. Later, she did the same thing when he'd reappeared with a small pistol. A revolver, maybe a .38, he now carried in his pocket as a constant threat.

The plane was circling back.

"If the pilot sees we're aground," Lydia said as if equally concerned, "I'm afraid he might hail the Coast Guard. The smart thing to do—it's up to you, of course—is go out on the deck and give him a thumbs-up. Or I can. But it's better if he sees a man, don't you think?"

"This piece-of-shit chart plotter," Donner said, and smacked the screen for allowing them to bulldoze onto a sandy shoal that Lydia had tried to warn him about. "This is your fault for second-guessing every goddamn thing I do. Hands off the controls 'til I get back."

The moment the cabin door slammed, she tried the VHF radio. Morse code squawks, *S-O-S*, with the mic key. Donner had cut the antenna cables and disabled all satellite EPIRB devices, but it was possible a static message might get out.

Stainless fixtures in the cabin vibrated as the plane roared low overhead, then banked north toward a mangrove archipelago of coral flats.

Squawk-squawk-squawk . . . Squawk-squawk-squawk . . . S-O-S . . . S-O-S . . .

No response.

Lydia gave it up as hopeless. Switched off the radio and was re-cradling the mic when, at the edge of visibility, the aircraft appeared to dip its wings, a quick port and starboard. Subtle, all but imperceptible to a limo rat like Efren Donner.

Was that possible? No . . . the pilot had no way of knowing her situation. He would have confirmed reception by circling at least once. And why bother after getting a thumbs-up from Efren, who looked distinguished in leisure attire, not insane like last night when he'd come to her bed still bloody and wearing a freakish wooden mask?

Replaying it made her want to vomit. Not that he'd touched her, which would have been even worse. His intent was to humiliate. Lydia was the homely, helpless loser—a role she had endured before. Donner was less convincing as the movie god who was her only hope.

The man's behavior swung from nasty to insane.

In a leather bag was an array of drugs, including coke, meth, and syringes. In college, Lydia had peddled both enough to know. The seesaw highs and spiraling indecision of an addict were all a form of rage that could be gently redirected but never confronted head-on.

Like now, Lydia at the wheel when Donner slammed the cabin the door, saying, "The nosy fuck, flying that low. I ought to report him. Shit . . . Or do you think he's a cop?"

Paranoia was another weakness to be used.

"He would've come back. But god I hope not." Nikon binoculars added a few seconds of drama before she put them away. "I think he's gone, but you never know. We've got to get off this bar, Efren. The tide's falling. We could be stuck here all night. Want me to give it a try?"

"Captain Fugly, the expert, I forgot," he said. "Like you wouldn't love for a bunch of Bahamian cops to show up." But then, after a nervous glance out the window, he asked, "How do you know the tide's falling? Don't try to play me, Lydia. I've been played by some of the best and they were a hell of a lot smarter than you."

"We made a deal," she replied. "They'd arrest me, too, goddamn it. You don't think I want this over with? We both know I've had more experience in boats this size. And you're right about the chart plotter. It sucks."

"There, see? I told you it wasn't my fault," he said. "Stop second-guessing me . . . Bitch." He turned a nautical eye to the tide as if assessing the situation. "Okay. What do you want me to do?"

Donner had become increasingly dependent on her boating skills. The rental yacht was equipped to be user-friendly. Push-button navigation that could take a novice from point A to point B without incident. Waypoints included all the popular stops on the tourist trail, but don't stray into isolated areas unless you actually know how to run a boat and understand the markers, both day and night.

Like last night. On the trip from Marl Landing to Cat Island, she had saved him from the fatal error of crossing between a tug

----

and the barge it towed. Fifty yards of unlit steel cable was impossible to see, but a triad of white lights on the tug and a yellow light astern had warned her in time. The man, frazzled by coke and violence, had nearly broken down in tears. She'd paid for his display of weakness later—the horror scene with blood and a mask.

There'd been no mention of the incident this morning until now, when he added, "Do you expect me to salute? . . . I asked you a question. Are you deaf or just buying time?"

"I was checking the gauges," Lydia said. "We need to jettison our aft freshwater tank, at least a hundred gallons. That might lift the stern enough to free our props. You can reverse the flow switch in the bilge unless you'd rather I—"

"I'm not exactly a novice," he said. "That was my next move anyway. God, Lydia, just shut your mouth and do what I tell you, okay?"

"Sorry, Efren," she said, afraid to spark another mood swing.

When he was gone, she ducked under the wheel and used a spoon to tap a throttle linkage bar. The throttle was connected to the hot, cramped engine room, where poor Leonard was locked below. At every opportunity, they'd communicated in this way. And every time, she feared he would not reply.

But he did reply. *Tap . . . Tap-tap-tap*. Not Morse code. Simply a confirmation he was still alive.

As for the boy, no way of knowing. She hadn't been allowed to check on him in more than an hour. That might change depending on what happened next.

All gauges were digital. The numbers began to spin when Donner finally found the right valve. An automatic pump jettisoned eighteen gallons of fresh water per minute. A southerly breeze helped lift the stern. It also threatened to strand the vessel beamside to the shoal. She waited to feel the stern swing before firing the engines, and immediately shifted into reverse.

The hull shuddered. A prop banged a chunk of coral. With engines in neutral, there was another wait until she was sure, then throttled hard when the sonar indicated the water was deep enough to continue toward a channel marker that no sober person would've missed.

Donner reappeared. The frantic movement of his hands, the twitching, did not reflect his superior manner. "I told you it would work. How much water did we have to dump?"

"About a hundred gallons. Look, I've got the autopilot all set, so take over. I want to check on the kid. And something else—really, there's no need to keep Leonard locked down there."

He came toward her, saying, "A hundred gallons is all? Move your ass."

Lydia got out of the man's way but could not avoid the stink of him—sweat, cologne, the butane acidity of the meth he'd just smoked.

"At eight-point-four pounds per gallon, that's just about half a ton," she reminded him. "Almost the same as what Jimmy stashed. Seriously, I'm done cooperating if you don't make at least a few concessions."

"Capt. Fugly." He smiled. "Is that a threat?"

"It's a win-win, Efren," Lydia said, forcing a smile herself. "Instead of enemies, why not be partners?"

"Because you haven't told me a goddamn thing. Not really. Mooring buoys, my ass—we've checked enough public anchorages. I think you're full of shit."

No, there were two charted mooring areas—and one not on the chart—still unchecked. What she hadn't shared were the details. Jimmy Jones, while a student at MIT, had worked part-time at a place that manufactured commercial mooring buoys. The buoys were used worldwide—a big floating ball connected to a chain and a heavy weight below. It was a quick way to secure a boat where there was insufficient dockage. The size and shape of the mooring weights varied. Pyramid weights were the most common—and the heaviest. What Jimmy had pilfered were two dozen mushroom anchors because they were light enough to carry, and more effective, and they might come in handy down the road.

A few months before he was arrested, they did. A mushroom anchor resembles a metal dish attached to a long stainless shank. When covered by sand—or filled with molten gold and set—the design withstood ten times the strain of conventional mooring weights.

"The cops couldn't figure out why I spent four days anchored in the area," Jimmy had told her. "Went ashore every night, got drunk, and every night afterward on a different island—them following me the whole time. Same'll happen to you, Lydianne,"

- - - - - - - - - - -

which he sometimes called her. "Just keep in mind, they ain't no smarter than us."

Said with a Southern inflection, the word *us* had seemed as binding as the phrase *I do*. Dear, dear Jimmy. He'd made love like a Labrador retriever—a few quick humps, then come trotting back with some pointless gift in his mouth as if apologizing.

Not at all like Leonard—the second lover she might fail to save from the crazy man who stood at the wheel, glaring.

"I told you the truth, Efren," she said. "A mooring area somewhere near Cat Island. That's all I know."

"Four hundred mil in gold," he chided. "Sure, babe."

"I never said that. You know how Jimmy was. He loved making fools of reporters and the government guys, bureaucrats, who were hounding him." As she said it, Leonard, as he'd once been, popped into her mind.

"How much did he really hide? Gotta be at least two hundred mil or my Central American friends wouldn't waste their time."

"He didn't say an exact amount. It's not like I could have brought a chart to visitation, and the guards monitored everything. You know that."

"Mooring buoys," Donner scoffed. "Fabulous—Jesus Christ." He looked ahead and slammed the twin throttles forward, hoping the scrawny little know-it-all would fall ass backwards, but Lydia didn't.

"Stay in the channel," she said.

"Fuck you. Even a redneck like Jimmy wasn't dumb enough to

----

hide the shit in plain sight where boats come and go. Tell me the truth or I'll—" He reached for the pistol, but in the wrong pocket, while the boat again veered toward the shoals. "Shit, I mean it." Finally, he got the pistol out and said, "How about this? If there's nothing at the next spot, I kill the kid. The spot after that, I kill your boyfriend. Only one more strike, babe, you're out. Sound fair?"

Lydia wanted to make eye contact but knew better.

"You've been very fair about everything, Efren. I know I'm not easy to work with." She started toward the stairs.

"A pain in the ass, more like it. Where do you think you're going?"

"Below, to keep us from being charged with murder along with everything else. Try to trust the autopilot, okay?"

She felt the man's craziness on her back as she exited the cabin.

When Leonard couldn't drink any more water, he squinted up into the sunlight and asked, "How's the boy?"

His voice was raspy, hard to understand above the noise of twin engines and the wind.

"Better," Lydia lied, "but you both need a doctor. Leo, what I'm thinking is"—she looked up and confirmed Donner was watching from the cabin, the boat on autopilot—"I'm going to try to talk him into leaving you someplace safe where an ambulance can—"

"Can't hear you," Leonard said, and tried to stand. In the

engine hold, a narrow space separated the drive shafts. On the wall was a Halon fire suppression system, fuse boxes, electrical conduit, in a compartment only five feet high. He got his hands on the rim, and she helped him up. "What's wrong?" he asked, easier to hear now that she was on her knees at deck level.

"Nothing," she said. "You look a lot better. Here . . . hold still. I brought a towel and disinfectant."

Gently, very gently, she dabbed at a face that was unrecognizable because of what Donner had done. "You need a bag of ice. Are you still nauseous?"

"Ice?" Leonard winced when he attempted to smile. "My turn, huh? Does he know the boy is her . . . that he's Kalik's grandson? I'm afraid they're going to blame me for everything. Honey, I need a weapon of some type. Do you know what he did with my—"

"Don't talk," Lydia said. "Please, just listen. I'm going to try to push him overboard, or knock him out, I don't know. He's got a bag full of drugs, so maybe I'll get him really stoned, then inject him with something." She glanced up: Donner, there in the window, the pistol against the glass as a warning. "But Leo, if I can talk him into leaving you and the boy someplace safe, then—"

Leonard shook his head, touched her face, and gazed through the slit of the eye that still functioned. "I'm not as bad off as you think. In fact, good enough to see you're still beautiful. Has that lunatic tried to—"

"Absolutely not. He hasn't touched me. All he wants is the gold Jimmy hid, so I told him where. Not exactly where, but close enough

----

to—" She stopped when she realized she had yet to share the truth with Leonard. "I'm sorry, I should have told you a long time ago."

"You . . . you and Jimmy Jones."

"Yes, but I had to narrow it down. We can split it when you're out of the hospital. But first—"

Leonard made a shushing noise and kissed her hand. "I don't give a damn about him or what he stashed. You listen to me. We're in this together. Tonight, whenever the timing feels right, sneak down here and let me out. First, look after the boy. Did he wake up?"

Lydia said, "He's breathing. The bleeding stopped. And his color seems better."

She was inventing more good news when Leonard remembered to say again, "Honey, I need a weapon of some type. Do you know what he did with the sword?"

There was a large mooring pond off Little San Salvador, an island that had been purchased by a cruise ship company and renamed Half Moon Cay. Boats and Jet Skis everywhere. Parasails, too. A vacation frenzy that would have been the last place authorities would have looked for half a ton of gold hidden in plain sight.

Lydia slipped over the side while Donner watched from the flybridge, engines running. She snorkeled around a few vacant buoys, tried a different area, then hefted herself onto the dive platform and shook her head.

- - - - - - - - - - -

"You spent less than ten minutes in the water," Donner said when they were under way. To the east was Cat Island. A few miles west was a smoky gray prominence that was Marl Landing.

She was toweling off, wearing a red two-piece, French-cut, that was one of several castoffs left by previous passengers. "I knew before I put my fins on. The weights Jimmy used are mushroom-shaped. All but the shanks and chain would be buried under sand. Pyramid weights—we'll be able to see them from up here, so that's how we do it from now on."

"Only stop if we don't see something," Donner said in a chiding way that was getting old. "Strike one," he reminded her. "I hope you're satisfied. But not here. Too many people. And it's getting late."

"You really think I give a shit about that kid?" she replied. "We've got plenty of time. Let's keep looking."

The man seemed to handle that okay. Maybe a little disappointed by her lack of feelings for a child he perceived as leverage. That faded when she eyed the goodie bag on the floor and said, "I don't suppose you're willing to share."

Now he was surprised. "So, Capt. Fugly wants to get hip, huh? What do you have in mind?"

"Weed, that's all I do. I'm a nervous wreck. Every boat out here has a VHF. My god, Efren, what if the cops are looking for us? They could be blasting the name and description of this boat all over the islands. Then what?"

His reaction: *Christ . . . she's right.* He snuck the throttles forward, trying to be cool, but lost it. "Yeah, no shit. Then what? My

----

Central American contacts have all kinds of juice with the cops, so maybe I'd better make a—" His attention shifted to the radio. "Damn it," he said, meaning he should have disconnected the antenna instead of cutting a cable that served three radios, a VHF on every deck. The crazy look returned, a glow in Donner's eyes. "This is all your fault. You and that goddamn runt of a boyfriend. He's the one who attacked me, him and the brat. What I should do is—" Red-faced, he pushed up from the captain's chair.

Lydia cut him off, saying, "I hated to admit it, but you're right." She knew where this was headed, so nudged the leather bag with her toe to shift the man's focus. "Look, we're both a little strung-out. What you said is exactly the way it happened and that's what I'll tell them. Honest to god, I will. But screw the cops for now, okay? Let's make at least one more stop."

"You're serious. Just like that, huh?"

"I plan to get what I came after. What country in Central America?"

"Oh Christ." He chuckled. "Here we go. Another sales pitch from little Miss Butt-Ugly."

"You don't think Jimmy could've had anyone he wanted?" she countered. "I might be able to help you that way, too. I don't care much about movies, but I know how to organize a business and get things done. I mean, really, why panic before we're sure there's a reason?"

Again, she nudged the bag, which didn't quite convince him, so she turned away, saying, "Go ahead while I finish," and did what

- - - - - - - - - - -

she had dreaded since selecting the red swimsuit. Unsnapped the bra with her back to him. Next, stepped out of the French-cut thong. Then used the towel, fluffed her hair, and went down the steps like they were partners with nothing to hide.

Thank god, the freak didn't follow her. But the finesse worked. Maybe worked a little too well, because when she returned fully dressed, Donner was waiting with a fatty already rolled and lit. He passed it, and assessed her smoking expertise, before saying, "I know a good place to lay low tonight."

"The villa you rented?" she asked.

It was too much to hope for.

"Your striptease act made me want something more secluded," he said, and grinned when she tried to hide her disgust. "It's a private compound my Latino associates rented. Dolphin Head, on the south end of Cat Island. I wasn't supposed to show up without the goods, but what the hell? It's not like there's a goddamn radio around that works."

"Then let's keep looking. We've got three hours before sunset, so why not?"

"Because I'm in a moviemaking kinda mood," he replied, singing the words, then gave her a hard look. "Stop playing me, babe. I want a closed set when I break in my new star."

20

y water, it was an hour run from the hotel to the south shore of Cat Island. Much quicker by car, so Ford drove fourteen miles to an area where, from the air, he'd spotted Efren Donner's boat snaking its way up a channel into Cutlass Bay.

At an isolated roundabout, the road sprouted east and west. He continued straight onto a rutted lane that ended among the ruins of a plantation house still shadowed by the days of cholera and slaves.

Superstition would guard the car. Wax myrtle trees would hide it from the road.

A good spot to park, as his contact in Nassau had suggested.

In the trunk was a four-piece Sage fly rod and a sportsman's pocket-laden vest. Years ago, he'd learned that even in war-torn countries a stranger with a fishing rod was dismissed as an affable fool, not a threat. Locals often dropped politics, and everything else, given a chance to offer advice and point the fool in a direction that required permission or the blessings of a fellow angler.

Ford was counting on it.

Wax myrtle ended at a path with a view of Cutlass Bay. It was a vast basin of sand and mangroves veined with turquoise and shielded by a bluff and miles of salt-bleached shoals. On an isolated point, elevated above the sea, was a rental estate called Dolphin Head, or Wind Drift—his contact in Nassau had been unsure. Names changed with every owner, but the place was a popular getaway for the few who could afford the price of privacy: A main house, two satellite cottages, a pool, and a gate that forbade entrance.

By car, only one way in. By water, a single narrow channel led to the only dockage for miles. Donner's boat was there, anchored away from the dock, its sleek black hull darker in the late-afternoon light.

This required Ford to return to the car and make a call on his new BTC throwaway phone.

When the sun was lower, he rigged the fly rod and waded toward the estate, ready to put on a show if anyone questioned his motives.

The motives of two men in dark suits slogging after him, water to their knees, were obvious, although best ignored. From the mangroves drifted a pointillism of cloud shadow that stirred a wake beneath a cloudless sunset sky.

A school of bonefish. Big-shouldered fish, long-bodied, dense as lead.

"Sir . . . hello? *Que onda, amigo!*" One of the security guys tried to get his attention, mixing English with Spanish.

Ford, stripping line, nodded eagerly and began to false-cast.

"Mister, we speaking for you!" The second man's voice was more strident.

Ford's green 9-weight line carved a question mark, then launched a tufted hook ahead of the schooling fish. The men stopped and watched the tourist, in his baggy, bulky vest, squat low. Watched him twitch the line, then lift a rod that bowed with sudden impact.

"Got one." Ford grinned, but sobered when he saw the bonefish—a big one—rocketing toward the men. For an instant, they froze . . . time enough for fish and line to thread between one man's legs. He whooped, leaped like he was protecting his nuts from a baseball, and fell. Funny, had he not surfaced wielding a mini machine pistol.

Nope, it was funny. Hilarious, his partner thought. No pretense of English now. Pure barrio Spanish. "You little pussy girl-boy," he howled. "Afraid a fish gonna bite your wee-wee off?"

The man with the gun was soaked. A little stunned. "God-damn, bro. Thing run right for my *cojones*, and you laughing? Shit."

His partner tried to imitate what had happened. A prissy ballerina leap, saying, "Yeah, but you recover smooth, man. Ready to shoot that fishy if the bitch comes after your wee-wee again." Staggering, it was so funny, and he nearly fell himself.

After years working in Latin America, Ford's mind shifted easily into Spanish. Whether to reveal this or not had to wait until he landed the fish. If he landed it. The bonefish had sizzled off a hundred feet and the reel was hot to the touch.

Ten minutes was enough to forge a temporary bond with the guys, land the fish, and remove the hook. "How much do you think it weighs?" he asked in Spanish.

"Nice one, man. But we got bigger in the 'Dor. You know El Salvador? The ocean, man, we got all kinds there."

So that's where they were from. The smallest, and sometimes meanest, country in Central America. It explained the gangbanger tats their jackets could not hide. But not the coiled earbuds. Or the heavy weaponry that was illegal for all but government-sanctioned agents.

"Never got any farther than Costa Rica," Ford replied. "I spent a month at a gringo Spanish school." He talked about the mountains there, the women, then offered the rod. "Want to try?"

"Can't, amigo, we working, you know? Go ahead, we already wet. And it's fun watching you."

"Ask the man some questions, too," the other hinted. "I can search him if you too busy talking shit."

Ford appeared confused for a moment. "Oh," he said, "you're police of some type. Here, I should've realized." From a pocket he handed over a plastic bag that contained his embossed research permit and a tourist fishing license purchased his first day in Andros Town.

The security guys conferred long enough for Ford's frazzled bonefish fly to be replaced with a new speck of tuft and Mylar.

"Says here you a fish doctor—that right, sir?"

"Just a biologist, down here on a research project," Ford replied. "I'm supposed to be working, too, so don't tell my boss you caught me having fun, okay?"

One of the men liked the slyness of that. "Sneakin' out but part of your job, far as the boss concerned. Yeah, that's cool. In El 'Dor—this is when I was a kid—we caught a hell of a lot of corvina just walking the beach. Hand lines, bro. Didn't need no fancy rods. Talk about good eating."

"What about catching gallo in the surf?" Ford asked. "Costa Rica, they'd tail right along the beach."

"Rooster fish, oh hell yes. But the Rica don't compare to the size we catch. Seriously, amigo." He took another look at the embossed

papers, then said, "Wow. The dude's got permission from the Crown. Like the Bahamas government, you know?"

His partner, the one who'd fallen, didn't like the sound of that. The machine pistol had disappeared into a holster. He eyed the biologist while tugging a cuff over a tattoo that took a moment to decipher. It was an elaborate insect with pincers—an ant.

Ford took pains not to notice by concentrating on another school of bonefish.

"We gonna have to search him anyway, Tito," the man said, and motioned to the dock and buildings across the bay. "Can't say who's staying there, sir, but they important dignitaries. You have a problem with that?"

"Help yourself." The biologist, in his baggy vest, still holding the rod, spread his arms and waited, which struck Tito as a waste of time and embarrassing.

"Man, this ain't no airport," he said to his partner, then asked Ford, "Bro, you carrying any weapons or shit?"

"Well . . . yeah, guess so." That startled them both until he starting plucking items from his vest . . . nail clippers, pliers, a sharpening stone, a forceps-looking instrument for removing hooks.

"Like we're damn TSA," Tito said. "Come on, Phillipé, let the man fish."

Phillipé, the humorless one with a tattoo of an ant on his wrist, stared and stepped closer. "Take off the vest, please, sir."

Ford did, handed it over, and continued to watch a school of

----

bones mudding toward Donner's boat—no movement aboard, but a flurry of activity among the buildings above. Stick figures on the move. Dust from a pickup truck that sped soundlessly inland. Also audible was the distant warble of a siren.

A radio squelched. Tito touched a finger to his ear and said, "Repeat that, please." He nodded, listening. "Yeah ... yeah. No ... just a *turista* fishing. Shit, you kidding. Don't let them in. We're on our way." Then spoke to his partner in a rapid guttural language that was K'iche' Mayan.

Phillipé tossed the vest back to the biologist, both guards suddenly in a hurry. "That's private property over there," he said. "Stay away, understand? I don't care who you are."

Ford asked, "Is something wrong?" It was pointless, over the noise of men trying to run in shallow water. Unnecessary as well. He didn't speak K'iche' but understood a phrase commonly used in Guatemala during the revolution: *Get-a' bal chee-wah!*

It was a command to attack or flee from an enemy—in this case, probably a Bahamian police car at the front gate requesting permission to enter.

Tito and Phillipé had approached him from behind but were returning to the compound via the shortest route possible, through the water. It was an opportunity to learn the terrain. Midway, sand became muck. The man with the unusual tattoo fell again. West of the point was a tidal trench, where the current swept seaward past the rented yacht. They were smart enough to skirt it and scramble up a limestone bank into trees, where there was probably no fence.

Ford continued to cast like he was pursuing another school of bonefish, but fixated on the boat. Someone was aboard, no doubt about it. Twice, curtains in the main cabin parted, then quickly closed. Trouble was, neither he nor his contact in Nassau had proof that a kidnapped child was being held there.

Legalities had to be considered. His contact was a Bahamian "diplomat," not a cop, so they'd come up with a plan. If the principals in residence had nothing to hide, a constable would be allowed through the gate without a search warrant. If not, tougher venues of access could be pursued.

Either way, they had to spook Efren Donner from a private dock into open water. Maritime law allowed a nation's Coast Guard to board and search any and all vessels under the flimsiest of pretenses. "Safety equipment," was the standard fallback. A faulty life jacket had helped detain far more felons than heroin or RPG rocket launchers found later in a ship's hold.

On the ridge near the houses, a dust contrail revealed the truck Ford had seen earlier. It was returning from the front gate unaccompanied by a Bahamian squad car—usually a white midsized Jeep. No surprise, not after hearing Tito say, "Shit no, don't let them in."

Still no activity above deck on Donner's boat. This was troubling. Twelve-year-old boys made noise. They were in constant motion. It suggested the boy was either not aboard. Or incapacitated. Or dead.

Josiah Bodden would not react kindly if he knew. Earlier in the

----

day, the man had offered his 28-foot Mako after learning the black-hulled yacht was in Cutlass Bay.

"Don't need the po-lice to do what you know is right," he'd said. Then had added a quote from Psalms. Something about God had trained his hands for war if revenge was justified.

The old preacher's statement regarding police was now moot. The same with the question he'd posed: Was it better to wait for a search warrant or go after the boy alone?

That decision had already been made.

Ford landed two more bonefish, the last just after sunset. There was sufficient light to convince an observer that he was an affable fool who—probably for foolish reasons—chose to disappear into the mangroves rather than follow a path to the road.

On the hike in, he'd hidden a waterproof bag. Fishing tackle went into the bag. Equipment he might need added weight to the vest, but not enough to arouse suspicion in a security guard who'd already searched it.

Ford stayed in the mangroves. Used the cover to move closer to Donner's boat. By dark, he was in a makeshift stand with a view. Below deck, lights flicked on, lights blinked off. Shadows glazed curtains in the main cabin, but still no activity outside.

- - - - - - - - - - -

An hour passed. Mosquito netting made it difficult to use an NV scope, which had to be pressed to the eye. So every few minutes he would swat and fan, then take another look. Star-black water was illuminated as if by a dazzling green sun. On the ridge, windows came alive with miniature people. Beams of infrared light guaranteed he was not the only one equipped with night vision.

Security at the compound included some modern toys.

Josiah had provided a handheld VHF radio, which was analog. Ford hadn't bothered to switch it on. Under ideal conditions, its maximum range was five miles at best. And what kind of idiot would respond after kidnapping a child and possibly two adults? After swatting more bugs he decided, what the hell, and hailed the boat by its cliché name on channel 16.

"Break-break for the vessel, *Island Time*. *Island Time*, do you read?" Twice he repeated the message.

In the main salon, a light came on. Curtains rustled.

Donner was monitoring the radio.

Ford tried again, saying, "Hailing the vessel *Island Time*. We have confirmed visual contact. Repeat, your location has been confirmed. Skipper, request you switch to channel twenty-two alfa and stand by for further instructions. Copy?"

A Coast Guard boarding party would have made a similar request prior to searching a private vessel.

Curtains parted. A man's faced peered out. Then a lot happened

----

fast. The cabin door opened and Donner stepped out, obviously wary. He signaled to someone inside, and Ford got his first look at Lydia Johnson. She appeared too tiny to warrant the attention of two nations—and possibly more, if he was right about a Salvadoran connection.

What happened next was difficult to watch. Donner summoned the woman aft, where a rubber dinghy was tied. When she balked, he threatened her with a fist. No . . . the butt of a small pistol. It was enough to convince her. She dropped out of sight as if falling to her knees. When she reappeared, a small, bald man was at her side.

Ford threw off the mosquito netting and watched Dr. Leonard Nickelby. The man moved like a cripple. Had to be helped down onto the dive platform, then into the rubber boat. Lydia hovered like a nurse while Donner started the engine and drove them ashore at top speed.

Where was the boy?

On the dock, three men wearing suits appeared. They, too, had been monitoring a radio. Not unexpected. What Ford hadn't anticipated was a device that instantly triangulated the location of his handheld VHF. A laser beam swept the water at his feet before he switched it off. He grabbed his bag and started inland through a tangle of roots and limbs. In a mucky area of briars near the path uphill he dumped the radio after powering it on.

Buy myself enough time to find the boy, he thought.

A more subtle finesse was backtracking through the mangroves

278

to the water, a custom dive mask and snorkel ready to go. It was a move no one should have expected.

One man did.

Ford's dive mask was fitted with a mount for underwater night vision. He had clamped the NV monoc in place when a familiar voice said from the bushes, "Went off and left your fly rod, amigo. Figured you'd be back."

Tito, a broad silhouette, stood behind him to his right. No flashlight, but a similar scope on a headband that masked one eye. Then Tito saw the elongated tube that was a silencer aimed at him and realized the biologist wasn't easily surprised.

"Be cool, bro. Just want to discuss the situation. You put that can on a Glock? A Beretta maybe, huh?"

Can was security-speak for a baffled sound suppressor.

"A Sig 9," Ford said. "Tell me now if your comm system is transmitting. I'd rather run than shoot you. It's something you'd have to experience to understand."

"Radio's off, amigo," Tito said, nodding like he did understand. "This is just you and me. I like Sigs, the trigger especially, but the whole double-action thing, you know? So I had to get used to this." He patted an unseen holster, meaning a Glock, which was common in the trade. "You really a biologist?"

Ford hoped the guy's calm, easygoing manner signaled the possibility of a deal. "If I was smart, I'd ask for your weapons," he said. "What would you do?"

"Shit, man, it was me? Go home, get drunk, and be out first thing looking for a new place to fish. But not here." Tito referenced window lights across the bay. "You ever do security for a dictator? Some of the dudes he hires . . . man, I don't know. I'm starting to wonder myself if the money's worth prison in the States. Or worse. You know the expression 'Send El Caucho'?"

Caucho was a cheap plastic raincoat. Ford said, "To keep the blood off. What, they always send someone with a machete? Your partner Phillipé would probably be good at it."

"Marabuntas," Tito said, which was the name of a street gang and also a predatory jungle ant. "Yeah, MS-13, it's the way they do things, man. Old-school, the Indio way. Hang a man's head on a hook, light candles all around. Spooky shit I didn't spend seven years in Armada Recon to learn. Not just Phillipé either—all them out there looking for you." He shrugged like it was out of his hands. "As you know, a man's got to make a living."

It was a subtle proposition. In response, Ford holstered the pistol and said, "Let's find a place to sit down. I've got bug spray if you need it."

Tito used what was left in the can while he explained. At sunset, he'd watched Ford through binoculars and had to wonder why a scientist carrying papers from the Bahamian government would crawl into the mangroves instead of using a footpath.

"So I come here to check while the others staked out a white Toyota near the road. I found this where you dropped it." He

----

handed over a Sage fly rod case. "A man casts as good as you, I knew you'd be back. As for your other intentions . . ."

It was his way of referencing a high-tech dive mask and a sound-suppressed pistol.

Ford nodded toward dock lights that glistened a quarter mile away. "A boy was kidnapped yesterday. I think he might be aboard a boat anchored over there."

"That's it?"

"Some view kidnapping as a crime."

"Hey, the only reason we're talking is I got a three-year-old at home, so go easy on something I don't know nothing about. I'm talking about the man paying me. Are you here because of him and his *junta miembros*?"

"Nope. Absolutely nothing to do with whoever it is you were hired to protect."

Tito laughed. "Man, you are so lucky, if that's true. You talking about the gringo movie director's boat, huh?"

"He's the one. Efren Donner. I don't suppose you went aboard and—"

"A *maricón* like that, who cares? He's bad news, bro. Showed up uninvited but didn't bring nothing to the party. Like an insult, understand? That shit don't fly with a certain generalissimo, so maybe what happens to the dude is El Caucho gonna pay him a visit. That's all I can say unless we can, you know, work something out."

"We can," Ford said.

They did.

- - - - - - - - - - -

O n his belly, he crabbed through the shallows to a trench where the tide swept seaward past Donner's boat. No need to swim. The current pulled him along, just a portion of his stocking cap and mask showing. At the channel's edge was a sandy delta where night herons, spooked by the intrusion, growled like lions and vaulted skyward.

On the dock, a security guard lit a cigarette, indifferent to the behavior of birds.

Ford used his feet as rudders and caught the boat's swim platform before the tide could vent him past the dock into the channel. For a minute or so, he waited in the crackling silence of barnacles, then pulled himself aboard. Slipped over the transom and didn't stand until he popped the cabin door, pistol drawn. Master switches were on the wall to the right. He killed the lights and again waited in silence for someone inside or ashore to react.

Tito had offered, but couldn't promise, thirty minutes, maybe longer, before his guys allowed Donner and the others to return.

Ford noted items he normally would have searched: a leather medical bag, a briefcase, an electronics suite, and—most tempting of all—a chart plotter. But he continued down the steps to the aft master cabin, where the AC was on high. His dive mask began to fog. He tilted it to his forehead and used a light with a red filter that confirmed Efren Donner preferred a very different assortment of masks. All kinds—plastic and feathers, and a tribal-looking African mask with straw hair.

The boy was in the crew quarters, a closet-sized room, on a lower bunk. Ford had to take a calming breath because of what he saw. When he scooped the child up, he whispered, "Your grandfather's waiting."

The boy fidgeted as if in a dream and slurred, "Sir, you be jumbey-fucked if he not."

Three life jackets, tandem-lashed, carried them out to sea.

21

Efren Donner knew he was in trouble when the guy he'd been dealing with, the generalissimo's majordomo, asked, "If we've got her, why do we need you?" Meaning Lydia, which was okay, but why so snotty about it?

Donner knew. He'd used variations on the same line to stiff street dudes or some gofer who'd hustled his ass off organizing a project but who didn't have the brains to protect his assets before pitching the idea.

"Not bad," Donner would say. "But if the talent's already on board, why do I need you?"

That simple. Clean, like a knife.

Wannabe actors didn't care about a friend or mentor or butt buddy who got dumped along the way. Like a flock of crows, casualties went unnoticed. Sign the contract or there's the door. Better yet, the couch. Verbal pitches, titles, log lines were not copyrightable. So send a one-paragraph treatise, registered mail, to an attorney before the dumbass street dude tried to get smart.

"Theft of intellectual property," the contingency bar hacks would claim.

No, it was Hollywood—New York or Miami Beach. Atlanta was moving up, too. That's the way the business worked, which, he hoped, was his ace in the hole.

A patio outside the main house, with tiki torches, is where Donner gave the generalissimo's guy a hard-on stare and replied, "You don't need me, fine. Good luck peddling bananas while I shoot my next movie in Nicaragua. Honduras, maybe—those people hate your country, from what I hear." Which didn't play well, so he added, "Not that I wouldn't be disappointed. I thought we had a deal."

The guy, a twenty-some-year-old colonel wearing medals and a uniform straight out of *The Birdcage*, said, "You speaking to these certain parties without our permission?"

"No. Strictly hypothetical."

"What does this *hypothetical* mean?"

Christ, he had to explain that to a man authorized to carry a fancy pistol but who spoke English like a pimple-faced teen.

"Let me ask you, Señor Donner, what is the importance of"—

----

a notebook had to be consulted—"Dr. Leonard Nickelby? Is he Ms. Johnson's, how you say, *experto* for the salvage?"

Off on a totally different tangent. Patience was required. "Nickelby doesn't know shit. And he's a pain in the ass."

"Of no use, in other words?"

"Exactly in those words," Donner replied. "Back to what I was saying. You guys brought me to the dance, which is why I haven't spoken to anyone else. Why would I?"

"Honduras, señor, did you know they once started a war because of a soccer match?"

"Total right-wing assholes, I agree. Anyway, I'm so impressed by you, your people, the generalissimo's commitment to creating a first-rate film industry, that I already have backers for a project. Two hundred million. Tropical jungle, the world's most beautiful stretch of beach—that's the setting. I have to shoot it somewhere. And shitty as Honduras probably is, if they appreciate what a man like me can bring to the table—"

"You promised us four hundred million," the colonel interrupted. "Instead, you show up with nothing. Only trouble. First the police. Next, possibly, the Coast Guard." No eye contact. The man was too busy texting on his phone.

Donner felt his stomach knot—the descent, with no coke handy as a backup. "I already explained that. Look, you want the truth? I came here uninvited because I picked up a local kid, he's hurt bad. So sue me for trying to help a little boy instead of leaving him out there to drown."

"You saved a child?"

"Yes! That's why I need to get back to my boat. What you don't seem to understand is, I actually care about you people . . . I mean, all people who've gotten the shitty end of the stick. Equality is what I'm all about, man."

The colonel stared while speaking Spanish into a handheld radio, then said in English, "We'll see."

He got up and went through sliding glass doors into a room filled with smoke and salsa music. A few minutes later, came out, just close enough to say, *"Embustero,"* smiling, not angry.

Donner took it as a compliment. So wasn't prepared when the colonel added, "There is no boy."

"What?"

"My men checked."

"But . . . he has to be there."

"No, señor," the twenty-some-year-old colonel said, cold-eyed, done with the subject. "I suggest you return to your vessel and see for yourself. What is the expression in Hollywood? 'Don't call us until we call you'?"

Kiss my ass, is what he wanted to say, but not here, not alone in a compound that was fenced, security ninjas stationed along a downhill path to the dock. That was scary in itself. Had the punk colonel sent a text to one of them?

Donner paused at the top of the path, where lights were strung to show the way, then decided it was safer to do the unexpected. Cross-country, he set off through the trees and down a rutted

----

incline. A view of the water guided him until he came to a mountain of junk—the island garbage dump. A service road angled toward what seemed the right direction, but, goddamn, was it dark, like a tunnel roofed with leaves.

He turned anyway, walking faster, almost jogging . . . then stopped. Blocking his exit was a man. His silhouette shiny, as if clothed in plastic, and carrying something long like a machete.

"How's it going, Efren?"

The voice was unfamiliar or distorted by a sudden roaring in the film producer's ears, like on the island three weeks ago when he'd been so goddamn scared that he'd run from an imaginary killer who might not have been imaginary.

"Phil?" he called. "That you, ol' buddy?"

The silhouette responded, "Phillipé to you, asshole," then had the fun of asking, "Now who sucks?" after he'd sprinted in pursuit and caught Donner from behind.

Leonard said to Lydia, "Is that a coyote howling?"

All she knew or cared about was that the guard outside their door had jogged toward the distant sounds, joined by two others, their gun belts glistening as they crossed the patio where the tiki torches blazed.

"Come on, let me help you," she said. "We might not get another chance."

- - - - - - - - - - -

"I'm not a cripple," he responded, and did pretty well keeping up until they were almost to the dock. "Damn headache." He stood hunched over and touched his temple. "Just a little dizzy, that's all. I wonder where Efren is?"

Lydia listened to the silence. It had been silent for a while. She noted the dock, an empty chair, usually occupied, and an ashtray, where a cigarette smoldered. "Honey, they'll be back soon. You can lie down when we're aboard."

Leonard said, "You're right. Fuck Efren," and helped her push the dinghy into water deep enough to start the engine.

"The boy . . . I hope he's okay."

Lydia said, "Keep your head down, Leo. They have guns. Get ready with that line."

The air, the stars, the wash of waves outside the channel, descended like a weight during the minutes it took to land the dinghy and ready a yacht that was not theirs. The weight was fear. A tangible pressure every moment she was topside, her body visible, an easy target from shore. The forward anchor chock had to be cleared by hand. There wasn't time to hoist the dinghy aboard. It would have to be left behind, but the cradle had to be secured or waves would turn it into a wrecking ball.

Back and forth she went, then, finally, at the main controls, started the twin diesels and flipped the anchor retrieval switch. As the winch tractored the boat forward, Leonard hollered from below, "We can't leave yet. Shut it off, shut it off!"

Lights on the dock were commercial-grade, mustard yellow.

Three men were there. One waved frantically in a threatening way.

Lydia's hand was poised above the ignition keys but she decided no, it was too late. She called, "I can't. What's wrong?"

"He's gone . . . goddamn it, the boy's gone. Someone took him." Leonard came up the stairs in a rush—a hunchback, half his face bloated in the shadows—and nearly fell when the anchor popped free. The hull jolted when she put the engines in neutral, and a breeze pushed them toward rocks at the channel's edge. "Shit," Leonard said, meaning the men, not the rocks. "I don't care. We can't leave him."

Lydia warned, "Grab something," and throttled forward enough to keep them off the shoals. The boat swung. A starboard window panned the dock, where one man was climbing into the dinghy she'd set free. Another had a rifle trained on them while the third spoke into a radio. "Leo, we have to go."

"Not until I get my goddamn—"

Engine noise blotted out the rest when she again jammed the levers forward. The sudden thrust lifted the bow, blocking her view, while the deck tilted aft. She heard the banging of a door and looked back to see Leonard outside the cabin on his knees like he'd been thrown there. The only way to level off was to increase speed. She did, yelling, "Hold on."

A boat the length of a semi responds like a plane during takeoff. For long, sickening seconds, her view was of stars and an anchor pulpit that gradually descended to reveal a line of unlit

----

markers. They were in the channel, at least, but still a few hundred yards from a hedge of charcoal trees that might shield them from the dock. A quarter mile beyond was Dolphin Head, the rocky point where the compound sat elevated above the sea.

Behind her, Leonard yelled something. Yelled again, only the words *following us* decipherable. She glanced to see him exiting the engine hold with a weapon he'd hidden earlier—the antique sword. It was in response to what was behind them: the dinghy closing fast in their wake. At the tiller, the driver stood holding a bowline for balance as if waterskiing.

The image of a Jet Ski chasing a slow truck came to mind. But what could the guard do, should they refuse to stop?

The answer was still visible on the dock, where a rifle tracked their escape. The rifle fired twice. Seaworthy windows are double-paned, yet glass exploded into the cabin. A third shot shattered the window to her right.

Lydia screamed, "Leo, please get down," and buried the throttles. For a time, she steered by memory. When a blur of mangroves swept past, it seemed safe to stand—but too late to react to a marker that should have been portside, not starboard. The hull bucked when it hit bottom. She was thrown forward but clung to the wheel and turned sharply, which freed one spinning prop to plow toward the channel.

The sudden deceleration surprised the man in the dinghy behind them. At night, a black hull blends with the horizon. He tried to swerve, but not in time. A second impact knocked Lydia

----

from her seat and showered the boat with a chaos of vague shapes, sounds, and water.

Where were the damn light switches? Calling, "Leo . . . Leo, are you okay?" she shifted to neutral and began flipping toggles near the wheel.

Leonard responded, "Don't do it, I'm warning you right now," like he was speaking to a third person.

Finally, the right switch. The aft deck was illuminated, yet it took a moment to process what she saw. The rubber boat hung from a railing where its outboard had snagged after skipping over the transom. Standing against the transom was a man wearing a cheap plastic rain slicker over slacks and a turtleneck. He was dazed and bleeding from the nose but still powerful enough to swing a saw-toothed machete—and he did, making a slashing lunge at Leonard, then grabbed the transom as if waiting for his head to clear.

"Don't make me do this," Leonard yelled, then had to back away when the man lunged again—a man with a bizarre tattoo on his wrist, Lydia noticed for the first time.

It was not Prof. Nickelby who turned to her with an antique saber at ready. And the man she'd fallen in love with would not have ordered, "Turn out that goddamn light. I've had enough."

But Lydia had changed, too.

"Leave him there and hang on," she called. "Maybe you won't have to."

At the controls, she killed the lights and plowed a span of

----

shallows before jettisoning the dinghy with a burst of twin throttles. Maybe the man, too.

It was a detail that, even later, Capt. León thought too dangerous to discuss.

When they cleared the channel, the weight of what they had done descended. Murder, a stolen boat scarred by violence and blood—and a missing child that had to be explained.

"Let's get rid of these right now," she said, and tossed Efren Donner's goodie bag overboard. "He'll blame us for everything, Leo, you know that. Those men will never stop looking for us."

"Not just them," he said. "The feds will try to nail you for what Jimmy Jones did just on Donner's say-so. I know how those stiffs think, and they've got nothing better to do."

He would've done the same in a previous life.

The list of felonies they might be charged with grew as stars rotated on the horizon. Marl Landing was still an hour away, according to the GPS, when Lydia decided, "We can never go back, you know."

Leonard, cleaning his saber with a towel, replied, "Why would we?"

- - - - - - - - - - -

22

hen Celeste, a Cat Island dive master in training, asked
Tomlinson if he'd ever experienced feelings of love un-
derwater, she was puzzled by his answer, which was, "Do
you mean with a partner?"

"Say what?"

He repeated the question.

"Are you talkin about . . . ?"

He nodded.

The girl was still confused. "What other way can it be, unless
you're one of them that prefers . . ." She paused and dismissed the
notion as absurd—the man was too obviously, yet charmingly, a
lover of women.

"As in, with another person," he explained. "When you've logged as much bottom time as me, decompression stops can get freaky. Occasionally, you have to, you know, let your mind soar and take matters into your own hands."

"There's something I haven't tried." She smiled. "But I'm willing to . . . Whatever it is you're talking about . . . Don't that sun feel hot on your shoulders? Man, I can feel it down my spine."

She stretched, yawned, and listened to the boney American hipster reply, "For sure, like sticking one's fun receptors into a light socket. Back when I was a boy, I pissed on an electric fence. Changed my whole outlook on life. Yeah, you should definitely give it a try."

"Say what? Where I'm gonna find a fence 'round here that's—"

"No, getting off while you're decompressing."

"Does that mean . . . ?"

"Hope so. It's all about maintaining sanity during periods of solitude. See, I've got this pal who's constantly going off, leaving me in the lurch. Underwater, on land, I can't tell you how many countries. Like now." He had to look around to get his bearings. They were anchored inside a reef south of Andros, close enough to glimpse Cat Island if he were to climb the mast of the 42-foot sailboat he'd chartered out of Fernandez Bay near the airport. "He's somewhere up the rim looking for the guy I told you about—after ordering me back to the States like I'm some flunky."

"Your friend that's looking for the treasure hunting thief?" she said.

"Straightest dude you can imagine, most of his life."

"Your friend?"

"The thief. An office drone—until he disappeared. But let's not get into that. As far as my friend's concerned, I could be slobbering drunk in some godforsaken South Beach bar."

"But you're not."

"Drunk? Nope, only a couple of beers. That reminds me—" A tiny leather bag appeared from beneath his tank top.

The woman scolded him, whispering, "We ain't smokin' no kef before a dive, crazy man. We're not alone. And I've got to take this serious. But later, maybe?"

Celeste gave the last part a saucy inflection. Standing on the forward deck, lean legs honey brown in a crimson thong, and a white T-shirt, its *Jack Bay Dive Shop* logo elevated by the angle of her breast. Pretty face, smile, and eyes that pierced the heart.

The smile vanished when her instructor, Tamara Constance, came up the gangway carrying a clipboard and an extra regulator. "Why y'all talking instead of finishing the checklist?" she asked, frowning. Then removed some papers from the clipboard and found a pen. "You need to sign these. This is my dive spot, Celeste. Exclusive, which means once you get your ticket—if you graduate—you still have to call for permission. And no talking about what you saw down there. Understand?"

"Yes, Ms. Constance."

"It's Captain Constance in public," the woman said, softening a bit. "Just Tamara will do out here."

She didn't speak as gently when she got Tomlinson off by

----

himself. "Marion was right about you. Don't be messing with that young girl's heart."

"You're jealous." He smiled.

"The hell I am. Being professional, is what it's called. Something you wouldn't know about."

"View it as part of the curriculum," Tomlinson suggested. "Come on. Like I'm the only client who's gonna hit on her? Celeste needs to learn there are boundaries in life. Some people, it's years before they understand we weren't sent to this planet to have fun." He chuckled to signal he was only semi-serious and bumped her with his shoulder. "This isn't as exciting as being holed up in a Nassau hotel room, is it?"

Tamara said, "Shut your mouth." She refused to be embarrassed by what had happened between them after a few drinks at the bar on Queen's Staircase. Then happened again at the Victoria, a hotel that catered to the posh and others worthy of around-the-clock security. "That's something else you can't talk about," she added. "Or did you blab to him already?"

"Doc?" Tomlinson said. "Ask him yourself. He's supposed to pick me up around five." This was a good excuse to look at his watch and suggest, "If we're gonna get a third dive in, we'd better suit up. Or not. I'd bet I'm right about the elephant tusk and the rest, especially the bracelet you lost."

It was a slave ship, he had theorized. Copper bracelets—*manillas*, as they were known—were still used in West Africa as currency.

"But it's your call, skipper," he conceded.

- - - - - - - - - - -

The old preacher waved from the ground and was on the landing strip ready to help secure the blue-on-white amphib when they exited, Ford carrying a heavy bag, Tomlinson just his dive gear.

"Best keep your plane out of sight," Josiah said, referring to an open, tin-roofed hangar. "These here is dangerous times, gentlemen, and will continue to be so until they find that sonuvabitch who kidnapped our grandson. Can you believe they still ain't found his boat?"

Tomlinson was perceptive enough to realize that his Masonic brother had spent the last few days dealing in confidence with his pal the biologist. It was in the wink-wink subtext of their exchange, Doc saying, "It's not the first boat to disappear in these waters," to which Josiah responded, "Lord knows, and not the last. Not the biggest either. This here's a boat-losing island, gentlemen. Up at the church we got proof you've never seen, if you're interested."

Ford, finished with the subject, adjusted the bag on his shoulder. "We don't have a lot of time, so why don't you two stay here and catch up? I'll be on the footbridge getting ready."

It had been nearly a week since exchanging the secret handshake. When Tomlinson offered his hand, the old man pulled him close and spoke mouth-to-ear, a fraternal rite that communicated urgency and also demanded a promise. For a full minute they stood that way.

"So mote it be," Tomlinson responded, serious about the exchange, and a little teary, too. "Can I see him?"

"Need you to understand something first. I was hoping to show Dr. Ford as well, but . . . is he real bad jumbied about something?"

Worried, seemed to be his meaning. Tomlinson looked in the general direction of the bridge, where oceanic white tips gathered daily to feed. "Hell yes, preacher. I'm a tad jumbied myself . . . Oh, wait. Do you mean upset? Hmm . . . Could be the clerk at Arthur's Town screwed the pooch by giving Doc his mail. Yeah . . . makes sense. He seemed cheery on the flight over, but with the linear types you never know."

"Linn-eer-what?" Josiah's rheumy grape-blue eyes showed puzzlement. "Brother, when Genesis says *Let the earth bring forth herbs and grass*, the Good Lord had cattle in mind, not a man I'm trying to talk sense to. The question I have is about trust."

"Who? Me or Doc?"

"Both," Josiah said. "I'll show you."

The church smelled of moss and springwater. Inside, windows reshaped sunlight into a series of arches that followed thirteen pews to an altar. Artifacts from a shipwreck formed a triangular shrine: ballast rock, a bell, a dusty Bible, a trunk that held swords and scraps of dehydrated leather.

The front pew opened on invisible hinges. Josiah reached in,

- - - - - - - - - - -

saying, "Way back we held lodge meetings here, but this is something no foreigner, brother or not, has been allowed to see. I was hoping to grant the same privilege to your scientist friend."

A parchment logbook, wood endplates bound with straps, was placed on a table. The elaborate script on the cover was illegible. Except for the date: 1784.

Josiah opened it just enough to see a page crammed with flourishes, stemmed vowels, errors dotted with ink spots. Words and syntax were archaic: *Your Breast from the borde if that ye be wyse / Lest ye take hurte a'ter dawgwatch . . .*

Meaningless words, out of context. At the bottom of the page the author had signed in a bold hand: *Entarred this day of Our Lorde, Capt. J. Marley Bodden.*

"Marley Bodden," Tomlinson said, smiling. "As in, Marl Landing. And you're a direct-descended. Very cool, Rev."

Josiah closed the book. "He was captain of a ship out of Glasgow, the *Cailleach*. In those years, they burned or cast out witches, which is contrary to God's Word. Also goes against the convictions of our craft, as you know."

"Your grandfather how many times removed?" Tomlinson asked. Then decided, "It doesn't matter. The craft—he was a Freemason."

"His officers were members of Kilmory Lodge as well—there's a chapel there with Knights Templar graves. I'd like to see it before I die, but . . ." The man patted the book and continued, "Capt. Bodden was a brother of the craft, but he sure weren't no saint.

Off the Abacos, a papist ship had lost its sails. Was foundering. The *Cailleach* was bound for Cuba, but they captured the ship instead—killed every able man aboard, which is the gravest of sins. Then decided—"

"A Spanish galleon," Tomlinson said, thinking about Fitzpatrick's story—the *El Cazador*'s sister ship, which had fled toward Cuba.

"Yes, a galleon out of Vera Cruz. They towed it south, where a storm put them both on a reef—" Josiah nodded to the island's windward side. "That reef. Capt. Bodden, two of his officers, fifteen crew, and thirty-one women survived out of a manifest of seventy-five souls. There was a Taino village here. The Indios were so sick with cholera, they welcomed anyone, even witches, if they had a knowledge of medicine."

"Castaways." Tomlinson was picturing it in his head. "They had to assimilate, live off the land, but didn't want to be rescued. Why? Because of the men they killed? Or what that galleon was carrying?"

Josiah shrugged, returned the book to its hiding place but left the pew open. "Three hundred years have weakened the pages, brother, but not the truth. This book contains what foreigners might use against us—and the source of our survival. Wealth, some would say. That secret has to be protected."

"The Marl people's private stash." Tomlinson nodded. "Enough to tell the greed mongers and cops—modern times, too—to kiss your ass. Brother, I'm envious. What they brought ashore has financed—"

"Nope. They too smart to salvage the valuables all at once," the old man said. "With all the robbers in them days? These days, too. They burnt the vessels to the waterline and let the wind and coral hide what they decided should be taken as needed. Over the years, hiding boats and such is something we good at."

Tomlinson loved the agrarian wisdom of harvesting silver as if picking beans. "Brilliant. Really. Just wade out to wherever the galleon is scattered and—" He paused, mindful of Ford's Shark Zapper. "Hold on . . . Every generation your people have to wade out a little farther. By now, to make a withdrawal, they're risking water that's deep enough to—"

"The deacons," Josiah agreed. "They our protectors, so we honor them with tithes, as it states in the Book. And your friend Dr. Ford, smart as he is, ain't one to promise something unless he understands. That's what I hope you'll pass along."

The logbook rested in a Tupperware container to keep it dry. Other items were hidden there: silver plates, a gold chalice, a sack of something heavy—oxidized Spanish coins, perhaps. A more ancient object demanded attention. It was a wooden scythe, doubled-edged with sharks' teeth and lashed to a bamboo handle.

"Whew, that bad boy belongs in a museum," Tomlinson said.

Josiah seldom sounded stern, but he did when he replied, "No, brothah. That there's a blessed Taino axe. I keep it handy in case foreigners start poking around where they shouldn't." A smile defused the implied threat.

Tomlinson took a step back anyway. "You set me up, Rev.

Brought a box of fish ashore to clean, knowing it would lure me close enough—like a trap."

The smile broadened. "As a precaution, *Be sober, be ever vigilant*, in the words of the great fisherman. Must admit, I was relieved to find you're a master of the craft—and quoting from the Good Book didn't hurt you none either. Purely was a joy to find a brothah I'd never met."

The old man closed the pew. "Now that you know," he said, "come see what's worth protecting."

They didn't walk far. A rocky incline provided a view of the windward shore—the least attractive side to settle because of rocks and salt spray. Also the least accessible by sea. Waves pounded an outside reef and pushed streamers of foam toward land. Palm trees shaded a curvature where the island bowed.

"Wind ain't good for anything but privacy and growing coconuts," the old preacher said. "Come on."

They zigzagged downhill toward the sea. In an arid area of cactus, wild green plumes sprouted from a crater. A ragged man was there with a cart. "Fine, fine," he said in greeting. Josiah replied, "Fine, fine," then explained, "That there's what's called a banana hole. You hungry?"

Tomlinson was peeling his third when they stopped again. Through the palms, close enough to smell wood smoke, was a house. Old wattle-and-daub, whitewashed with lime. Its heavy thatched roof needed repair, judging from the ladder and a woman sitting with her back to them weaving palm fronds. A tiny woman,

----

short mousy hair that had been braided into spikes island style. Nearby was a pile of lumber, screens, and other items needed to make the hut livable.

Josiah postponed questions by touching a finger to his lips.

By the time a short, bald man appeared . . . then a boy, who took the man's hand as if convalescing, Tomlinson didn't need to ask.

Among the lumber was a heavy black panel that had been painted, but not enough. Still legible was the name: ISLAND TIME.

23

F ord was in the water when he saw Tomlinson coming down the hill. The expectation that Josiah would follow caused a gaggle of children to scatter—back to their bicycles, their chores, their gray book bags that matched neatly pressed school uniforms.

"That's got to piss you off," he said, wading ashore, mask tilted, fins in hand. Strapped to his leg, the shock cable trailed like a six-foot snake.

Tomlinson replied, "What do you mean?" but couldn't wait to share the news. "They found the boy. He's here, I saw him. Aside from a concussion, the resident juju woman says he'll be okay. I don't know why Josiah didn't tell you."

"Didn't need to," Ford replied. "The doctor I flew in three days ago said the same on our way back to Nassau. I was talking about school uniforms. A free spirit like you can't approve."

"Uniforms? Geezus, stick to the subject. Instead of letting me fret my ass off, you could've at least mentioned the boy was alive. And why are you here instead of the bridge? I left Josiah there half an hour ago, man, told him I'd find you."

The biologist made light of it, saying, "And, by god, you did. Hold your horses while I pack my stuff."

It was better not to reveal what he'd just seen. Not yet. Maybe ever. Ford had chosen this spot near the fish co-op after speaking with a woman who officially was still missing, and the old man who'd waited for him and the boy off Dolphin Head in a battered 28-foot Mako.

"Years ago," the old preacher had told him the next morning, "some foreigner stuck a bunch of them mooring buoys along here like he was doing us a favor. Just appeared overnight. But guess how long they lasted before all them lines was cut?"

This was in response to Ford's interest in several commercial-grade buoys, yokes still attached, that were piled among other junk near the warehouse.

Buoys—but no mooring weights.

"Do you remember the guy's name?"

"The foreigner?" They'd been on their way to recheck the Mako, so the question was unexpected. "Hell if I know. Or care. Some rich fella trying to help us poor dumb natives, most likely.

306

You want them marker weights, sir, they all yours. We ain't got no use for 'em.'"

This, in Ford's mind, was proof that Josiah was unaware of what Jimmy Jones might have hidden in this sharky stretch of water.

For several very busy days the biologist had waited for a chance to dive the spot alone. Snorkel gear was all he needed to confirm the lines that had been cut were still there, but so heavy with barnacles the rope lay in coils twenty feet below. Six bounce dives later, enough sand had been fanned away to expose five mushroom-shaped anchors. A dozen or more remained covered, and would've stayed that way, even if Tomlinson hadn't intruded.

Ford zipped his gear bag and was using a towel when his hipster pal retrieved a knife and scabbard left on the ground.

"Why didn't you bring your good one?"

"My Randall? It's worth about a grand and I don't trust customs agents. I always pick up something cheap on the road—you know that."

Tomlinson clicked the knife free. "Talk about cheap," he said, inspecting the blade, "looks like they missed with the spray paint."

"A throwaway," Ford agreed, and took the knife. It was his way of ignoring flecks of gold on the blade that were not specks of paint. Then changed the subject as they walked toward the footbridge. "I've got a big decision to make, ol' buddy."

"Sure, pretend you're in a good mood, then nail me when my guard's down," Tomlinson said. "Don't blame me, *hermano*. I told that damn clerk at Arthur's Town not to hand over your mail unless—"

"That's not what I mean. But while we're on the subject, she thinks jail's too good for you and so do I."

"Hannah?"

"Her and probably a lot of other women. The decision I have to make, though, has to do with Lydia Johnson. What did you think when you saw them?"

"Geezus, Doc, is there anything you don't know? I can't even comment. *A blood secret kept in death and beyond,* is how a certain Brotherhood might phrase it. But you didn't hear it from me."

"That's what I'm asking you. Are those two safe here? No one cares about Dr. Nickelby, even his wife according to a talk I had with Fitz. She dropped the idea of pressing charges in return for scuba lessons, apparently."

"No way."

"The best revenge, I guess, is finding a way to stay happy."

Tomlinson liked that. "There you go—the beauty of a broken heart is that fault lines heal no matter who's at fault. Fitz called her?"

Ford dismissed the subject with a shrug. "Lydia's the one I'm worried about. There are some high-tech people still looking for her. On the other hand, she could try to cut a deal with the Treasury Department. I can't go into detail, but she'd have to . . . Well, let's just say turn over some key information."

"Trust the feds—are you high?" Tomlinson considered the

- - - - - - - - - - -

idea absurd. "No one's gonna find them here, man, even that prick Efren Donner. Why? Because Lydia and Leonard Nickelby no longer exist. Not as modern manifestations—a heavy concept for a guy like you to understand, I know. Think of it this way. If caterpillars can do the unexpected, so can people. Hell, you and Josiah are so tight suddenly, I'm surprised you didn't attend the adoption ceremony a few nights back."

Ford had, in a way—viewed it at a distance, from the porch of a coral pink villa that more often than not was used to lure enemies close enough to assess—and sometimes strike.

Sixteen mushroom-shaped mooring anchors weighted with gold lay in the shallows nearby. They were unknown, unsuspected by anyone but Ford, an underpaid biologist who had recently received good news in the mail. He'd already done the math. A conservative estimate based on Lydia's best guess was one hundred pounds per anchor multiplied by the price of gold in troy ounces—about one-point-five mil apiece.

"That helps," Ford said. "I'm going to stay another week or so and work on my shark project. It's kind of nice here, you know? No Internet, no interruptions. Yeah, might even stay longer."

Tomlinson gave his pal an odd look. "What's wrong with you?"

"Nothing. I've got Fitz's logbook and the coin boxed on the plane. I suggest you stick them in your carry-on when you fly home, commercial. Oh, and give everybody my regards. And don't let my damn dog run away again."

The dude was repressing. The envelope containing Hannah

Smith's letter was thin enough to reveal a paragraph or two, thanks to a bright light and a magnifying glass.

"Drop the act, Marion," Tomlinson said, and stepped closer to face his friend. "I didn't snoop—not intentionally. Call it intuition, if you like, but I'm pretty damn sure Hannah dumped you for . . . what, like the third time? Suppressed emotion is a killer, *hermano*, so shallow up and talk to me."

The biologist found that funny for some reason. "Let's do call it snooping. But take it from a professional, you're a half-assed snoop at best. Hannah didn't dump me, she just doesn't want to marry a man who, well, travels as much as me."

"Disappears with guns and shit, you mean," Tomlinson said in translation. "And you're okay with that?"

"Can you blame her? You missed the part you'd have to open the envelope to read. She gave me a second chance." Smiling, with the footbridge in sight—already a massive shark in the turquoise eddy below—Ford explained, "I'm going to be a father—again. And this time, I'm not going to blow it."